REX STOUT, the creator of Nero Wolfe, was born in Noblesville, Indiana, in 1886, the sixth of nine children of John and Lucetta Todhunter Stout, both Quakers. Shortly after his birth the family moved to Wakarusa, Kansas. He was educated in a country school, but by the age of nine he was recognized throughout the state as a prodigy in arithmetic. Mr. Stout briefly attended the University of Kansas but he left to enlist in the Navy and spent the next two years as a warrant officer on board President Theodore Roosevelt's yacht. When he left the Navy in 1908, Rex Stout began to write free-lance articles and worked as a sightseeing guide and an itinerant bookkeeper. Later he devised and implemented a school banking system that was installed in four hundred cities and towns throughout the country. In 1927 Mr. Stout retired from the world of finance and, with the proceeds from his banking scheme, left for Paris to write serious fiction. He wrote three novels that received favorable reviews before turning to detective fiction. His first Nero Wolfe novel, *Fer-de-Lance*, appeared in 1934. It was followed by many others, among them, *Too Many Cooks, The Silent Speaker, If Death Ever Slept, The Doorbell Rang*, and *Please Pass the Guilt*, which established Nero Wolfe as a leading character on a par with Erle Stanley Gardner's famous protagonist, Perry Mason. During World War II Rex Stout waged a personal campaign against Nazism as chairman of the War Writers' Board, master of ceremonies of the radio program "Speaking of Liberty," and member of several national committees. After the war he turned his attention to mobilizing public opinion against the wartime use of thermonuclear devices, was an active leader in the Authors Guild, and resumed writing his Nero Wolfe novels. Rex Stout died in 1975 at the age of eighty-eight. A month before his death he published his seventy-second Nero Wolfe mystery, *A Family Affair*. Ten years later, a seventy-third Nero Wolfe mystery was discovered and published in *Death Times Three*.

The Rex Stout Library

REX STOUT

Over My
Dead Body

Introduction
by John Jakes

BANTAM BOOKS
NEW YORK • TORONTO • LONDON • SYDNEY • AUCKLAND

A NERO WOLFE
MYSTERY

*This book is fiction. No resemblance is intended
between any character herein and any person,
living or dead; any such resemblance is
purely coincidental.*

OVER MY DEAD BODY

A Bantam Crime Line Book / by arrangement with
the author

PUBLISHING HISTORY

Farrar and Rhinehart edition published 1940
Bantam reissue edition / January 1994

ISBN 978-0-553-23116-8

Published simultaneously in the United States and Canada

Bantam Books are published by Bantam Books, a division of Random House,
Inc. Its trademark, consisting of the words "Bantam Books" and the portrayal
of a rooster, is Registered in U.S. Patent and Trademark Office and in other
countries. Marca Registrada. Bantam Books, 1540 Broadway, New York,
New York 10036.

Introduction

I met Rex Stout in the aftermath of a crime. Beg pardon, alleged crime. The creator of Mr. Wolfe and Archie didn't believe any crime had been committed.

The year was 1962; the place, Rochester, New York. I was working there as a copywriter in an ad agency whose major account was Eastman Kodak, irreverently known as Big Yellow. I was also one of the youngest, if not the youngest, board members of the Friends of the Rochester Public Library. This was the first of several Friends groups I became associated with out of my general love of, and need for, libraries, and it stands out as one of the most vigorous and progressive.

The crime, so-called, was not the kind that figures in one of these fine Stout reprints. It was what some term a victimless crime. But to the authorities in Rochester, especially the district attorney, whose press statements seemed to reek of puritanical hellfire and political ambition, it was a crime of the most dangerous kind.

To wit: selling a book.

The book was the Grove Press edition of Henry Miller's *Tropic of Cancer*. Sale of the allegedly obscene book was prohibited in New York State and a lot of other states as well. The alleged perp was a smallish, mild-appearing bookseller, whom I'll call Norman B. Norman B. ran a large independent store not far from the massive granite block of the main library, on the bank of the Genesee River. Along with the usual array of semilurid girlie magazines and sexy paperbacks, in which the raciest word was something like "nipples," the bookstore offered Miller's novel for sale.

Which got Norman B. in a peck of trouble.

Now I honestly don't remember whether he was actually served with an arrest warrant, or just ordered by the D.A. to get rid of the Miller or else. But I do remember the quick response. Certain members of the Friends, including several stouthearted technical writers from Kodak, formed an ad hoc group called Audience Unlimited. Its purpose was to advertise and write letters objecting to the law coming down hard on Norman B. and, more pertinently, on the freedom to read. Yours truly was part of the new group.

Norman B. himself immediately took countermeasures, instituting a legal action to overturn the *Tropic* ban. In 1964 the case was decided in his favor by the New York State courts, some four months after the U.S. Supreme Court ruled the book not obscene.

In the midst of the *Sturm und Drang* unleashed by the *Tropic* affair, Mr. Stout came to town.

He came not to defend Norman B. or Henry M. but as a guest speaker at the sixth annual Friends Literary Award presentation. The award that year was given to Lewis Stiles Gannett, a native of Rochester and a journalist, author, and at that time editor of Doubleday's marvelous Mainstream of America series of historical studies.

The award ceremony was held in the great main hall of the Rochester library, with a small social gathering preceding. As a Friends board member, I was invited to attend the reception. The words "high excitement" hardly describe my state; the honored guest was a Famous Name Writer, and I was a devoted fan of his mysteries.

I vividly recall my first sight of Rex Stout, who was at that time seventy-five. His hair was white and so was his splendid long beard, and I remember thinking that he looked like an American cousin of Shaw. Of course he was a godlike figure to me—I was thirty, slogging along fairly unsuccessfully with one third-rate pulp novel after another. But I approached him, shook his hand, muttered a few words, and I remember that he was friendly and humorous: kindness personified.

He was less friendly and humorous when it was his turn to speak. Of course he was appropriately warm and complimentary to his friend Gannett. But then he launched into a jeremiad against book-banners. He said, "Efforts to censor what people read are not justified under the American system." He thrilled me with his remarks. The audience gave him an ovation when he finished.

Which brings me around to the real point of this Introduction.

Rex Stout was a lifelong champion of writers, and a lifelong foe of those who would take advantage of them or suppress their work. As a highly successful writer himself, he obviously believed in giving something back to the profession for the benefit of others who weren't so successful.

Virtually his whole life testifies to this. Stout became a member of the Authors League in 1915. He was president of the League, the umbrella organization for the Authors Guild and the Dramatists Guild, from 1951 to 1955 and again from 1961 to 1969.

He served the Authors Guild as president from 1943 to 1945 and was a member of the Guild Council from 1942 until the time of his death in 1975. As the Guild's

Bulletin said in its obituary, "He was always ready to give of his time and spirit to Guild business." Of his many activities, probably none was more important than his presidency of the Authors League Fund, which helps professional writers who happen to fall into dire financial distress.

A man named Olin Miller has said, "Writing is the hardest way of earning a living, with the possible exception of wrestling alligators." That's more than a little self-serving; millions of men and women in other jobs would make the same statement about their work. But it's also true that writers have few defenders beyond themselves.

That's why the Authors League was formed, and its two guilds as well.

That's why Rex Stout gave so much of himself to Guild and League causes.

That's why he came to Rochester and spoke out against the immoral banning of Miller's novel. (Who knows what he thought of the book? He might have hated it; I've never been wild about it myself. But it was a serious book, and if you allow the yahoos to ban one such, you open the door to suppression of all of them—and a lot of other art besides. Which is hardly big news but is, regrettably, a recurring problem.)

Rex Stout gave me great pleasure through his novels. I expect he has done the same for you and will certainly do so again in *Over My Dead Body*.

But he also gave me great pride in my chosen profession and a sure knowledge that, someday, if ever I could, I had to give something back too.

I'll never forget the day Rex Stout came to Rochester. If you'd been there, you wouldn't either.

—John Jakes

Over My Dead Body

Chapter 1

The bell rang and I went to the front and opened the door and there she was. I said good morning.

"Pliz," she said, "I would like to see Misturr Nero Wolfe."

Or you might have spelled it plihz or plizz or plihsz. However you spelled it, it wasn't Middle West or New England or Park Avenue or even East Side. It wasn't American, and naturally it irritated me a little. But I politely invited her in and conducted her to the office and got her a chair, and then extracted her name, which I had to ask her to spell.

"Mr. Wolfe will be engaged until eleven o'clock," I told her, with a glance at the wall clock above my desk, which said ten thirty. "I'm Archie Goodwin, his confidential secretary. If you'd like to save time by starting on me . . ."

She shook her head and said she had plenty of time. I asked if she would like a book or magazine, and she shook her head again, and I passed her up and resumed at my desk, where I was heading up a bunch of hybridizing cards for use upstairs. Five minutes later I had finished and was checking them over when I heard her voice behind me:

"I believe I would like a book. May I?"

I waved at the shelves and told her to help herself and went on with the checking. Presently I looked up when she approached and stood beside me with a volume in her hand.

"Misturr Wolfe reads this?" she asked. She had a nice soft low voice which would have sounded all right if she had taken the trouble to learn how to pronounce words. I glanced at the title and told her Wolfe had read it some time ago.

"But he stoodies it?"

"Why should he? He's a genius, he don't have to study anything."

"He reads once and then he is through?"

"That's the idea."

She started for her chair and then turned again. "Do you read it perhaps?"

"I do not," I said emphatically.

She half smiled. "It's too complicated for you, the Balkan history?"

"I don't know, I haven't tried it. But I understand all the kings and queens got murdered. I like newspaper murders better."

She turned off the smile and went and sat down with the book, and appeared to be absorbed in it a few minutes later when, the checking finished, I jiggled the handful of cards neatly together and departed with them, and mounted the two flights of carpeted stairs to the top floor and the steeper flight to the roof level, where the entire space was glassed-in for the orchids except the potting room and the corner where Horstmann slept. Passing through the first two rooms, down the aisles with silver staging and concrete benches and thousands of pots holding everything from baby seedlings to odontoglossums and dendrobiums in full bloom, I found Nero Wolfe in the warm room, standing with his thumbs on his hips, frowning at Horstmann, who in turn was scowling reproachfully at an enormous coelogyne blossom with white petals and orange keels. Wolfe was muttering:

"A full two weeks. At the very least, twelve days. As Per Hansa says, I don't know what God expects to accomplish by such management. If it were only a question of forcing—well, Archie?"

I handed Horstmann the cards. "For that batch of miltonias and lycastes. The germination dates are already in where you had them. There's a female immigrant downstairs who wants to borrow a book. She is twenty-two years old and has fine legs. Her face is sullen but well-arranged and her eyes are dark and beautiful and worried. She has a nice voice, but she talks like Lynn Fontanne in *Idiot's Delight*. Her name is Carla Lovchen."

Wolfe had taken the cards from Horstmann to flip through them, but he stopped to send me a sharp glance. "What's that?" he demanded. "Her name?"

"Lovchen." I spelled it, and grinned. "Yeah, I know, it struck me too. You may remember I read *The Native's Return*. She seems to be named after a mountain. The Black Mountain. Mount Lovchen. Tsernagora. Montenegro, which is the Venetian variant of Monte Nero, and your name is Nero. It may be only a coincidence, but it's natural for a trained detective—"

"What does she want?"

"She says she wants to see you, but I think she came to borrow a book. She took that *United Yugoslavia* by Henderson from the shelf and asked if you've read it, and do you stoody it, and am I reading it and so on. She's down there with her pretty nose in it. But as I say, her eyes look worried. I had a notion to tell her that because of the healthy condition of the bank account—"

I turned it off because he was ignoring me and giving his attention to the cards. Reflecting that that was an unusually childish gesture even for him, since it lacked only three minutes till eleven o'clock, the hour when he invariably proceeded from the plant rooms to the office, I snorted audibly, wheeled, and went for the stairs.

The immigrant was still in the chair, reading, but had abandoned the book for a magazine. I looked around for it to return it to the shelf, but saw that she had already done so; it was back in its place, and I gave her a good mark for that because I've noticed that most girls are so darned untidy around a house. I told her Wolfe would be down soon, and had just got my notes cleared away and the typewriter lowered when I heard the door of his personal elevator clanging, and a moment later he entered. A pace short of his desk he arrested his progress to acknowledge the visitor's presence with a little bow which achieved only one degree off the perpendicular, then continued to his chair, got deposited, glanced at the vase of cattleyas and the morning mail under the weight, put his thumb to the button to summon beer, leaned back and adjusted himself, and sighed. The visitor, with the magazine closed on her lap, was gazing at him through long lowered lashes.

Wolfe said abruptly and crisply, "Lovchen? That is not your name. It is no one's name."

Her lashes fluttered. "My name," she said with a half smile "is what I say it is. Would you call it a convenience? Not to irritate the Americans with a name like Kraljevitch?"

"Is that yours?"

"No."

"No matter." Wolfe sounded testy—as far as I could see, for no reason. "You came to see me?"

Her lips parted for a soft little laugh. "You sound like a Tsernagore," she declared. "Or a Montenegrin if you prefer it, as the Americans do. You don't look like one, since Tsernagores grow up and up, not out and all around like you. But when you talk I feel at home. That's exactly how a Tsernagore speaks to a girl. Is it what you eat?"

I turned my head to enjoy a grin. Wolfe demanded, almost bellowing at her, "What can I do for you, Miss Lovchen?"

"Oh yes." Her eyes showed the worry again. "I was forgetting on account of seeing you. You are a famous man, I know that, of course, but you don't look famous. You look more like—" She stopped, made a little circle with her lips, and went on, "Anyway, you're famous, and you have been in Montenegro. You see, I know much about you. *Hvala Bogu.* Because I want to engage you on account of some trouble."

"I'm afraid—"

"Not my trouble," she continued rapidly. "It's a friend of mine, a girl who came with me to America not long ago. Her name is Neya Tormic." The long black lashes flickered. "Just as mine is Carla Lovchen. We work together at the studio of Nikola Miltan on 48th Street. You know, perhaps? Dancing and fencing are taught there. You know him?"

"I've met him," Wolfe admitted gruffly, "at the table of my friend Marko Vukčić. But I'm afraid I'm too busy at present—"

She swept on in front. "We're good fencers, Neya and I. Corsini in Zagreb passed us with foils, épée, and sabre. And the dancing, of course, is easy. We learn the

Lambeth Walk in twenty minutes, we teach it to rich people in five lessons, and they pay high, and Nikola Miltan takes the money and pays us only not so high. That is why, in this foolish trouble Neya has got into, we can pay you not so much as you might expect from some people, but we can pay you a little, and added to that is the fact that we are from Zagreb. It's not a little trouble Neya has got into, it's a big one, through no fault of hers, because she is not a thief, as anyone but an American fool would be aware. They'll put her in jail, and you must act quickly, at once—"

Wolfe's face was set in a grimace, showing that he was in the throes of an agitation away beyond his chronic reluctance to bother his mind about business when the bank balance was up in five figures. Displaying a palm at her, he tried to expostulate:

"I tell you I'm too busy—"

She hopped right over it. "I came instead of Neya because she has important lessons this morning, and it is necessary we should keep our jobs. But you will have to see her, of course, so you will have to go there, and anyway Miltan is arranging for everyone to be there together today, this afternoon, to settle it. It's the biggest nonsense anyone could imagine to suppose that Neya would put her hand in a man's pocket and steal diamonds, but it will be terrible if it happens the way Miltan says it will happen if the diamonds are not returned—but wait—you must let me tell you—"

My mouth was standing open in astonishment. After two hours on his feet in the plant rooms, when he came to the office at eleven o'clock and got lowered into his chair, with me there to annoy him pleasantly and the beer-tray freshly delivered by Fritz Brenner, Wolfe was ordinarily as immovable as a two-ton boulder. But now he was rising; he was risen. With a mutter that might have been taken either for an excuse or an imprecation, and with no glance at either of us, he stalked out of the room, by the door that led to the hall. We watched him go and then the immigrant turned and let me have her eyes wide open.

"He gets sick!" she demanded.

I shook my head. "Eccentric," I explained. "I suppose you might call it a form of sickness, but it's nothing tangible like concussion of the brain or whooping-cough. Once when a respectable lawyer was sitting in that very chair you're in now—Yes, Fritz?"

The door which Wolfe had closed behind him had opened again and Fritz Brenner stood there with a bewildered look on his face.

"In the kitchen a moment, please, Archie."

I got up and excused myself and went to the kitchen. Preliminary preparations for lunch were scattered around on the big linoleum-covered table, but it was obvious that Wolfe had not been suddenly seized with a violent curiosity about food. He stood at the far side of the refrigerator, facing me in a determined manner that seemed entirely uncalled for, and told me abruptly as I entered:

"Send her away."

"My God!" I admit I blew up a little. "She said she'd pay something, didn't she? It's enough to freeze the blood of an alligator! If you read it in her eyes that her friend Neya did actually glumb the glass, you might at least—"

"Archie." It was about as hostile as his voice ever got. "I have skedaddled, physically, once in my life, from one person, and that was a Montenegrin woman. It was many years ago, but my nerves remember it. I neither desire nor intend to explain how I felt when that Montenegrin female voice in there said '*Hvala Bogu.*' Send her away."

"But there's no—"

"Archie!"

I saw it was hopeless, though I had no idea whether he was overcome by terror or was staging a stunt. I gave it up and went back to the office and stood in front of her.

"Mr. Wolfe regrets that he will be unable to help your friend out of her trouble. He's busy."

Her head was tilted back to look up at me, and a little gasp left her mouth open. "But he can't—he must!" She jumped to her feet and I backed up a step as her eyes flashed at me. "We are from Tsernagora! She is—my friend is—" Indignation choked it off.

"It's final," I said brusquely. "He won't touch it. Sometimes I can change his mind for him, but there are limits. What does '*hvala Bogu*' mean?"

She stared. "It means 'Thank God.' If I see him, tell him—"

"You shouldn't have said it. It gives him the willies to hear a Montenegrin female voice talk Montenegrin. It's a kind of allergy. I'm sorry, Miss Lovchen, but there's not a chance. I know him from A to P, which is as far as he goes. P is for pigheaded."

"But he—I must see him, tell him—"

She was stubborn enough herself so that it took five minutes to persuade her out, and since the only prejudice I had acquired against Montenegrin females up to that point was based merely on pronunciation, which is not after all vital, I didn't want to get rough. Finally I closed the front door behind her and went to the kitchen and announced sarcastically:

"I think it's safe now. Stay close behind me and if I holler run like hell."

Wolfe's inarticulate growl, as I wheeled and headed for the office, warned me that there was barbed wire in that neighborhood, so when he came in a few minutes later and got re-established in his chair I made no effort to explain my viewpoint any further. He drank beer and fiddled around with a pile of catalogues, while I checked over a couple of invoices from Hoehn's and did some miscellaneous chores. When a little later he asked me to please open the window a crack, I knew the tension was relaxing toward normal.

But if either or both of us had any idea that we were through with the Balkans for that day, it wasn't long before we had it jostled out of us. It was customary for Fritz to answer the doorbell from eleven on, when I was in the office with Wolfe. Around twelve thirty he came in, advanced the usual three paces, stood formally, and announced a caller named Stahl who would not declare his business but stated that he was an agent of the Federal Bureau of Investigation.

I let out a low whistle and ejaculated cautiously "Aha!" Wolfe opened his eyes a trifle and nodded, and Fritz went for the caller.

We hadn't bumped into a G-man before in the course of business, and when he entered I did him the honor of swiveling clear around for a look. He was all right, medium-sized, with good shoulders and good eyes, a little skimpy in the jaw, and he needed a shoeshine. He told us his name again and shook hands with both of us, and took from his pocket a little leather case which he flipped open and exhibited to Wolfe with a reserved but friendly smile.

"My credentials," he explained in an educated voice. He certainly had fine manners, something on the order of a high-class insurance salesman.

Wolfe glanced at the exhibit, nodded, and indicated a chair. "Well, sir?"

The G-man looked politely apologetic. "We're sorry to bother you, Mr. Wolfe, but it's our job. I'd like to ask whether you are acquainted with the Federal statute which recently went into effect, requiring persons who are agents in this country of foreign principals to register with the Department of State."

"Not intimately. I read newspapers. I read about that some time ago."

"Then you know of that law?"

"I do."

"Have you registered?"

"No. I am not an agent of a foreign principal."

The G-man threw one knee over the other. "The law applies to agents of foreign firms, individuals or organizations, as well as to foreign governments."

"So I understand."

"It also applies, here, both to aliens and to citizens. Are you a citizen of the United States?"

"I am. I was born in this country."

"You were at one time an agent of the Austrian government?"

"Briefly, as a boy. Not here, abroad. I quit."

"And joined the Montenegrin army?"

"Later, but still a boy. I then believed that all misguided or cruel people should be shot, and I shot some. I starved to death in 1916."

The G-man looked startled. "I beg your pardon?"

"I said I starved to death. When the Austrians came and we fought machine guns with fingernails. Logically I was dead; a man can't live on dry grass.

Actually I went on breathing. When the United States entered the war and I walked six hundred miles to join the A. E. F., I ate again. When it ended I returned to the Balkans, shed another illusion, and came back to America."

"*Hvala Bogu,*" I put in brightly.

Stahl, startled again, shot me a glance. "I beg your pardon? Are you a Montenegrin?"

"Nope. Pure Ohio. The ejaculation was involuntary."

Wolfe, ignoring me, went on, "I would like to say, Mr. Stahl, that my temperament would incline me to resent and resist an attempt by any individual to inquire into my personal history or affairs, but I do not regard you as an individual. Naturally. You represent the Federal government. You are, in effect, America itself sitting in my office wanting to know something about me, and I am so acutely grateful to my native country for the decencies it still manages to preserve . . . by the way, would you care for a glass of American beer?"

"No, thank you."

Wolfe pushed the button and leaned back. He grunted. "To your question, sir: I represent no foreign principal, firm, individual, organization, dictator, or government. Occasionally I pursue inquiries here, professionally as a detective, on requests from Europe, chiefly from Mr. Ethelbert Hitchcock of London, an English confrere, as he does there for me. I am pursuing none at present. I am not an agent of Mr. Hitchcock or of anyone else."

"I see," Stahl sounded open to conviction. "That's definite enough. But your early experiences in Europe . . . may I ask . . . do you know a Prince Donevitch?"

"I knew him long ago. He's getting ready to die, I believe, in Paris."

"I don't mean him. Isn't there another one?"

"There is. Old Peter's nephew. Prince Stefan Donevitch. I believe he lives in Zagreb. When I was there in 1916 he was a six-year-old boy."

"Have you communicated with him recently?"

"No. I never have."

"Have you sent money to him or to anyone or any organization for him—or the cause he represents?"

"No, sir."

"You do make remittances to Europe, don't you?"

"I do." Wolfe grimaced. "From my own funds, earned at my trade. I have contributed to the Loyalists in Spain. I send money occasionally to the—translated, it is the League of Yugoslavian Youth. Prince Stefan Donevitch assuredly has no connection with that."

"I wouldn't know. What about your wife? Weren't you married?"

"No. Married? No. That was what—" Wolfe stirred, as under restraint, in his chair. "It strikes me, sir, that you are nearing the point where even a grateful American might tell you to go to the devil."

I put in emphatically, "I know damn well I would, and I'm only a sixty-fourth Indian."

The G-man smiled and uncrossed his legs. "I suppose," he said amiably, "you'd have no objection to putting this in the form of a signed statement. What you've told me."

"On a proper occasion, none at all."

"Good. You represent no foreign principal, directly or indirectly?"

"That is correct."

"Well, that's all we wanted to know." He got up. "At present. Thank you very much."

"You're quite welcome. Good day, sir."

I followed him out, to open the front door for America and make sure he was on the proper side of it when it was closed again. Wolfe could get sentimental about it if he wanted to, but I don't like any stranger nosing around my private affairs, let alone a nation of 130 million people. When I returned to the office he was sitting back with his eyes closed.

"You see what happens," I told him bitterly. "Just because you rake in two fat fees and the bank account is momentarily bloated, in the space of three weeks you refuse nine cases. Not counting the poor little immigrant girl with a friend who likes diamonds. You refuse to investigate anything for anybody. Then what happens? America gets suspicious because it's un-American not to make all the money you can, and sicks a Senior G-man on you, and now, by God, you're going to have to investigate yourself! You don't need—"

"Archie. Shut up." His eyes opened. "You're a liar. Since when have you been a sixty-fourth Indian?"

Before I could parry his counterattack Fritz appeared to announce lunch. I knew it was to be warmed-over duck scraps, so I was off at the gun.

Chapter 2

During meals Wolfe ordinarily excludes business not only from his conversation but also from his mind. But that day it appeared that his thoughts were straying from the food, though I didn't see how they could have been on business, since there was none on hand. He did his share of demolition to the remains of three ducks—his old friend Marko Vukčić had dined with us the day before—but there was an air of absent-mindedness in his ardor as he tore the backbones apart and scraped the juicy shreds off with his gleaming white teeth. It somewhat prolonged the operations, so that it was after two o'clock when we finished with the coffee and waddled back to the office. That is, he waddled. I strode.

Then, instead of resuming with the catalogues or playing with some other of his toys, he leaned back and clasped his hands over the duck repository and shut his eyes. It wasn't a coma, for several times during the hour he sat there I saw his lips push in and out, so I knew he was hard at work on something.

Suddenly he spoke.

"Archie. What made you say that girl wanted to borrow a book?"

So he hadn't been able to get his mind off of Montenegrin females. I waved a hand. "Persiflage. Chaff."

"No. You said she asked if I had read it."

"Yes, sir."

"And if I study it."

"Yes, sir."

"And are you reading it."

"Yes, sir."

He nearly opened his eyes. "Did it occur to you that she was finding out if either of us would be apt to look at that book in the immediate future?"

"No, sir. My mind was occupied. I was sitting down and she was standing in front of me and I was thinking about her curves."

"That is not thought. Those nerves are in the spinal column, not the brain. You said it was *United Yugoslavia* by Henderson."

"Yes, sir."

"Where was it when you returned to the office?"

"On the shelf where it belongs. She had put it back herself. For a Monteneg—"

"Get it, please."

I crossed the room and got it down and took it to him. He rubbed the cover caressingly with his palm, as he always did with a book, and then turned it with its front edge facing him, squeezed it tight shut and held it for a moment, and suddenly released the pressure. Then he opened it around the middle and took out a piece of paper that was there between the leaves. The paper was folded, and he unfolded it and started reading it. I sat down and set my teeth on my lip to hold in what might otherwise have come out. I set them hard.

"Indeed," Wolfe said. "Shall I read it to you?"

"Oh, please do, yes, sir."

He began an incoherent jabber and splutter that didn't even sound human. I knew he expected me to butt in with an outcry, so I set my teeth again. When he had finished I grinned at him.

"Okay," I said, "but why couldn't she tell me to my face how handsome and seductive I was and so on instead of writing it down and sticking it in that book. Especially that last—"

"And especially writing it in Serbo-Croat. Do you speak Serbo-Croat, Archie?"

"No."

"Then I'll translate. It's dated at Zagreb, 20th August, 1938, and bears the Donevitch crest. It says, roughly, 'The bearer of these presents, my wife, the Princess Vladanka Donevitch, is hereby empowered without reservation to talk and act in my name, and attach my name and honor by her signature, which appears herewith below my own, in all financial and political matters and claims pertaining to me and to the Donevitch dynasty, with particular reference to Bosnian forest concessions and to the disposal of certain credits at present in the care of Barrett & De Russy, bankers of New York. I bespeak for her loyalty from those who owe it, and co-operation from those whose interests ride with mine.'"

Wolfe folded the paper and imprisoned it under his palm. "It is signed Stefan Donevitch and Vladanka Donevitch. The signatures are attested."

"Good." I glared at him. "He even spent two bits on a notary. Let's take one thing at a time. How did you know that thing was in that book?"

"I didn't know it. But her questioning you—"

"Sure. Your curiosity got aroused. Check that off.

Do you mean to say that that girl is a Balkan princess?"

"I don't know. Stefan married only three years ago. I got that from this book. Don't badger me, Archie. I don't like this."

"What don't you like about it?"

"I like nothing about it. Of all the activities of man, international intrigue is the dirtiest. The Balkan mess, as it is today, I know only superficially, but even on the surface the maggots of corruption may be seen writhing. The regent who rules Yugoslavia deviously courts the friendship of certain nations. He is a Karageorgevitch. Prince Stefan, the head of the Donevitch clan now that old Peter is dying, is being used by certain other nations, and he is using them for his own ambition. And now look at this!" He slapped the paper with his palm. "They bring this to America! If it could be used to destroy them all, I would use it!"

He puffed. "Bah!" He made a gesture of spitting, which I had seen him do only once before in the years I had lived under his roof. "Pfui! Bosnian forest concessions from a Donevitch! As soon as I saw that girl and heard her voice I knew the devil was around. Confound them for crossing the ocean and stepping on this shore—confound her for coming here, here to my office, and soiling one of my books with this—this nauseous—"

"Hold it," I cautioned him. "Breathe deep three times. How do you know she put it there? It's been months since you've had that book down, and maybe somebody—"

"Who? When?"

"Lord, I don't know. Vukčić is a Montenegrin—"

"Gibberish."

I waved a hand. "All right, then the immigrant girl

did it, and she's either an obnoxious Balkan princess or she's not, and so what and why? Is she in cahoots with evil forces in America, and will Mr. Stahl come back with a search warrant and find it and throw you in the coop? Is it a plant? Or did she swipe it from the princess and come here to cache it—"

"Archie."

"Yes, sir."

"Address an envelope to Miss Carla Lovchen in care of the Nikola Miltan studio—get the address from the phone book. Put this thing in it and mail it at once. I don't want it here. I'll have nothing to do with it. I don't want—I send money to those young people over there because I know it's hard for even a Montenegrin to be brave on an empty stomach, but it's their stable now, not mine, and they'll have to clean it out. This is the first time—well, Fritz?"

Fritz Brenner, entering, advanced his three paces and announced:

"A young lady to see you, sir. Miss Carla Lovchen."

I made a noise. Wolfe blinked at him.

Fritz held to his formal stance, waiting. He had to wait a full two minutes, for Wolfe sat motionless, his lips puckered up, his forehead creased with a frown. Finally:

"Where is she?"

"In the front room, sir. I always think—"

"Shut that door and come here."

Fritz obeyed and was standing by the desk. Wolfe turned to me: "Address an envelope to Saul Panzer at his home and put a stamp on it."

I elevated the typewriter and followed instructions. As I put the stamp in the corner I inquired, "Registered or special?"

"No. Neither. That's another point for America,

mail gets delivered intact and promptly. Let me have
it." He inserted the folded paper in the envelope,
licked the flap and pressed it down. "Here, Fritz, go to
the box at the corner and drop it in. Immediately."

"The young lady—"

"We'll attend to her."

Fritz departed. Wolfe cocked an ear and waited
until the sound of the street door opening and closing
reached us, and then told me, "Remember to phone
Saul and tell him to expect that envelope and to take
care of it." He slid *United Yugoslavia* across the desk.
"Put this away before you bring her in."

I returned the book to its place on the shelf and
then went to the front room for her. "This way, please.
Sorry you had to wait." As I stood back to let her
precede me into the office, I inspected her build and
swing and the set of her head from the fresh viewpoint
of the princess theory, but the first strong impression
I had had of her was the way she said pliz, and to me
she was still an immigrant girl and in my opinion
always would be. Anyway, judging from various pictures of princesses I had seen, from brats on up, I was
inclined to give her the benefit of the doubt and
assume that she had swiped that paper from the
rightful owner.

She thanked me for the chair and I returned to my
own. I had a notion to warn her to lay off on the *hvala
Bogu* stuff, but decided that Wolfe was in no mood for
the light touch. He was upright in his chair with his
eyes narrowed at her.

"I sent you a message this morning, Miss
Lovchen," he said dryly, "by Mr. Goodwin, that I
would be unable to help you out in your trouble. Your
friend's trouble."

She nodded. "I got it. I was disappointed, very

much, because we're from Yugoslavia and we know you have been there, and we're strangers and there was no one else to go to." She kept the lashes up, her dark eyes at him straight. "I told Neya—my friend— and she was disappointed too. It is a very extremely serious trouble. We talked it over, and there is only one thing to do, and that is you must get her out of it."

"No." Wolfe was still dry, and positive. "I can't engage to do that. But I would like to ask—"

"Pliz!" She snapped it out. "It must be done quick now, because they will all be there at five o'clock to settle it, and that man is not only an American fool, he is the kind of man who would simply make trouble anywhere. And somehow there is a terrible mistake. There is no one we can go to but you. So we talked it over and I said the only thing to do is to tell you the very good reason why you must help her, and she agreed to it because she had to. The reason is that my friend, Neya Tormic, is your daughter."

Wolfe's eyes popped open to a new record. Not liking the sight of that, I transferred my astonished stare to the girl.

Wolfe exploded: "My daughter? What's this flummery?"

"She is your daughter."

"My daugh—" Wolfe was speechless. He found a piece of his voice:

"You said her name is Tormic."

"I told you her name in America is Neya Tormic just as mine is Carla Lovchen."

Wolfe, erect, was glaring at her. She glared back. They stayed that way.

Wolfe blurted, "I don't believe it. It's flummery. My daughter disappeared. I have no daughter."

"You haven't seen her since she was three years old. Have you?"

"No."

"You should. Now you will. She's very good-looking." She opened her handbag and fished in it. "I suspected you wouldn't want to believe me, so I got this from Neya and brought it along. Here." She reached to hand him a paper. "There is your name where you signed it . . ."

She went on talking. Wolfe was scowling at the paper. He went over it slowly and carefully, holding it at an angle for better light from the window. His jaw was clamped. I watched him and listened to her. What with the paper hid in his book and now this, it began to look as if the Montenegrin female situation held great promise.

He finished inspecting the thing, folded it with deliberation, and stuck it in his pocket.

Miss Lovchen extended a hand. "No, you must give it back. I must return it to Neya. Unless you take it to her yourself?"

Wolfe regarded her. He grunted. "I don't know anything about this. The paper's all right. That is my signature. It belonged to that girl. It still does, if she lives. How do I know it wasn't stolen?"

"For what?" She shrugged. "You're suspicious beyond anything to be expected. Stolen to be brought across the ocean for what? To have an effect on you, here in America? No, you are famous, but not as famous as all that. It was not stolen from her. She sent me to show it to you and to tell you. She is in trouble!" Her eyes flashed at him. "What are you in your opinion, a rock on Durmitor for a goat to stand on? You will see your grown daughter for the first time perhaps in a jail?"

"I don't know. I am not in my opinion a rock. Neither am I a gull. I couldn't find that girl when I went back to Yugoslavia to look for her. I don't know her."

"But your America will know her! The daughter of Nero Wolfe! In jail for stealing! Only she didn't steal! She is no thief!" She sprang up and put her hands on his desk and leaned across at him. "Pfui!" She sat down again and flashed her eyes at me to let me know she was making no exceptions. I winked at her. Admitting the princess theory and counting me as a peasant, I suppose it was out of character.

Wolfe sighed, long and deep. There was a silence during which I could hear both of them breathing. At length he muttered:

"It's preposterous. Grotesque. No matter how many tricks you learn, life knows a better one. I've put many people in jail, and kept many out. Now this. Archie, your notebook. Miss Lovchen, please give Mr. Goodwin the details of this trouble your friend had got into." He leaned back and shut his eyes.

She told it and I put it down. It looked to me, as it unfolded, as if somebody's confidence in someone's daughter might turn out to be misplaced. The two girls taught both dancing and fencing at Nikola Milt-an's studio on East 48th Street. It was an exclusive joint with a pedigreed clientele and appropriate prices for lessons. They had got their jobs through an introduction from Donald Barrett, son of John P. Barrett of Barrett & De Russy, the bankers. Dancing lessons were given in private rooms. The salle d'armes, on the floor above, consisted of a large room and two smaller ones, and there were two locker rooms, one for men and one for women, where clients exchanged street clothes for fencing costumes.

One of the fencing pupils was a man named Nat Driscoll. She pronounced it Nawht. He was middle-aged or more and fat and rich. Yesterday afternoon he had informed Nikola Miltan that upon going to the locker room after completing his fencing lesson, which had been given by Carla Lovchen, he had seen the other female fencing instructor, namely Neya Tormic, standing by the open door of the locker, in the act of returning the coat of his street suit, on its hanger, to its hook within the locker; and that she had then closed the locker door and departed by the door to the hall. Upon inspection, to which he had proceeded as soon as possible, he had found that his gold cigarette case and wallet, the contents intact, were in the pockets where they belonged, and it was not until after he got dressed that he remembered about the diamonds, in a pillbox, which should be there too. They were gone. He had carefully explored each and every pocket. They were not there. He demanded their immediate recovery.

Miss Tormic, summoned by Nikola Miltan, denied any knowledge of the diamonds, and further denied that she had opened Mr. Driscoll's locker or touched his clothing. The accusation, she said, was outrageous, infamous, and false. She had not been in the locker room. Had she been in the locker room for any conceivable purpose, it would not have been to go through men's clothes. Had she gone through a man's clothes, it would not have been Mr. Driscoll's clothes; it was beyond the bounds of possibility that she should have the faintest interest in the contents of Mr. Driscoll's pockets. She had been justly and somewhat violently indignant.

She had submitted to a search of her person, performed by Jeanne Miltan, Nikola's wife. Every-

body at that time in the studio, on both floors, employees and clients alike, had been questioned by Miltan,
and a search of the premises conducted. Driscoll
stated positively he had seen Neya Tormic's face, from
the side, as she stood by the locker, and furthermore
that she was wearing her fencing costume. Neya and
Carla had both insisted that they be searched again
before leaving the studio to go home. Miltan was half
frantic at the threat of disgrace to the reputation of his
place and had successfully resisted Driscoll's demand
that the police be called. In the morning—this day—he
had spent two hours pleading with Neya to tell where
the diamonds were, what she had done with them, to
whom she had given them, who was her accomplice,
and had met with the disdain which his assumption
deserved. In a desperate effort to solve the affair
without police or publicity, he had arranged for everyone concerned, all who had been on the premises
yesterday afternoon, to meet in his office at five
o'clock today. In Neya Tormic's presence he had told
his wife that he would engage the services of Nero
Wolfe; and Neya, knowing Nero Wolfe to be her father,
had promptly stated that he would be present in her
behalf. But Neya had a strong disinclination to reveal
her identity to her father, for reasons understandable
to him, and therefore Carla, hotfooting it for Wolfe's
office, had been instructed not to divulge it.

That was the crop. Miss Lovchen, looking at her
wrist and stating that it was five minutes to four,
added that Wolfe must come immediately. Fast.

Without moving, even his eyelids, Wolfe growled:

"Why didn't Mr. Driscoll challenge Miss Tormic on
the spot, seeing her with his coat?"

"He was naked. He came from the shower bath."

"Is he too fat to be seen even at the risk of losing diamonds?"

"He says he is modest. He also says he was too surprised to speak, and she moved rapidly and went away at once. Then his wallet and cigarette case were there, and he forgot about the diamonds until he was dressed. He is not nearly as fat as you are."

"I wouldn't expect him to be. Do the lockers have keys?"

"Yes, but there is much carelessness. The keys lie around. That part is very confused."

"You say Miss Tormic did not steal the diamonds?"

"I do say that. Never did she."

"Did she take something else from Mr. Driscoll's clothing? Something he fails to mention? Letters, papers, even a piece of candy perhaps?"

"Nothing. Nothing at all."

"Did she go to the locker room?"

"What would she go there for?"

"I don't know. Did she?"

"No."

"Fantastic." Wolfe's eyes threatened to open. "How long have you known she is my daughter?"

"All my life. I have been . . . her friend, very close. I knew about you—about your—I knew your name."

"About my deplorable intransigence, you would say." Wolfe's tone was suddenly savage. "Ha! You juicy girls with your busts swelling with ardor for the heroics of past centuries! Pah! Do the rats still gather crumbs from under the Donevitch table?"

"We are—" Her chin went up and her eyes showed fire. "They preserve honor! And they will share glory!"

"They will someday share obloquy. Blind and selfish fools. Are you a Donevitch?"

"No." Her bust was swelling, but not apparently with ardor.

"What's your name?"

"Carla Lovchen."

"What's your name at home?"

"I am not at home now." She flung out a hand impatiently. "What is all this? All this about me? Do you realize what I have told you about Neya? About your daughter? Does it help for you to sit there and sneer? I tell you, you must do this at once or there will be the police!"

Wolfe sat up. I was thinking it was about time. The clock on the wall said two minutes past four, and his daily routine, which included an afternoon session to the plant rooms from four until six, was supposed to be unalterable by fire, flood or murder. I was flabbergasted when, although he glanced at the clock, he merely sat up straight.

But his tone was brisk. "Archie, please conduct Miss Lovchen to the front room and return for instructions."

She started to sputter. "But there's no—"

"Please." He was curt. "If I'm to do this let me do it. Don't waste time. Go with Mr. Goodwin."

I was off and she followed. I deposited her in front and shut the door on her, and, returning to the office, shut that one too.

Wolfe said, "I'm late. This won't do. There's no point in getting a line on Mr. Driscoll or anyone else until you've been there and reported. I shall have to phone Mr. Hitchcock in London before I go upstairs. The book with his private number, please."

I got it from the safe and gave it to him.

"Thank you. Go up there with her. You will see Miss Tormic. The assumption, from this document, is that she has the right to bear my name. If so, I reject the possibility that she stole diamonds from a man's coat. Start from that."

"She says she wants the document back."

"I'll keep it for the present. Apparently you will encounter a single yes and a single no in contradiction. Neglect nothing and no one. Nikola Miltan himself is from the peninsula, South Serbia, old Macedonia. Look at Miss Tormic and talk to her. Your first concern is the rumpus about the diamonds. Your second is that paper which Miss Lovchen hid in my book. If you can't resolve the contradiction about the diamonds and Mr. Driscoll insists on the police, bring him here to me."

"Oh, sure. How and in how many pieces?"

"Bring him. You're good at that."

"Much obliged ever so much. But the fact is I guess you'd better pay me off. I'm resigning as of this moment."

"Resigning from what?"

"You. My job."

"Rubbish."

"No, boss, really. You told the G-man you have never married. Yet you have a daughter. Well—" I shrugged. "I'm not a prude, but there are limits—"

"Don't jabber. Go on up there. She was an orphan and I adopted her."

I nodded skeptically. "That's a good trick, but pretty transparent. What do you think my mother would say—" But I saw his whole face tighten and knew I was getting close to out-of-bounds, so I asked casually, "That's all?"

"That's all."

I got my hat and coat from the hall, and the immigrant princess from the parlor, and went out to the roadster, parked at the curb. As I shifted into high, headed for Park Avenue, I reflected that Wolfe was prepared to go to almost any length to protect his family, since he was at that moment spending twenty bucks on a transatlantic phone call to London, though I didn't see how that was going to help things any.

Chapter 3

Up to a certain point, the five o'clock gathering at Nikola Miltan's studio for some old-fashioned fun with the game of diamonds, diamonds, who's got the diamonds, was a howling farce. Therefore, I admit, it took on a different aspect.

The swank of the place was more real than apparent. There was nothing shabby about it, but it didn't give you an impression of being dolled up to impress the customers. I trailed around after Carla in her effort to locate Neya, and so got a look. It was one of the old four-story houses. On the ground floor were a reception room and a large office and a couple of small ones; one flight up, a long hall with a gray carpet, with doors leading into the private rooms for dancing lessons; two flights, the salle d'armes, with two medium-sized rooms, one big one, and the showers and locker rooms; and at the top, living quarters for Miltan and his wife. Those I didn't see, then. Neya was finally flushed in the women's locker room. Carla brought her out to where I was waiting in the hall and introduced me, and we shook hands. Neya Tormic said:

"Can you do something about this awful thing, Mr. Goodwin? The awful lie that man tells? Can you? You must! I was hoping that Nero Wolfe . . . my father . . ."

Her voice had a foreign purr in it, but she pronounced words a little better than Carla. God knows she didn't look anything like Nero Wolfe, but of course a girl that looked like him would be something that you would either pass up entirely or pay a dime to look at in a side show. And then—um—he had adopted her. Her eyes were as black as Carla's and she was about the same height, an inch over medium, but her chin, in fact her whole face, went more to a point, and the whole idea of her, the way she talked and stood and looked at you, was a queer combination of come-hither and don't-touch-me. Having known her father a long while, I suppose I gave her the preliminary once-over with more interest than any other female I had ever met, and my first verdict was that she had real quality, both of mind and of matter, but that a definite judgment would have to wait for further analysis. She noticed me taking in her costume, a green robe, belted and carelessly closed in front, showing underneath a white canvas blouse and slacks, with gym shoes and rolled-up socks.

"I was giving a lesson," she said. "Miltan wanted me to. He doesn't want any fuss. Nobody does but that fool Driscoll. A liar like that—we would know how to deal with him in my country. Carla tells me that he—that my father has been told about me, and of course you have too. I do not wish anyone else to know. Why didn't he come?"

"Nero Wolfe? Bad case of pernicious inertia. He never goes anywhere anytime for anybody."

"I am his adopted daughter."

"So I understand. And you've been here in New

York a couple of months and his address is in the phone book."

"He abandoned me. I was taught to hate him. I had no wish—"

"Until you got into trouble. I got the impression that you abandoned him at the age of three. But let's skip that, I was sent here to keep you out of jail and time's short. You look intelligent enough to know that I've got to have the truth and all of it. What were you doing with Driscoll's coat?"

Her chin went up and her eyes withered me. "Nothing. I didn't touch his coat."

"What were you doing in the men's locker room?"

"I wasn't there."

"Is there any other girl around that looks like you?"

"No. Not enough—no."

"Not enough for Driscoll to see her and think she was you?"

"No."

"What were you doing yesterday afternoon at the time Driscoll says he saw you with his coat?"

"I was giving Mr. Ludlow a lesson."

"Fencing?"

"Yes, épée."

"In the large room?"

"No, the small one at the end."

"Who is Mr. Ludlow?"

"He is a man who comes to take lessons with the épée."

"Are you sure you were with him at the time Driscoll says he saw you frisking his coat?"

"Yes. Mr. Driscoll went to Miltan at twenty minutes to five. He said it had taken him about fifteen minutes to dress. I began the lesson with Mr. Ludlow at four o'clock, and we were still there when Miltan sent for me."

"And you didn't leave that room during that time?"

"No, I did not."

Carla Lovchen put in, "But Neya! Do you forget that Belinda Reade says she saw you outside, in the hall, a little before half past four?"

"She lies," Neya said calmly.

"But the man that was with her saw you too!"

"He also lies."

My God, I thought, it's a good thing Wolfe isn't here to see his daughter put on an exhibition like this. It looked very much as if the family reunion would take place in jail.

"How about Ludlow?" I demanded. "Does he lie too?"

She hesitated, her brow wrinkling, and before she got her answer ready another voice broke in. It was a male voice, and its owner had appeared from around the corner which led to the stairs. He was about my age and size, with a good pair of light-colored eyes, and a gray suit of a distinctive weave hung on him in a way that made it obvious the fit had not been managed by waving a piece of chalk at a stock job.

"I was looking for you." He came up to us, with a conventional smile. "Miltan wants you in the office. This ridiculous affair."

Carla Lovchen said, "Mr. Ludlow, this is Mr. Goodwin."

We shook, and I met his eyes and liked them, not on account of any candor or friendliness, but because they showed sense.

I inquired, "Ludlow?"

"Right. Percy Ludlow."

"Miss Tormic gave you a fencing lesson yesterday afternoon?"

"That's right."

"Then you're the man I want to see. Was she with you continuously from four o'clock till half past?"

His brow went up and he smiled. "Well, really. All I know about you is that your name is Goodwin."

"I represent Miss Tormic. She has engaged Nero Wolfe. I'm his assistant."

He glanced at her and caught her nod. "Well! Nero Wolfe? That ought to do it. I was told that Miss Tormic said yesterday that she was with me continuously."

"Yeah. What do you say?"

His brow went up again. "I couldn't very well call Miss Tormic a liar. Could I? Let's go down to the office. Driscoll isn't there yet, but he should be, any minute—"

"Then she was with you? You realize that in that case she can't possibly be held on Driscoll's charge?"

"Oh, yes, I quite realize that. But unfortunately there are those two people who claim to have seen her in the hall." He pointed. "Right there, not ten feet from the door of the locker room. And of course Driscoll too."

He was moving. I obstructed him. "Look here, Mr. Ludlow, if you'll assure me that you'll stick to it—"

"My dear chap! Assure you? This sort of thing must be handled—anyhow, a dozen or more people have been made acquainted with this charge against Miss Tormic, and whatever is said they should hear. To clear it up, you know."

They were all moving, for the stairs, and I couldn't obstruct all of them, so I went with the current. It was so loony that it dazed me. Carla looked worried and Ludlow looked bland. As for Neya, her attitude could have come only from the sublime assurance of innocence or the sublime asininity of a nincompoop, or mix it yourself. Here she had a witness who might have been wheedled into standing fast with a class A alibi and she wasn't even bothering to toss him a suggestion. As I trailed them downstairs and entered the office with them, I was trying to figure out a method of enticing Driscoll down to 35th Street, for it certainly seemed likely it would come to that.

The office was the big room at the rear of the ground floor. There was a large red carpet and a couple of desks, and chairs scattered around. The walls were decorated with pictures of people dancing and fencing, or standing holding a sticker, with a large one of Miltan in some kind of a uniform, and with swords and daggers hanging here and there. I knew the picture was Miltan because Carla Lovchen took me across and introduced me to him and his wife. He was small and thin, next door to a runt, but wiry-looking, and had black eyes and hair and a moustache which pointed due east and west. He looked and acted harassed, and as soon as he shook hands with me darted off somewhere. His wife, in spite of her New York clothes and her 1938 hair-do, looked like one of those colored pictures in the *National Geographic* entitled "Peasant Woman of Wczibrrcy Leading a Bear to Church." At that, she was handsome if you like the type, and she had shrewd eyes.

I went and stood by a glass cabinet which displayed an assortment of curios and implements, among them a long thin rapier with no edge and a blunt point which apparently wasn't a rapier, since a card leaning against it said "This épée was used by Nikola Miltan at Paris in 1931 in winning the International Championship." I looked around. He was across the room, chinning with a broad-shouldered six-footer maybe thirty years old, with a slightly pushed-in nose and a vacant look to go with it. I looked further. If by chance Wolfe's long lost daughter hadn't pinched Driscoll's diamonds, it was probable that the person who had was among those present. Carla Lovchen's voice came, beside me:

"But you . . . you aren't doing anything."

I shrugged. "Nothing I can do. Not right now. What's Miltan waiting for?"

"Mr. Driscoll isn't here yet."

"Did he say he would be here?"

"Of course he did. He only agreed to wait until now to go to the police."

"Who's that guy Miltan's talking to?"

She looked. "His name is Gill. He's a dancing client. It was he who was with Belinda Reade yesterday when they saw Neya in the hall. They say they did."

"Which one's Belinda Reade?"

"Over there standing by a chair. The beautiful one, with hair like yellow amber, talking to the young man."

"Check. Baby doll with a new silk dress and pipe the earrings. Not to mention the young man. I seem to recognize him from perhaps the movies. Who is he?"

"Donald Barrett."

"The son of John P. Barrett of Barrett & De Russy, who got you girls a job here?"

"Yes."

"Who are those other girls?"

"Well . . . the three in the corner, and the one sitting by the end of the desk, teach dancing. That one talking now with Mrs. Miltan is Zorka."

I boosted the brows. "Zorka?"

"Yes, the famous couturière. She charges four hundred dollars for a dress. That would be over twenty thousand dinars."

"She looks like a picture in our Bible at home of the dame that cut off Samson's hair, I forget her name, but it wasn't Zorka. Does she sell diamonds at her place?"

"I don't know."

"She wouldn't those, anyway. Who's the chinless wonder with his—hold it. Miltan's going to make a speech."

The épée champion, with Percy Ludlow standing beside him, was in the middle of the room trying to collect eyes. Some of them didn't get it and he claimed their attention by clapping his hands. Two of them went on talking and his wife shushed them.

"If you please." He sounded as harassed as he looked. "Ladies and gentlemen. If you please. Mr. Driscoll has not arrived. It is very disagreeable, asking you to wait. He should be here. Mr. Ludlow has something to say."

Percy Ludlow looked around at the faces with complete aplomb. "Well," he observed in a conversational tone, "really I don't quite see that we should hang around waiting for Driscoll. It's his row, you know. I've an explanation to make that I'd like you all to hear, because all of you know of Driscoll's absurd accusation regarding Miss Tormic. You'll understand it better if you'll observe the clothes I'm wearing. This is the suit I had on yesterday. Didn't any of you notice anything peculiar about it?"

"Certainly," said a voice promptly, fluttering the *r* like a moth on a marathon. "I did."

He smiled at her. "What did you notice, Madame Zorka?"

"I noticed that the material is of the same pattern, perfectly, as the one Mr. Driscoll was wearing."

Two additional female voices chimed in simultaneously, "So did I," and other voices murmured.

Ludlow nodded. "Apparently Driscoll agrees with me on tailors." His tone sounded as if there were something about that faintly deplorable. "The fabric is identical. I wondered that none of you mentioned it yesterday. Perhaps you did, but not to me. Of course the coincidence explains why, when Miss Tormic went to my locker to get my cigarettes from my coat, and Driscoll saw her, he thought the coat was his own. My locker adjoined his."

There was a round of ejaculations. Eyes moved from his face to that of Neya Tormic and back again. I felt Carla Lovchen's fingers gripping my elbow, but I didn't react because I was trying to keep my brain cleared for action.

Ludlow continued in the same easy tone, "Yesterday when Miss Tormic was suddenly confronted with Driscoll's ugly accusation, naturally she was flustered. Impulsively and perhaps foolishly, she denied having been in the locker room. Hearing that denial, I was a little flustered myself. It would have produced a most unfortunate impression if I had contradicted her on the spot, so I temporized and confirmed her statement that she had been with me continuously in the end room. But as it turned out, that was no go. Driscoll was positive that it was Miss Tormic he had seen with his coat. Miss Reade and Mr. Gill both declared that they had seen her in the hall near the door of the locker room shortly prior to four thirty. So it was clear that the only thing for it was the truth, which is that while we were fencing yesterday the strap of my pad broke and I had to change it, and we felt like a cigarette and found that we had none, and while I was changing the pad she took my key and went to the locker room for my cigarettes."

I had left his face and was concentrating on Neya's, but I couldn't read it. It wasn't alarmed nor angry nor pleased; I would have said it was more puzzled than anything else; but that seemed unlikely, so I scored myself zero. There was a buzz around the room which stopped when Miltan remarked, more to space than to any audience, "So! So she was there!"

Ludlow nodded negligently. "Oh, yes, she was there, but it was my coat she had, not Driscoll's. No doubt of it, because she returned with my cigarette case and lighter. We had a few puffs together, and we were fencing again when word came that Miltan wished to see Miss Tormic—"

He stopped, and lost his audience. The door had opened, and two men entered. The one in front was a gray-haired guy with a full cargo of dignity and an air that invited respect, and behind him, practically hiding behind him, was a plump specimen about fifty-one years old with thick lips and bald eyebrows. They came on in and Miltan met them.

"We've been waiting for you, Mr. Driscoll—"

"I'm sorry," the plump one stammered, edging around. "Very sorry . . . unh . . . this is Mr. Thompson, my lawyer—Mr. Miltan . . ."

As the gray-haired one extended a hand for the shake he conceded the point without reservation or qualification. "I am Mr. Driscoll's counsel. I thought it best to come personally—this regrettable affair—extremely regrettable—will you kindly introduce me to Miss Tormic? If you will be so good . . ."

That was done by Miltan, who looked a little bewildered. The lawyer's bow was courteous and respectful, as was his verbal acknowledgement; Neya stood motionless and silent. He turned. "These people—are these the persons whom Mr. Driscoll—before whom he accused Miss Tormic—"

Miltan nodded. "We've been waiting for him, to—"

"I know. We're late. My client was reluctant to

come, and I had to persuade him that his presence was necessary. Miss Tormic, what I have to say is addressed primarily to you, but these others should hear it—in fact, they must hear it, in justice to you. First for the facts. When Mr. Driscoll left his home yesterday morning he had in his pocket a pillbox containing diamonds which he intended to take to a jeweler to be set in a bracelet. From his office he phoned the jeweler and discussed the matter. His secretary took the box of diamonds to arrange for their delivery. They are at the jeweler's now. Here, later, Mr. Driscoll, lamentably and inexcusably, but innocently, forgot that his secretary—"

A clatter of comment from all corners interrupted him. He smiled at Neya but got nothing in return. Driscoll had a handkerchief out, wiping his brow, trying to find a place to look without meeting a pair of eyes. Miltan sputtered:

"Do you mean to say that this infamous—this irresponsible—"

"Please!" The lawyer had a hand up. "Please let me finish. Mr. Driscoll's lapse of memory was inexcusable. But he was honestly convinced that he had seen Miss Tormic with his coat—"

"It was my coat," Ludlow snapped. "Of the same pattern. I have it on."

"I see. Well. That explains that. Was it in the same locker?"

"The one adjoining." Ludlow was severe. "But Mr. Driscoll should know that before making a grave accusation—"

"Certainly he should." The lawyer conceded everything again. "Even the coincidence of the coats is no excuse for him. That's why I insisted on his coming, to make his apology to Miss Tormic in the presence of all of you. His reluctance is understandable. He is extremely embarrassed and humiliated." He eyed his client. "Well?"

Driscoll, gripping his handkerchief, faced Neya Tormic. "I apologize," he mumbled. "I'm damn sorry." The mumble became abruptly and surprisingly an outraged roar. "Of course I'm sorry, damn it!"

Someone giggled. Nikola Miltan said grimly, "You certainly should be sorry. It might have been disastrous, both for Miss Tormic and for me."

"I know it. I've said I'm sorry and I am."

The lawyer put in smoothly and sweetly, "I hope, Miss Tormic . . . may we hope for an expression from you—of forgiveness? Or . . . er . . . quittance?" He took an envelope from his pocket. "In fact, I thought it would be as well for you to have Mr. Driscoll's written apology to support his oral one, so I brought it along"—he got a paper from the envelope—"and I brought also a quittance, just an informal sentence or two, which I'm sure you will want to sign for him in return—"

"Just a minute." It was me entering on my cue. "I represent Miss Tormic."

The way he went on guard like lightning, facially, was a treat. He demanded, "Who are you, sir? A lawyer?"

"Nope, I'm not a lawyer, but I speak English and I represent Miss Tormic and we're not before a court. She isn't signing anything."

"But my dear sir, why not? Merely an informal—"

"That's the trouble, it's too informal. For instance, what if Miltan here gets sore about this fracas, though it's not her fault, and she loses her job? Or what if this thing had been turned loose around town and she can't catch up with it? Nothing doing on the quittance."

"I have no intention," Miltan put in, "of dismissing Miss Tormic. But I agree that it is not necessary for her to sign anything. I am quite sure she will have no desire to make trouble for Mr. Driscoll." He looked at her.

She spoke for the first time. "No, certainly." She sounded darned unconcerned for a girl who had just escaped being thrown in the hoosegow as a sneak thief. Almost indifferent, as if her mind was on something else. "I will make no trouble."

The lawyer pounced on her. "Then, Miss Tormic, if you feel that way, surely you have no objection to signing—"

"Damn it, let her alone!" It was his own client tripping him up. Driscoll glared at him. "Damn a lawyer anyway! If I'd had the nerve to face it, I'd have done just as well if I'd come alone!" He confronted Miltan. "Now I've apologized! I'm sorry! I'm damn sorry! I like this place. I've been overweight for years. I'm damn near fat! I've monkeyed around with exercises and health farms and damn fool games throwing a ball and riding a horse as tall as a skyscraper, and the first thing I've ever done to sweat that is any fun is what I do here! I may be a rotten fencer but I like it! I don't care whether Miss Tormic signs a paper or not, I want to be friends with Miltan!" He whirled. "Miss Lovchen! I want to be friends with you! Miss Tormic is your friend and I acted like a damn fool. I am a damn fool. Will you fence with me or won't you? I mean right now!"

Somebody snickered. People moved. The lawyer looked dignified. Carla said, "I work for Mr. Miltan. I'll follow his instructions." Miltan said something conciliatory and diplomatic, and it was apparent that Mr. Driscoll wasn't going to be deprived of his fun. I faded into the background. The chinless wonder, whose name I hadn't got, a blond guy with thin lips and an aggressive nose who stood and walked like a soldier, went up to Neya with a thin smile and said something evidently meant to be agreeable, and was followed by Donald Barrett for a similar performance. Mrs. Miltan crossed to her and patted her on the shoulder, and then she was approached by Percy Ludlow. They spoke together a minute, and she left him and headed for me.

I grinned at her. "Well, a pretty good show. I hope you didn't mind my horning in. Nero Wolfe never lets a client sign anything except a check drawn to his order."

"I didn't mind. I say good-bye. I am going to fence with Mr. Ludlow. Thank you for coming."

"Your eyes glitter."

"My eyes? They always glitter."

"Any message for your father?"

"I think—not now. No."

"You ought to run down and say hello to him."

"I will someday. Au revoir then."

"So long."

Turning to go, she bumped into the lawyer and he apologized profusely. That accomplished, he addressed me:

"Could I have your name, sir?"

I told him.

He repeated it. "Archie Goodwin. Thank you. If I may ask, in what capacity do you represent Miss Tormic?"

I was exasperated. "Look here," I said, "I am willing to stipulate that a lawyer has a right to live, and I'm aware that even when he's dead no worm will enter his coffin because if it did he'd make it sign some kind of a paper. I suppose if you don't get that thing signed you'll have a tantrum. Give it to me."

From the envelope, which he was still clutching in his hand, he extracted the document and handed it over. A glance showed me that his two informal sentences were in fact five legal-size paragraphs. I got out my pen and with a quick flourish signed on the dotted line at the bottom, "Queen Victoria."

"There," I said, and shoved it at him, and moved off before he could react, considering how dignity slows a man up.

The room was about empty. Miltan's wife was over by a desk, talking with Belinda Reade. Carla Lovchen, along with the others, had disappeared, presumably to let the rich fat man enjoy some fun. He must have been a pip of a swordsman, I reflected, as I got my hat and coat from the rack and meandered to the hall and out the street door to the sidewalk.

My wrist told me it was a quarter to six. Wolfe would still be up in the plant rooms, and he wasn't enthusiastic about being disturbed regarding business while there, but I considered that this wasn't business, properly speaking, but a family matter. So I found a drugstore with a phone booth and called the number.

"Hello, Mr. Wolfe? Mr. Goodwin speaking."

"Well?"

"Well, I'm in a drugstore at 48th and Lexington. It's all over. It was a farce in three acts. First she, meaning your daughter, seemed to be more bored than bothered. Second, a chap named Percy said she was frisking his coat for cigarettes, not Driscoll's for diamonds, which appeared to be news to her, judging from her expression. Third act, enter Driscoll with a trouble hound and a written apology. There hadn't been any diamonds in his coat. None had been stolen.

His mistake. Sorry and damn sorry. So I'm headed for home. I may add that she doesn't resemble you a particle and she is very good-look—"

"You're sure it's clear?"

"It's cleared up. Settled. I wouldn't say it's entirely clear."

"You went there with two problems. What about the second one?"

"No light on it. Not a glimmer. No chance to sniff around on it. There was a mob present, and when the meeting broke up both Balkans went off to give fencing lessons."

"Who is the man named Percy?"

"Percy Ludlow. My age, and a good deal like me—courteous, gifted, of distinguished appear—"

"You say my—she seemed to be bored. Do you mean to imply—is she stupid?"

"Oh, no. I mean it. Maybe she's a little complicated, but she's not stupid."

Silence. No talk. It lasted so long that I finally said, "Hello, you there?"

"Yes. Get her and bring her here. I want to see her."

"Yeah, I thought so. I expected that. It's a perfectly natural feeling and does you credit, but that's why I phoned, to explain that I asked her if she had a message for you and she said no, and I said she ought to drop in on you to say hello and she said she would someday, and now she's in there crossing blades with Percy—"

"Wait till she's through and bring her."

"Do you mean that?"

"I do."

"I may have to carry her or—"

He hung up, which is a trick I detest.

I went to the fountain and got a glass of grapefruit juice, and while drinking it considered persuasions to use on her short of force, but developed nothing satisfactory, and then strolled back along 48th Street to the scene of operations.

Nikola Miltan and his wife were the only ones in the office. It looked to me as if she had been headed for the door when I entered, but when I took off my hat and coat and put them on the rack, explaining that I wanted to see Miss Tormic when she was disengaged, apparently she changed her mind and decided to stick around. Miltan invited me to have a chair, and I sat down not far from the desk where he was, while his wife opened a door of the big glass cabinet and began rearranging things which didn't need it.

"I have met Mr. Nero Wolfe," Miltan offered politely.

I nodded. "So I understand."

"He is a remarkable man. Remarkable."

"Well, I know of one guy that would agree with you."

"Only one?"

"At least one. Mr. Wolfe."

"Ah. A joke." He laughed politely. "I imagine there are many others. In fact—what is it, Jeanne?"

His wife had uttered a foreign exclamation, of surprise or maybe dismay. "The *col de mort*," she told him. "It's not here. Did you remove it?"

"I did not. Of course not. It was there—I'm sure—"

He got up and trotted over to the cabinet, and I arose and wandered after him. Together they stared at a spot. He stretched, and then ducked, to inspect the other shelves.

"No," she said, "it's not there. It's gone. There is

nothing else gone. I was in favor long ago of having a lock put on—"

"But my dear." Miltan looked defensive. "There is no sensible reason that could possibly exist why anyone would want to take that *col de mort*. It was a nice curiosity, but of no particular value."

"What's a *col de mort*?" I asked.

"Oh, just a little thing."

"What kind of a little thing?"

"Oh, a little thing—look." He put an arm through the open door of the cabinet and placed a finger upon the point of an épée which was displayed there. "See? It's blunt."

"I see it is."

"Well, once in Paris, years ago, a man wanted to kill another man, and he made a little thing with a sharp point, very cleverly, which he could fit over the end of the épée." He took the weapon from the shelf and dangled it in his hand. "Then, with the thing fitted on, he made a thrust in quarte—"

He made a lunge at an imaginary victim in my neighborhood, so unexpected and incredibly swift that I side-stepped and nearly tripped myself up, and was perfectly willing to concede him the championship. Just as swiftly he was back to normal position.

"So." He smiled, and returned the weapon to its place. "A thrust in quarte gets the heart, theoretically, but that time it was not theory. A member of the police who was a friend of mine gave me the little thing as a curiosity. The newspapers called it *col de mort*. Neck—no, not neck. Collar. Collar of death. Because it fitted the end of the épée like a collar. It was amusing to have it."

"It's gone," said his wife shortly.

"I hope not gone." Miltan frowned. "There is no

reason for it to be gone. There has been enough talk of stealing around here. We will find out. We will ask people."

"I hope you find it," I told him. "It sounds cute. Speaking of asking people, I was about to ask you if it would be okay for me to have a little chat with whoever it is that cleans up the fencing rooms."

"Why . . . what for?"

"Oh, just a little chat. Who does the cleaning?"

"The porter. But I can't imagine why you should want—"

His wife interrupted him, with her eyes on me. "He wants to find out if cigarette stubs and ashes were found in the room where Miss Tormic and Mr. Ludlow were fencing yesterday," she said calmly.

I grinned at her. "If you will pardon a personal remark, Mrs. Miltan, I might have known from your eyes that you had that in you."

She merely continued to look at me.

"For my part," Miltan declared, "I don't see why you should want to know about cigarette stubs and I don't see how my wife knew you wanted to. I am slow-witted."

"Well, you have to be slow at something, to even up for your speed with that sticker. May I see the porter?"

"No," Jeanne Miltan said bluntly.

"Why not?"

"It isn't necessary. I don't know what is in your mind, but I saw you looking at Miss Tormic, you who were supposed to be here as her friend. If you want to know whether she and Mr. Ludlow were smoking cigarettes, ask her."

"I will. I intend to. But how could I do her any harm by discussing the matter with the porter?"

"I don't know. You may mean no harm. But this affair of yesterday and today is ended. It was bad. It could have turned out very badly for our business. It is a very delicate matter, the tone of a place like this. A breath may destroy it. Even if you mean no harm to Miss Tormic or to us, I shall tell the porter not to answer your questions if you do see him. I am plain-spoken. Nor may you go to the salle d'armes and inspect the pads to see if the strap of one is broken."

"What makes you think I wanted to?"

"Because I don't take you for a fool. If you were curious about the smoking, naturally you would also be curious about the broken strap."

I shrugged. "Okay. Anyhow, you used the right word. I was just curious. As you know, I'm a detective, and I guess we get into bad habits. But if you're aware of the reputation of Nero Wolfe, you're also aware that he dishes out trouble only to people who have asked for it."

She gazed at me a moment, turned and closed the sliding door of the cabinet, and then returned to me. "This morning," she said, "my husband was saying that he would engage Mr. Wolfe to investigate the disappearance of Mr. Driscoll's diamonds. Miss Tormic was present. She declared that she had engaged Nero Wolfe to act in the matter in her behalf. Shortly afterwards her friend, Miss Lovchen, asked permission to go out on an errand. It is not only detectives who are curious. I am sometimes curious. If I were to ask—"

She stopped with her mouth open, her body stiffening. Miltan spun on his heel to face the door to the hall. I did the same. The yell that had split the air sounded like something that you might expect but would certainly resent if you found yourself alone in a jungle at night.

When the second yell came all three of us were running for the door. Miltan was ahead, and in the hall he bounded for the stairs with us after him. There were no more yells, but sounds of commotion, steps and voices, came from above, and on the second-floor landing we were impeded by people who popped out of doors. Miltan was a kangaroo; I couldn't have caught him for a purse. At the top of the second flight we were brought to a halt by obstructions. A colored man was wriggling, his arms held by the chinless wonder; Nat Driscoll, in his shirt but no trousers, was jumping up and down; the two Balkans, in fencing costumes, were backed against the wall; Zorka, in gold-leaf undies and that was all, was standing apart and systematically screaming. Before Miltan could make any progress or I could get around him, I felt myself brushed aside and Jeanne Miltan was there.

"What?" she demanded in a tone that would have stopped a hurricane. "Arthur! What is it?"

The colored man stopped wriggling and rolled his eyes at her and said something I didn't get, but apparently she did, for she started off on a lope down the hall. I was close behind her and there were steps behind me. She went to the last door, the end room. It was standing open and she passed through, taking the curve without slowing down. She jerked to a halt, saw it there on the floor, and walked over to it. I was beside her. It was Percy Ludlow, lying on his side, so tilted that he would have been on his back if he hadn't been propped up by the protruding point of the épée which was sticking clean through him.

Chapter 4

Jeanne Miltan said something foreign and then stood and stared down at it with her face frozen. I heard a gasp from Miltan behind me, and other noises, and turned and saw them ganged in the doorway.

"Keep out of here," I said. "All of you."

I stooped over for a quick look and straightened up and told Jeanne Miltan, "He's dead." She said peevishly, "Of course he is." A scream came from the doorway and I yelled in that direction, "Shut up!" and went on to Mrs. Miltan, "Somebody must stay here, and the police of course, and nobody must leave."

She nodded. "You phone the police. In the office. Nikola, you stay here. I'll go down to the hall—"

She was moving, but I stopped her. "I'd rather not. You do the phoning. It's your place and you saw it first. I'll take the street door. Don't let anyone in here, Miltan."

He looked pale as he mumbled. "The *col de mort*—"

"No, it's not there. The end of the épée is bare and blunt."

"It can't be. It wouldn't go through."

"I can't help that, it's not there."

Jeanne Miltan was headed for the door and I followed her. They made way for us. Carla Lovchen was going to say something to me and I shook my head at her. The chinless wonder grabbed at my elbow and I dodged him. People had come up from the floor below and Nat Driscoll came running down the hall with his shirttails flying. At the head of the stairs I wheeled to announce: "Don't go into the end room, anybody. Ludlow's in there dead. Nobody is to leave the building." I saw Donald Barrett moving in my direction and the chinless wonder behind him. "If you two guys would herd everyone downstairs into the office it might simplify matters."

I disregarded the chatter that broke out and beat it down the steps, with Mrs. Miltan following me. On the ground floor she went to the rear, to the office, and I went to the front, to the door to the street vestibule. I was tempted to keep on going, right on through, and get to a phone and call up Nero Wolfe, but I decided it would be a bad move. If I once got out I might not get back in again, or, if I did, it would be under conditions not nearly so favorable as they were now. Guarding the portal, loyal and true, was the best bet.

From where I stood I could see the inmates straggling down the stairs. They were mostly silent and subdued, but a couple of the female dancing teachers were jabbering. Belinda Reade, the baby doll with a new silk dress, came along to me instead of turning towards the office and said in a determined voice that she had a very important appointment to keep. I told her I had one too so we were in the same boat. Donald Barrett, who was hovering in the background, approached.

"See here," he said, "I know I'm caught in this God-awful mess. Frightful stink and I'm helpless just because I'm here. But Miss Reade—after all—are you a cop?"

"No."

"Then my dear fellow, just turn your back and talk to me a moment—and she can just slip out and go to her appointment—"

"And before long a dozen dicks will slip out and trace her and haul her back. Don't be silly. Have you ever been intimate with a murder before? I guess you haven't. The worst thing you can do is make them start looking for you. They get upset. Take my advice and—just a minute, Miss Tormic."

The two Balkans were there, three paces off. The glances that passed back and forth among the four of them, in one second, obviously meant something to them but not to me. Belinda Reade said, "Come on, Don," and he followed her in the direction of the office. I surveyed the pair of girls. Carla had put a long loose thing with buttons over her fencing costume. Neya had on the green robe, carelessly closed as before, with one hand inside its folds apparently clinging to it.

"There's no time to talk," I snapped. "You may be a couple of goons. I don't know. But I'm asking you a damn straight question, and maybe your life depends on giving me a straight answer." I took Neya's eyes with mine. "You. Did you kill that man?"

"No."

"Say it again. You didn't?"

"No."

I switched to Carla. "Did you?"

"No. But I must tell you—"

"There's no time to tell me anything. That's the hell of it. But anyhow you can—there they are! Beat it! Quick, damn it!"

They scampered down the hall towards the office

and were gone by the time the cops got through the vestibule. It was a pair of flatfeet. I opened the glass-paneled door and when they were in the hall let it close again.

"Hello. Precinct?"

"No. Radio patrol. Who are you?"

"Archie Goodwin, private detective from Nero Wolfe's office, happened to be here. I was sitting on the lid. I'll keep." I pointed. "Back in the office is Mrs. Miltan and others, and two flights up is a corpse."

"God, you're snappy. Sit on the lid a little longer, will you? Come on, Bill."

They tramped to the rear. I stood and played with my fingers. In about two minutes one of them tramped down the hall again and went upstairs. In another two minutes there were fresh arrivals in the vestibule, three dicks in plain clothes, but one glance was enough to tell that they were precinct men, not homicide squad. I gave them a brief picture of it. One of them relieved me at the door, another went for the stairs, and the third went to the office and took me with him.

The radio flatfoot was there, holding his tongue between his teeth while he wrote down names in a notebook. The precinct dick spoke with him a moment and then started in on Mrs. Miltan. I sidled off and made myself unobtrusive alongside the coat rack, resisting a temptation to edge around and get in a few words of advice to the Montenegrin females before the homicide squad arrived, which was when the real fun would start. I decided not to take a chance on starting a mental process even in a precinct man. The clients and employees were scattered all around the office, some sitting, some standing, with no sound coming from them except an occasional muttering. While I was making the round of their faces, without any real expectation of seeing anything interesting or significant, I suddenly saw something right in front of my eyes that struck me as being both interesting and significant. My coat was there on the rack where I had left it, so close my elbow was touching it, and what I saw was that the flap of the left-hand pocket had been pushed inside and the pocket was gaping on account of something in it. That was wrong. I didn't patronize the kind of tailors Percy Ludlow had, but I was born neat and I don't go around with my pocket flaps pushed in; and besides, that pocket had been empty.

My hand had started for it instinctively, to reach in for a feel, but I caught the impulse in time and stopped it. I looked around, but as far as I could see no one had me under special observation, either furtive or open. There was no time for a prolonged test of that nature, for the homicide squad would be busting in any minute, maybe less than a minute, and once they arrived the right of self-determination wouldn't stand a chance.

I reached up and took the hat and coat from the rack and started for the hall door, and had taken three steps when I was halted by a loud growl from behind:

"Hey, you, where you going?"

I turned and spoke loudly but not offensively to the suspicious glare from the precinct dick, "The management is not responsible for hats and coats, and these are mine. There'll be a lot of company coming and I'd prefer to put them in a locker."

I moved as I spoke, and sailed on through the door. There was one chance in three that he would actually abandon Mrs. Miltan and take after me, but he didn't. In the hall, I didn't even glance toward the left, where the watchdog stood at the entrance, knowing that it was out of the question to bluff a passage to freedom.

Instead I turned right, and it was only five steps to a narrow door I had noticed there. I opened it and saw an uncarpeted wooden stair going down. There was a light switch just inside, but without flipping it on I shut the door behind me and it was pitch-dark, black. With my pencil flashlight for a guide, I descended to the bottom of the stair, quietly but without wasting any time. Playing the light around, I saw that I was in a large low-ceilinged room lined with shelves and with stacks of cartons and shipping cases occupying the middle floor space. I stepped around them and headed for the rear, where I could see the dim rectangles of two windows a few feet apart. I must have been a little on edge, because I stood stiff and motionless and stopped breathing when the beam of my light, directed toward the floor, showed me something sticking out from behind a pile of cartons that I wasn't expecting to see. It was the toe of a man's shoe, and it was obvious from its position and appearance that there was a foot in it and the foot's owner was standing on it. I kept the light on it, steady, and in a few seconds I breathed, moved the light upwards, and put my right hand inside my coat and out again. Then I said out loud but not too loud:

"Don't move. I'm aiming a gun at where you are and I'm nervous. If your hands are empty stick them out beyond the edge. If they're not empty—"

A sound came from behind the cartons that was something between a moan and a squeal. I let my right hand fall and stepped forward with a grunt of disgust and put the light on him, where he was flattened against the pile of cartons.

"For the love of Mike," I said, absolutely exasperated. "What the hell are you scared of?"

He moaned, "I seen him." His eyes were still rolling. "I tell you I done seen him."

"So did I see him. Look here, Arthur, I have no time to waste arguing with you about primitive superstitions. What are you going to do, stay here and moan?"

"I ain't going back up there—don't you try it—don't you touch me, I'm telling you—"

"Okay." I laid the light on a carton, returned the pistol to my holster, and put on my coat and hat. Then I retrieved the light. "I'm going out the back way to see that no one escapes. The best thing you can do is stay right where you are."

"I mean don't I know it," he groaned.

"Fine. Have you got the key for that door?"

"They's a bolt, that's all."

"What's outside, a court with a high fence around it?"

"Yes, sir."

"Any door in the fence?"

"No, sir."

Overhead, namely on the floor of the office directly above, I heard the tread of dozens of heavy shoes on heavy feet. The company had come. I even thought I detected the sound of Inspector Cramer's number twelves. As I moved, I had a piece of luck; the beam of my light passed over a boy's-size stepladder standing by the shelves. I went for it, arranged for a diversion by warning Arthur to yell for help if he heard anyone else coming down, found the rear door and unbolted it, and skipped through with the stepladder.

The court was fairly large, maybe 30 x 40, and paved with concrete, and the solid board fence was two feet over my head. There was plenty of light from the windows of the buildings. I trotted across to the rear, leaned the ladder against the fence, mounted, and looked over into the adjoining court. It was the same size as the one I was in, with a miscellaneous clutter of vague objects scattered around and one object not so vague: a bulky person dressed in white, including an apron and a chef's cap, apparently doing breathing exercises from the way he stood there and puffed. Ten feet back of him a blaze of light came from a door standing open.

I grabbed the top of the fence and pulled myself up and perched there, teetering. At the noise he looked up, startled, but before he could start screeching I demanded:

"Did you see that cat?"

"What cat?"

"My wife's cat. A yellow, long-haired fiend. It got loose and jumped out a window and climbed this fence. If you—" I lost my balance and toppled over and landed flat on the concrete on his side. As I picked myself up I cussed appropriately. "If I find the little darling I'll strangle the damn thing. If you've been standing here you must have seen it."

"I didn't see it."

"You must have. Okay, then you didn't, but it came here. It must have smelled the grub in the restaurant—"

I was on my way and kept going. He started after me, but with slow acceleration, so I went through the open door unimpeded. It was a large room, full of noise, cookery smells, and activity. Without coming to a stop I inquired above the noise, "Did a cat come in here?" They stared at me and a couple shook their heads. There was one with a loaded tray, in waiter's uniform, headed for a swinging door, and I got on his heels and followed him through. At the other end of a pantry corridor another swinging door let us into the restaurant proper—purple and yellow leather, gleaming chromium, gleaming white tables—with waiters fussing around waiting for the evening's customers. One of them blocked me and I snapped at him, "Catching a cat," and went on around. In the foyer the sucker usher gave me an astonished look and the hat-check girl started for me instinctively, but I merely repeated, "Catching a cat," and kept going, on through two more doors and then up to the sidewalk.

I was, of course, on 49th Street. My impulse was to hoof it around a couple of corners to 48th Street and get the roadster, but it was parked only a few yards from the entrance to Miltan's, so I voted unanimously for discretion and hopped into a taxi. On its cushion, bumping along downtown on Park Avenue, I maintained the discretion by not attempting to explore my overcoat pocket, considering that if things got complicated and aggravating enough the taxi driver might be asked questions about what he had seen in his mirror. So I just sat and let him bump me down to 35th Street and cross-town to the number of Wolfe's house.

As I passed through the front hall I tossed my hat on a hook but kept my overcoat on. In the office, Wolfe sat at his desk, and in front of him was the metal box that was kept on a shelf in the safe, to which he alone had a key, and which he had never opened in my presence. I had always supposed that it contained papers too private even for me, but for all I knew it might have been stuffed with locks of hair or the secret codes of the Japanese army. He put something into it and shut the lid and frowned at me.

"Well?" he demanded.

I shook my head. "No soap. I might have been able to bring her if I had had a chance to exert my charm, but on account of circumstances beyond my control—"

"Circumstances forcing you to return here alone?"

"Not exactly forcing, no, sir. You may remember that on the phone I mentioned a bird named Percy Ludlow who said that your daughter was getting his cigarettes out of his coat at his request. Well, somebody murdered him."

Wolfe glared. "I am not in a mood for buffoonery."

"Neither am I. I ruined my coat falling off of a fence on purpose. At two minutes after six, Miss Lovchen and Miss Tormic were upstairs giving fencing lessons and various other people were doing other things. Miss Tormic was supposed to be giving a lesson to Percy Ludlow. I was downstairs in the office with Mr. and Mrs. Miltan. We heard yells and ran up two flights into a commotion of assorted people. In the fencing room at the end we found Percy Ludlow on the floor with an épée running through him from front to back and eight inches beyond. Miltan stayed there on guard and his wife went to the office to phone for the police and I took charge of the front door. The first two cops on the scene were radio patrol, the next three were precinct bums, and the homicide squad arrived around 6:24."

"Well?"

"That's all."

"All?" Wolfe was as nearly speechless as I had ever seen him. "You—" He sputtered. "You were right there, inside there, and you deliberately ran away—"

"Wait a minute. Not deliberately. A cop relieved me at the door and another one took me with him to the office, where the inmates had gathered. I happened to be standing near the rack where I had hung my coat and I noticed that the pocket was bulging open on account of something in it. When I had hung the coat up the pocket had been empty. Maybe someone had merely mistaken it for the wastebasket. On the other hand, there was a murderer in the room, and Miss Tormic had presumably been fencing with the victim, and I was there as the representative of Miss Tormic. The attitude that might be adopted by the homicide squad in face of those facts would certainly be distasteful, in case there was a general search and the object in my pocket wasn't wastepaper. So I descended to the basement and left by the back door and fell over a fence and took a taxi."

"And what was the object?"

"I don't know." I removed my coat and spread it on his desk. "I thought it would be more fun to look at it with you. To the tips of my fingers it felt like a piece of canvas." I was widening the mouth of the pocket and peeping in. "Yep, it's canvas." I inserted fingers and thumb and eased it out. It was rolled tight. As I unrolled it, it became a heavy canvas gauntlet, with reinforced palm, and a little metal dingus slid off onto the desk.

"Let's don't touch that," I suggested, and bent over to inspect it. At its middle it was about a quarter of an inch thick. At one end it had three claws, or fingers, and at the other it tapered to a single point, sharp as an ice pick. I straightened up with a nod.

"Uh-huh, I thought so."

"What the devil is it?"

"My God, look at it! It's the *col de mort*!"

"Confound you, Archie—"

"Okay, but let it alone." I told him about the disappearance of the curio from Miltan's cabinet and the history of it. He listened with his lips compressed.

When I was through he demanded, "And you think this was used—"

"I know damn well it was. The end of the épée that killed Ludlow was blunt, and Miltan said it couldn't possibly have been thrust through him that way. So this thing was removed afterwards. It looks as if it would slide right off. I doubt if I need to point out those stains on the glove where this was wrapped up in it."

"Thank you. I can see."

"And you can also see that it is a woman's glove. It looks big on account of the way it's made, but it's not big enough—"

"I can see that too."

"And you can see that if I had stayed there and that contraption had been found in my pocket, or if I had tried to hide it—"

I stopped because his lips were working and he had shut his eyes. It didn't take long, maybe thirty seconds, then he reached for the button and pushed it. When Fritz appeared he was in a cap and apron similar to those worn by the man in the court who hadn't seen my wife's cat.

"Turn out the light in the hall and do not answer the door," Wolfe told him.

"Yes, sir."

"If the phone rings, answer it in the kitchen. Archie is not here and you don't know where he is or when he will return. I am engaged and cannot be disturbed. Draw the heavy curtains in the front and the dining room, but first—is there a full loaf of the Italian round?"

"Yes, sir."

"Bring it, please, with a small knife and a roll of waxed paper."

When Fritz left I followed him, to hang my coat in the hall and shoot the bolt on the front door. As I returned I flipped the light switch, and in a moment Fritz returned with the required articles on a tray.

Wolfe told him to stand by and then attacked the loaf of bread with the knife, which of course was like a razor, as Fritz's knives always were. He described a circle four inches in diameter in the center of the loaf, and then dug in, excavating a neat round hole clear to the bottom crust but leaving the crust intact. Next he picked up the *col de mort* with the tips of his fingers, placed it on the palm of the glove, rolled the glove up tight, wrapped it in some waxed paper, and stuffed it into the hole in the loaf. He filled the extra space with wads of paper, and spread a sheet of paper smoothly over the top. With his swift and dexterous fingers, the entire operation consumed not over three minutes.

He told Fritz, "Make a chocolate icing, at once, and cover this well. Put it in the refrigerator. Dispose of the bread scraps."

"Yes, sir." Fritz picked up the tray and departed.

I said sarcastically, "Bravo. It's wonderful how your mind works. If that had been me I would just have gone up and chucked it in my bureau drawer. Of course it's more picturesque to disguise it as a cake, but it's an awful waste of chocolate, and who do you think is going to come looking for it? Do you think I'd have brought it here if anyone had any suspicion that I had it?"

"I don't know. But someone knows that you had it and that you brought it away—the person who put it there. Who had an opportunity to do that?"

"Everybody. They were all there in the office. While I was on guard at the street door."

"When you removed the coat from the rack and started off with it, were you looking at people's faces?"

"No, I was being nonchalant. There were two cops there and I had to get out of the room with it."

"You say Miss Tormic was supposed to be fencing

with Mr. Ludlow. Why supposed? Isn't it known whether she was or not?"

"It may be known, but not by me. I was down in the office with Mr. and Mrs. Miltan when the porter found the body and started a squawk. After that I had no chance to talk with Miss Tormic or anybody else."

The telephone rang. I plugged in the kitchen extension and we heard, faintly, Fritz's voice taking the call.

Wolfe leaned back and sighed. "Very well," he muttered. "Tell me about it. From the moment you got there until you left. No omissions."

I did so.

Chapter 5

At a quarter to ten we finally left the dining table, returned to the office, switched on the lights, and sat down to wait. Various developments had occurred. The doorbell had rung three times, unheeded, and the phone somewhat oftener. At the finish of the salad I had left Wolfe alone with the green tomato pie and gone to the darkened front room for a peek around the window curtain. Two men in plain clothes were on the sidewalk, standing there with their hands in their pockets looking chilly and frustrated. I gave them a Bronx cheer and went to the kitchen and used the phone. Johnny Keems and Orrie Cather were out, and I left a message for them to call the office. I got Fred Durkin and Saul Panzer and told them I was just making contact and they were to await possible orders, and informed Saul about the envelope he would receive in the morning mail. I took it for granted that the number which had been jotted on his memo pad by Fritz, who had been answering the phone as instructed, was the number of the Miltan studio, but I verified it anyway by looking in the book, and told Fritz to call it and convey the message that Mr. Wolfe and Mr. Goodwin were now both at home and at leisure. Then I went back to the dining room and joined Wolfe at coffee.

Our wait, after we returned to the office, was a short one. We hadn't been there more than five minutes when the doorbell called me to the front. As I opened the door I was expecting a brace of sergeants at the most, and was really surprised when I saw a single familiar figure confronting me, with a felt hat cocked over one of the half-buried irate eyes and an unlit cigar tilted up from a corner of the wide determined mouth.

"Honored," I declared, standing aside to give him passage. "Deeply honored."

"Go to hell," Inspector Cramer growled, entering. I shut the door and took his hat and coat and disposed of them, and followed him into the office.

Wolfe offered a hand, greeted him nicely, and said this was a pleasure he hadn't had for some months.

"Yeah. Quite a pleasure." Cramer sat down, took the cigar from his mouth, scowled at me, replaced the cigar at a better angle, and spoke.

"Where you been, Goodwin?" He was practically snarling. Before I could reply he went on, "Forget it. If I already knew you'd tell me and if I didn't you wouldn't." He removed the cigar again and leaned at me. "You're the most damn contrary pest within my knowledge. Twenty times I've had you under my feet when I was busy and had no use for you. Now I go to look at a murder and I am told that an important witness has calmly took his hat and coat and departed, and by God, it turns out to be you! The one time you're supposed to be there you're not! I've told you before that I'd throw you in the jug for a nickel. This time I'd do it for nothing!"

I inquired, "Did you find Arthur?"

"We found—none of your damn business what we found. What did you run away for?"

"Because I wanted to." I requisitioned a friendly grin for him. "Look, Inspector, you know perfectly well you're just being rhetorical. I ran away to keep from losing my job. Mr. Wolfe had sent me there on an errand with instructions to report back when the errand was finished. It was finished, and as you know, Mr. Wolfe doesn't take an excuse. By the way, I left my car there, parked on 48th—"

"Nuts. Why did you beat it?"

"I'm telling you. I would have been kept there till midnight, and for nobody's benefit, because there were a dozen people there who knew more than I did about the murder, and at least one of them a lot more." I let my voice rise a little in indignation. "I helped out all I could, didn't I? Didn't I guard the front door until the radio and precinct guys—"

I stopped short.

"Uh-huh." Cramer nodded grimly. "Just occurred to you, huh? Brain slowed up on you? I thought of that a long while ago, all by myself. What was it, Goodwin? What was it that happened between the time the precinct men arrived and the time you took your overcoat from the rack?"

"Nothing happened."

"Yes, it did. I want to know what it was."

"Nothing, except that when a cop relieved me at the door there was nothing I could do to help, and you know damn well what Mr. Wolfe is like if I let anything interfere with his business."

He glared at me. Then he slid back to a more comfortable position in the big leather chair, looked at Wolfe, and slowly shook his head. "I'm tired out," he said resentfully. "I was up most of last night on that

Arlen case, and I was going to bed at eight o'clock, and now here's this, and I find you're in on it even before it happens, and you can guess how pure and simple that makes it seem like."

"I can assure you," Wolfe said sympathetically, "that Mr. Goodwin's errand was neither to prevent nor to provoke murder. We really didn't know there was to be one."

"Oh, I know all about his errand. Driscoll's diamonds. To hell with that. Let's be reasonable. There was Goodwin, alone right at the front door for six or seven minutes after he came downstairs with Mrs. Miltan, before the radio men got there. Then they left him alone again until the precinct men arrived. He knew from the beginning what a murder investigation means for those on the premises when the squad gets on the job. If he wanted to get away and get to you to report, all he had to do was walk right out and get in his car and go. Instead of that, he waits until the precinct men come and one of them is stationed at the door, then he goes to the office and stands there and looks around, and all of a sudden he grabs his hat and coat, sneaks down to the basement, pulls a gun and scares the daylights out of a colored porter who—"

"He had no daylights left in him."

"Shut up. Tells the porter to stay where he is, takes a ladder to the rear court and climbs the fence and talks about his wife's cat and pretends to fall off, beats it through a kitchen and a restaurant on 49th Street, and jumps a taxi and tells the driver he likes to go fast. And he tells me nothing happened between the time the precinct men came and the time he reached for his coat! I ask you, what does that sound like?"

"It sounds like a delayed cerebral process. I am accustomed to it. Unfortunately."

"It sounds bughouse. And Goodwin's not bughouse."

"No, he isn't. Not quite. Will you have some beer?"

"No. Thank you."

Wolfe pushed the button, leaned back, and let the tips of his fingers meet at the apex of his middle mound. "Let's cut across, Mr. Cramer," he suggested helpfully. "You're busy and you need sleep. Regarding the point you have broached, as to what happened up there between this time and that time, Archie says he didn't want to be detained until midnight by the prolonged routine of your staff. I say delayed cerebration. If something significant really did happen it's obvious that we don't intend to tell you, at least not now, so let's pass on that. Next, if you ask why we kept ourselves incommunicado until half past nine, my reply is that I wished to get his complete report without interruption and that I abhor any disturbance during the dinner hour; further, that you had a large number of people up there to deal with and Archie could tell you nothing that you couldn't learn from them."

Fritz came with a tray, and Wolfe uncapped a bottle and poured. "Next? I suppose, why Archie was sent there? Because a girl named Carla Lovchen, whom we have never seen before, came this afternoon to engage me in the interest of a friend of hers named Neya Tormic, who had been accused of theft. That matter was cleared up by a statement from Mr. Driscoll, who appears to be a blundering ass. Next, you will doubtless ask, after that affair had been settled and Mr. Goodwin had departed, why did he return? Because he phoned me and I told him to. As you know, when I accept a commission I like to get paid. I try to stop this side of rapacity, but I like to collect, even when, as in this case, I have furnished more will than wit. I sent him back to see Miss Tormic. He was waiting for her in the office when the porter's yells were heard."

Cramer was slowly rubbing at his chin, looking stubborn and unconvinced. He watched Wolfe swallow the glass of beer and wipe his lips, and then turned to me:

"You're not bughouse, you know. Someday when I'm not busy I'd like to tell you what you are, but you're not bughouse. Now suppose you tell me a little story."

"Sure, I'll even tell you a big one. I was in the office talking with Mr. and Mrs. Miltan when we heard the yelling—"

"Oh, no. Back up. From the time you got there. I want the works."

I gave it to him, in my best style. I knew from the tone Wolfe had taken that the program was eagerness to oblige in inessentials, so I skipped none of the unimportant details. I covered the route. One of the little cuts I made was the brief passage between the Balkans and me while I was standing guard at the front door. When I got through Cramer asked me some questions that offered no difficulty, ending with a few more jabs regarding what had happened between the time when this and the time when that. My only addition to my former explanation was that I had started to get hungry.

He sat a minute and chewed his cigar, frowning, and switched to Wolfe.

"I don't believe it," he said flatly.

"No? What is it you don't believe, Mr. Cramer?"

"I don't believe that Goodwin's bughouse. I don't believe he left like that because he was homesick and hungry. I don't believe he went back there to collect a fee from Miss Tormic. I don't believe that as far as you're concerned it's washed up and you're not interested in the murder."

"I haven't said I'm not interested in the murder."

"Ho! Haven't you? Well, are you?"

"Yes." Wolfe grimaced. "Apparently I am. While Archie was on guard at the door Miss Tormic approached and asked him—me—to act in the matter in her interest. He accepted. I am committed, and the amount of profit that may be expected . . ." He shrugged. "I am committed. That was what happened that made Archie feel he should communicate with me promptly and privately. As you are aware, Mr. Cramer, I am quite capable of candor when the occasion presents—"

The inspector clamped his teeth on his cigar and said through them savagely, "I knew it!"

Wolfe's brows went up a millimeter. "You knew? . . ."

"I knew it the minute I learned Goodwin had been there and gone off to chase a cat. It had already begun to look like a first-class headache, and when I heard about Goodwin that cinched it. So you've got a client! And sure enough, by God, it has to be your client that was in that room fencing with him! It would be!" He rescued the cigar from his teeth with his left hand and hit the desk with his right fist, simultaneously. "Understand this, Wolfe! I came here in a mood of cooperation, in spite of Goodwin's tricky getaway! And what am I getting? Now you try to tell me that in the space of ten seconds, just like that, your man accepted a murder case for you! Nuts!" He hit the desk again. "I know what your abilities are, no one knows that better than I do! And like a fool I came here expecting a little disinterested discussion and you tell me you've got a client! Why have you always got to have a goddam client? Naturally from now on I can't believe a single solitary thing—"

My waving paw finally stopped his bellowing; the phone had rung and I couldn't hear. It was a request for him. With a grunt he got up and came to my desk for it, and I made way for him. For several minutes his part of it was mostly listening, and then apparently he was told something disagreeable, judging from the way he violated the law against the use of profanity on the telephone. He gave some instructions, banged the thing into its cradle, and said in a quiet but very sarcastic voice, "That's nice, now."

He went back to his chair and sat there a minute chewing his lip. "That's just fine," he said. "The case is as good as solved. I won't have to go to any bother about it."

"Indeed," Wolfe murmured.

"Yes indeed. Three Federals have blown in up there. Anybody might suppose that a murder in Manhattan is the business of the homicide squad of which I happen to be the head, but who am I compared with a G-man? If we throw them out on their tail, the commissioner will say tut-tut, we've got to co-operate. It has two pleasant aspects. First, it means an entirely new angle we haven't even suspected, and that's a cheerful idea. Second, whoever solves it and however and whenever, the G-men will grab the credit. They always do."

"Now, Inspector," I remonstrated. "A G-man is the representative of the American people, in fact it would hardly be going too far to say that a G-man is America—"

"Shut up. I wish you'd get an F.B.I. job yourself and they'd send you to Alaska. I can pull you in, you know."

"If you can it's news to me. Who made any law about an innocent man being overcome with repugnance at the sight of blood and taking a taxi home?"

"Where did you see any blood?"

"I didn't. Figure of speech."

"Metonymy," Wolfe muttered.

"Kid me. I like it." Cramer glared at Wolfe. "So you've got a client."

Wolfe made a face. "Tentatively I have. Archie accepted the commission. I say tentatively because I have never met her. When I've seen her and talked with her I shall know whether she's guilty or not."

"You admit she may be."

"Certainly she may be." Wolfe wiggled a finger. "May I make a suggestion, Mr. Cramer? If you want consilience. It would be doubly unprofitable for you to question me, since you have stated that you will believe nothing I tell you, and since all those people are strangers to me and I am completely ignorant of what went on."

"You say."

"Yes, sir, I say. But it might help for me to question you. It would certainly help me, and in the long run it might even help you."

"Great idea. Wonderful idea."

"I think so."

Cramer put his mangled cigar in the tray, got out another one and stuck it in his mouth. "Shoot."

"Thank you. First, of course, achieved results. Have you arrested anyone?"

"No."

"Have you found adequate motive?"

"No."

"Are there any definite conclusions in your mind?"

"No. Nor indefinite either."

"I see. No indictments from the mechanical routine—fingerprints, photographs, blabbing objects?"

"No. There's one object, and maybe two, that ought to be there and we can't find it. Do you know anything about fencing?"

Wolfe shook his head. "Nothing whatever."

"Well, the thing he was killed with is called an épée. It's triangular in section, with no cutting edge, and the point is so blunted that if you thrust at a man hard enough to go through him it would merely break the blade, which is quite flexible. In fencing they fasten a little steel button on the end, and the button has three tiny points. The points are only to show on your opponent's jacket when you've made a hit; the thick body of the button wouldn't permit the épée to pierce through the pad they wear or the mask over their face."

I said, "He didn't have any mask on."

"I know he didn't, so he wasn't actually fencing at the moment he was killed. Miltan says no one ever fences with the épée without a mask. The one Ludlow had been wearing was on a bench over by the wall. And the épée that was sticking through him had no button on it, just the blunted end, and it couldn't possibly have pierced him like that. But there was that thing in the cabinet in the office which Mrs. Miltan discovered was missing while your Mr. Goodwin was present. Which she calls a culdymore. You talk French; you can say it better than I can."

"*Col de mort.*"

"Right. Anyone could have taken it from the cabinet. The chances are a million to one it was used on the épée that killed Ludlow. At a distance of a few feet, and especially with the épée in motion, he would never have seen it was that and not the ordinary fencing button. But the culdymore was not on the épée. So it had been removed. So everyone was searched and twenty men went through that joint like molasses through cheesecloth. They didn't find it. One person and only one had left that building, namely Goodwin here. You don't imagine he took it with him for a souvenir?"

Wolfe smiled slightly. "I wouldn't suppose so. Thrown out of a window perhaps?"

"It could have been. They're still looking, in the damn dark with flashlights. Also for the other object which may be missing. Miss Tormic has an idea a glove is gone, one of the ladies'-size fencing gauntlets, from the cupboard in the locker room. Miss Lovchen and the dame that calls herself Zorka don't think so. Mrs. Miltan won't commit herself. Nobody seems to know for sure exactly how many there were."

"What about the button that had to be removed from the épée before the *col de mort* could be used?"

"They're all over the place. Right in the fencing rooms in drawers."

"Would the handle of the épée show fingerprints if it had been grasped without a glove?"

"No. Wrapped with cord or something for a grip."

"Well." Wolfe looked sympathetic. "The only two objects that might have helped aren't there. I'll promise you one thing, Mr. Cramer, if Archie did take them away I shall see that they are handed over to you as soon as we finish with them. But to go on, how many persons were in the building at the time the body was found?"

"Counting everybody, twenty-six."

"How many have you eliminated?"

"All but eight or nine."

"Namely?"

"First and foremost, the one who was fencing with him. Your client."

"I wouldn't expect that. If she is still my client after I see her I'll eliminate her myself. The others?"

"Mr. and Mrs. Miltan. They alibi each other, which would be a drug on the market at two for a nickel. The girl that came to see you, Carla Lovchen. That's four. She had been fencing with Driscoll, but they had quit and had gone to the locker rooms, and she could have sneaked to the end room and done it. Driscoll. He's unlikely but not eliminated. Zorka. She was in the big room on that floor with a young man named Ted Gill. He claims not to be a fencer and was in there with her learning how to start."

I said, "It was him that was with Belinda Reade yesterday when they saw our client in the hall as she was going to the locker room not to pinch Driscoll's diamonds."

"Right. Then there's the Reade girl and young Barrett. They were moving around and it's hard to tell. Of course if it's Donald Barrett you can have it. Also there's a kind of a man named Rudolph Faber."

"The chinless wonder."

"Not original but good. It's him, by the way, that's responsible for the fact that there's been no arrest. How many does that make?"

"Ten."

"Then it's ten. And no discovered motive in the whole damn bunch. I wouldn't—"

The phone rang. I performed and, after a moment, beckoned to Cramer.

"For you. It's the boss."

"Who?"

"The police commissioner, by gum."

He got up, said in a resigned tone, "Oh, poop," and came and took it.

Chapter 6

That telephone conversation was in two sections. During the first section, which was prolonged, Cramer was doing the talking, in a respectfully belligerent tone, reporting on the situation and the regrettable lack of progress to date. During the second, which was shorter, he was listening and apparently to something not especially cheerful, judging from the inflection of his grunts, and from the expression on his face when he finally cut the connection and returned to his chair.

He sat and scowled.

Wolfe said, "You were lamenting the lack of motive."

"What?" He looked at Wolfe. "Yeah. I'd give my afternoon off to know what you know right now."

"It would cost you more than an afternoon, Mr. Cramer. I read a lot of books."

"To hell with books. I am fully aware that you've got some kind of a line on this thing and I haven't; I knew that as soon as I heard about Goodwin. If it ever did any good to look at your face I'd look at it while I'm telling you that the commissioner just informed me that he had a phone call ten minutes ago from the

British consul general. The consul stated that he was shocked and concerned to learn of the sudden and violent death of a British subject named Percy Ludlow and he hoped that no effort would be spared and so forth."

Wolfe shook his head. "I'm afraid my face wouldn't help you any on that. My sole reaction is the thought that the British consul general must have remarkable channels of information. It's half past ten at night. The murder occurred only four hours ago."

"Nothing remarkable about it. He heard it on a radio news bulletin."

"The source of the news was you or your staff?"

"Naturally."

"Then you had discovered that Ludlow was a British subject?"

"No. No one up there knew much about him. Men are out on that now."

"Then obviously it's remarkable. The radio tells the consul merely that a man named Percy Ludlow has been killed at a dancing and fencing studio on 48th Street, and he knows at once that the victim was a British subject. Not only that, he doesn't wait until morning, when the usual conventional communication could be sent to the police from his office, but immediately phones the commissioner himself. So either Mr. Ludlow was himself important, or he was concerned in important business. Maybe the consul could supply some details."

"Much obliged. The commissioner has a date with him at eleven o'clock. Meanwhile how about supplying a few yourself?"

"I don't know any. I heard Mr. Ludlow's name for the first time shortly before six o'clock this afternoon."

"You say. All right, to hell with you and your client

both. I don't kick on any ordinary murder, it's my job and I try to handle it, but I hate these damn foreign mix-ups. Look at those two girls, they barely speak English, and if they want to monkey around playing with swords why can't they stay where they belong and do it there? Look at Miltan, I suppose some kind of a Frenchman, and his wife. Look at Zorka. Then look at that Rudolph Faber guy, he reminds me of the cartoons of Prussian officers at the time of the World War. And now the Federals are up there horning in, and this consul general informs us that even the dead man wasn't a plain honest-to-God American—"

"From old Ireland," I slipped in.

"Shut up. You know what I mean. I don't care if the background is wop or mick or kike or dago or yankee or squarehead or dutch colonial, so long as it's American. Give me an American murder with an American motive and an American weapon, and I'll deal with it. But these damn alien trimmings, épée and culdymores and consuls calling up about their damn subjects—and moreover, why I was fool enough to expect anything here is beyond me. I should have had you tagged and hauled in and let you wait in a cold hall until sunrise."

He appeared to be preparing to leave his chair. Wolfe displayed a palm.

"Please, Mr. Cramer. Good heavens, the corpse is barely cooled off. Would you mind telling me how Mr. Faber made himself responsible for the fact that there's been no arrest? I think that was how you put it."

"I might and I might not. Do you know Faber?"

"I've said all those people are strangers to me. I tell only useful lies, and only those not easily exposed."

"Okay. I would have arrested your client—I'm pretty sure I would—if it hadn't been for Faber."

"Then I'm in debt to him."

"You sure are. Except for lack of motive, which might have been supplied and still may be, it looked like Miss Tormic. She admitted she was in there fencing with Ludlow. There was no evidence of anyone else having entered the room, though of course someone could have done so unobserved. Miss Tormic said that when she left the room Ludlow said he would stay and fool with the dummy a while. A dummy is a thing fastened to the wall with a mechanical arm that you can hook a sword onto. She said she went to the locker room and left her pad and glove and mask, and then—"

"What about her épée?"

"She said she left it in the fencing room. There's a dozen or more in there on a rack. There was one with a button on it lying on the floor not far from Ludlow's body, presumably the one he had been using. Ludlow had no mask on, but of course it could have been slipped off after he was killed. I see no reason why it should have been, unless to make it look as if he hadn't been fencing at the moment it happened. Nor was there any reason for removing the culdymore as far as I can see except to play hide and seek with it. But about Faber. He was downstairs in a dancing room with Zorka until she went with Ted Gill to show him how to hold a sword. Then he went up and changed to fencing clothes, intending to get Carla Lovchen to fence with him as soon as she was through with Driscoll. He was hanging around the upper hall when Miss Tormic came out of the end room, and Ludlow was there too, opening the door for her to leave. Ludlow called to ask Faber if he cared to fence a little, and Faber said no. He says. Ludlow said all right, he'd practice his wrist on the dummy, and went back in the

end room, closing the door, and Faber and Miss Tormic
went to an alcove at the other end of the hall and sat
and smoked a couple of cigarettes. They were still
there when the porter entered the end room to clean
up, thinking it was empty, and saw the body and came
out squealing. They ran to see what it was, and other
people appeared from all directions."

Wolfe, who had closed his eyes, opened them to
slits. "I see," he murmured. "You couldn't very well
have arrested her after that, even if you had known
she was my client. From where they sat did they have
a view of the hall?"

"No, there's a corner."

"How long were they sitting there before the
rumpus?"

"Fifteen to twenty minutes."

"Did anyone see them?"

"Yes, Donald Barrett. He was looking for Miss
Tormic to ask her to have dinner with him. He went to
the door of the ladies' locker room and Miss Lovchen
told him Miss Tormic wasn't there. He found them in
the alcove, and was still with them five minutes later
when the yelling started."

"He hadn't looked for her in the end room?"

"No. Miss Lovchen told him she had stopped in the
locker room and left her pad and glove and mask, so he
presumed she wasn't fencing."

After a little silence Wolfe heaved a sigh. "Well," he
said irritably but mildly, "I don't see why the devil you
resent my client. She seems to be wrapped in a mantle
of innocence from head to foot."

"Sure, it's simply beautiful." Cramer abruptly got
up. "But . . . there's a couple of little things. So far as
is known, she and no one else was in that room with
him, and for the purpose of lunging at him with an

épée. Then the alibi Faber gives her is one of those neat babies that could be 99 per cent true and still be a phony. All you'd have to subtract would be the part about his seeing and speaking with Ludlow as Miss Tormic left the end room. I don't claim to know any reason why Faber—"

The interruption was the entrance of Fritz. Inside the door a pace he halted to get a nod from Wolfe, and then advanced to the desk and extended the card tray. Wolfe took the card, glanced at it, and elevated his brows.

He told Fritz to stand by, and looked up at Cramer, who was standing, speculatively.

"You know," he said, "since you're leaving anyway, I could easily finesse around you by having this caller shown into the front room until you're gone. But I really do like to cooperate when I can. One of your ten inmates up there has got loose. Unless they've let him go in order to follow him, which I believe is a usual tactic."

"Which one?"

Wolfe glanced at the card again. "Mr. Rudolph Faber."

"You don't say." Cramer stared at Wolfe's face for seven seconds. "This is a hell of a time of night for a complete stranger to be making an unexpected call."

"It certainly is. Show him in, please, Fritz."

Cramer turned to face the door.

I chalked up one for the chinless wonder. He may have been shy on chin, but his nerve was okay. While there may have been no reason why the unlooked-for sight of Inspector Cramer's visage should have paralyzed him with terror, it must have been at least quite a surprise, but he did no shrinking or blanching. He merely halted in a manner that should have made his heels click but didn't, lifted a brow, and then marched on.

Cramer grunted something at him, grunted a good night to Wolfe and me, and tramped out. I got up to greet the newcomer, leaving the front hall politeness to Fritz. Wolfe submitted to a handshake and motioned the caller to the chair that was still warm from Cramer. Faber thanked him and blinked at him, and then turned on me and demanded:

"How did you get away up there? Bribe the cop?"

I could have told, just looking at him, that that was the tone he would use asking a question. A tone that took it for granted any question he asked was going to be answered just because he asked it. I don't like it and I know of no way anybody is ever going to make me like it.

I said, "Write me special delivery and I'll refer the matter to my secretary's secretary."

His forehead wrinkled in displeasure. "Now, my man—"

"Not on your life. Not your man. I belong to me. This is the United States of America. I'm Nero Wolfe's employee, bodyguard, office manager, and wage slave, but I can quit any minute. I'm my own man. I don't know in what part of the world the door is that your key fits, but—"

"That will do, Archie." Wolfe said that without bothering to glance at me; his eyes were on the caller. "Apparently, Mr. Faber, Mr. Goodwin doesn't like you. Let's disregard that. What can I do for you?"

"You can first," said Faber in his perfect precise English, "instruct your subordinate to answer questions that are put to him."

"I suppose I can. I'll try it some time. What else can I do for you?"

"There is no discipline in your country, Mr. Wolfe."

"Oh, I wouldn't say that. There are various kinds of discipline. One man's flower is another man's weed. We submit to traffic cops and the sanitary code and so on, but we are extremely fond of certain liberties. Surely you didn't come here in order to discipline Mr. Goodwin? Don't try it; you'd soon get sick of the job. Forget it. Beyond that? . . ."

"I came to satisfy myself as to your position and intentions regarding Miss Neya Tormic."

"Well." Wolfe was keeping his voice oiled—controlling himself. "What is it in you that requires satisfaction? Your curiosity?"

"No. I am interested. I might be prepared, under certain conditions, to explain my interest, and you might find it profitable to help me advance it. I know your reputation of course—and your methods. You're expensive. What you want is money."

"I like money, and I use a lot of it. Would it be your money, Mr. Faber?"

"It would be yours after it was paid to you."

"Quite right. What would I have to do to earn it?"

"I don't know. It is an affair of urgency and it demands great discretion. That inspector of police who was here—can you satify me that you are not a secret agent of the police?"

"I couldn't say. I don't know how hard you are to satisfy. I can give you my word, but I know what it's worth and you don't. Before I went to a lot of trouble to establish my good faith, I would need satisfaction on a few points myself. Your own position and intentions, for instance. Is your interest a personal one in Miss Tormic, or is it—somewhat broader? And does it coincide with hers? It is at least, I suppose, not hostile to her, or you wouldn't have established that alibi for her when she was threatened with a charge of murder. But exactly what is it?"

Rudolph Faber looked at me, with his thin lips thinner, and then said to Wolfe, "Send him out of the room."

I started to deride him with a grin, knowing the reception that kind of suggestion always got, no matter who made it; but the grin froze on my face with amazement when I heard Wolfe saying calmly, "Certainly, sir. Archie, leave us, please."

I was so damn flabbergasted and boiling I got up to go without a word. I guess I staggered. But when I was nearly to the door Wolfe's voice from behind stopped me:

"By the way, we promised to phone Mr. Green. You might do so from Mr. Brenner's room."

So that was it. I might have known it. I said, "Yes, sir," and went on out, closing the door behind me, and proceeded three paces towards the kitchen. Where I stopped there was hanging on the left wall, the one that separated the hall from the office, an old brown wood carving, a panel in three sections. The two side sections were hinged to the middle one. I swung the right section around, stooped a little—for it had been constructed at the level of Wolfe's eyes—and looked through the peephole, camouflaged on the other side by a painting with the two little apertures backed by gauze, into the office. I could see them both, Faber's profile and Wolfe's full, and I mean full, face. Also I could hear their words, by straining a little, but it was obvious that they were both going on with the sparring with no prospect of getting anywhere, so I went to the kitchen. Fritz was there in his sock feet reading a newspaper, with his slippers beside him on another chair in case of a summons. He looked up and nodded.

"Milk, Archie?"

"No. Keep it low. The hole's uncovered. Tricks."

"Ah!" His eyes gleamed. He loved conspiracies and sinister things. "Good case?"

"Case hell. The second World War. It started this afternoon up on 48th Street. We'd better not talk."

I sat on the edge of the table for two minutes by my watch and then went to the house phone on the wall and buzzed the office. Wolfe answered.

"Well?"

"Mr. Goodwin speaking. Green says he has got to talk with you."

"I'm busy."

"I told him that. He said what the hell."

"You can give him the program as well as I can, and the reports we got yesterday—"

"I told him that too. He says he wants to hear it from you. I'll switch him onto your line."

"No, no, don't do that. Confound him anyway. You know I'm not alone—and that's a confidential—tell him to hold the wire. He's an unspeakable nuisance. I'll come there and take it."

"Okay."

I hung up and tiptoed back to the wood carving in the hall. In a moment the office door opened and Wolfe came out and shut the door. He got to me fast, whispered to me, "Quick on the signal," and glued his eyes to the peephole.

And I nearly missed connections. Rudolph Faber must have been in a hurry. Wolfe hadn't been at the peephole more than ten seconds before he jerked his hand up and waved it. I wasn't supposed to jump or run, so I trod the three paces to the office door, giving my steps plenty of weight, and flung the door open and kept going on in. Faber, in an attitude of arrested motion, was standing across the room from where his chair was, with his back to the bookshelves, but his hands were empty. He blinked at me once, but otherwise his face was impassive except for its inborn expression of superior and bullheaded meanness. With only one swift glance at him, I went to my desk and sat down, opened a drawer and took out a file of papers, and began going through them to look for something.

He didn't say a word and neither did I. I finished going through the file and started on another one, and was prepared to continue with that indefinitely, but it wasn't necessary. I was halfway through the second one when noises filtered in through the door to the hall, and pretty soon the door opened and I looked up and got another shock. Nero Wolfe was there, in overcoat, muffler, hat and gloves, with his applewood stick in his hand. I gawked at him.

"I'm sorry," he told Faber. "I must go out on business. If you want to go on with this, come tomorrow between eleven and one or two and four or six and eight. Those are my hours. Archie, we'll take the sedan. If you please. Fritz! Fritz, if you will help Mr. Faber with his coat . . ."

This time Faber's heels did click. I suppose they're more apt to when you're upset. He went, without having committed himself on the question of going on with it tomorrow.

When Fritz came back in Wolfe said, "Here, take these, please," and handed him stick, hat, gloves, muffler and overcoat. "Two bottles of beer." Hearing that, I put the files away in the drawer and went to the kitchen and got a glass of milk. When I returned to the office he was back at his desk, leaning back with his eyes closed. I sat and sipped the milk until the arrival of the beer made him straighten up, and then said:

"Genius again. He was going for *United Yugoslavia*."

Wolfe nodded. "He had his fingers on it when you opened the door."

"Lucky guess."

"Not a guess, an experiment. He was stalling. He wasn't saying anything and had no intention of saying anything. But he wanted you out of the room. Why?"

"Sure. Very good. But how did he figure on getting you out of the room too?"

"I don't know." Wolfe emptied the glass. "I don't manage his mind for him, thank God. I did go out, didn't I?"

"Yeah. Okay. So, did one of the Balkans send him to get that paper, or has he got Miss Tormic in his power because he's her alibi on the murder, or did he—by jiminy!" I slapped my thigh. "I've got it! He's Prince Donevitch!"

"Don't be amusing. I'm in no humor for it."

"I realize you're not." I sipped some more milk. "Where do we stand, anyway? Are we on a case or not? If so, what kind of a case?"

"I don't know. I don't like it. I don't like that paper. I don't like having that thing in the refrigerator disguised as a cake. We'll either have to find out who used it or turn it over to Mr. Cramer, and neither prospect is pleasing. And I have a responsibility. I adopted that girl."

"You don't even know whether it's her or not."

"I intend to find out. I sent you back to bring her here. You didn't do it."

"Well, boil my bones!" I glared at him. "Am I to infer that you insinuate that I should have lugged her along when I sneaked through the basement and fell over the fence and so forth? No. You're being aggravating, and God knows you're good at it. Do you want me to go get her right now?"

"Yes."

I gaped. "You do?"

"Yes."

I looked at him. He wasn't stringing me; he meant it. And not one red cent involved. It was at that moment that I decided never under any circumstances to adopt a daughter. Without another word I finished the milk and got up, and the next minute would have been gone if the phone hadn't rung.

I sat down and took it. "Office of Nero Wolfe. Archie Goodwin speaking."

"Ah, Meesturrr Gudwinnnn? Zees ess Madame Zorrrka."

"Oh, yeah." I passed Wolfe the sign to listen in on his phone. "I saw you up there this afternoon."

"Yes. Zat ees why I phone. What happen zis afternoon, eet ess terrible!"

"Right. Awful."

"Yes. Zee police, zey kestion me long time. I tell zem everysing but one sing. I deed not tell zem how I see Mees Tormic put something in your pocket."

"No?"

"But no. I sink eet ees not my beesiness and I do not want any trrrouble. But I am worried. Now I sink eet ees a murrrder, and I owe a duty. I must now tell zee police or I cannot sleep. I am duty bound."

"Sure, I see. Duty bound."

"Yes. But also I sink eet ees only fair I tell you before I tell zee police. Now I tell you. Now I tell zee police."

"Wait a minute, please. Let me get this straight. You're going to phone the police now?"

"Yes."

"And exactly what are you going to tell them?"

"Zat I see Mees Tormic put somesing in your pocket in zee coat hanging on zee rack and trying not to have anybody see. Zen pretty soon you take zee coat and go."

"Now, listen." I tried to laugh. "You sure are seeing things. Where are you now?"

"Zey let me go home. I am at my apartment, 78th Street. 542 East."

"Well, I'll tell you what I'll do. I'll get hold of Miss Tormic and we'll drop in to see you. If you think we're murderers, which we're not—"

"Oh, I'm not afraid. But I am worried."

"Don't you worry for a minute. We'll be there in less than an hour. You're sure you'll be there?"

"Certainly I will."

"The police can wait that long."

"But not longer, Meesturrr Gudwinnnn."

"Okay. Absolutely."

I shoved back the phone and stood up.

"There," I said, with no feeling because my feelings were too deep. "There you are. What else could I say?"

"Nothing," Wolfe muttered. "Now be quiet."

He shut his eyes and his lips began to push in and out. That went on for ten minutes. I sat and tried to figure out something milder than kidnapping, but my brain wouldn't work because I was too damn disgruntled. Finally he said quietly:

"Get Mr. Cramer."

That took a little doing, because the saps Cramer had left up at Miltan's studio had to go into a huddle before they would even admit he wasn't there. Next I tried his office at headquarters, and got him; apparently the base of operations had been moved down there. Wolfe took it:

"Mr. Cramer? I have a little something on that Ludlow case. No, it's somewhat complicated. I think the best idea would be for you to have a man collect Madame Zorka and Miss Tormic and bring them to my office as soon as possible. No, I want to co-operate, but I hardly think any other procedure would be feasible. No, I haven't solved the case, but this is a development that I am sure will interest you. You know whether I may be depended on for that sort of thing. You'll come yourself? Fine."

He hung up and rubbed his nose with his forefinger. I blurted, "And whoever goes to get Zorka, she'll spill the entire bag of beans before they get here—"

"Let me alone, Archie. Take that confounded thing out of that idiotic cake and put it back in your pocket the way it was."

I gave up. And obeyed blindly. Talk about discipline.

Chapter 7

Neya Tormic was the first to arrive for the party.

It was close to midnight when I went to answer the bell, saving Fritz the trouble of putting his slippers in commission and glad of a chance to stretch my legs even that much.

"Hullo," I said in polite surprise, for three of them crossed the threshold and I knew all of them. First Neya Tormic, then Carla Lovchen, and bringing up the rear, Sergeant Purley Stebbins. Purley and I had often been enemies and even friends once or twice. While I helped with wraps he said:

"This other one coupled on and I would have had to use force to separate her. So I thought if she's not wanted we can do the separating here."

"Sure," I agreed, "let Cramer do it. He ought to be here any minute. You go on to the kitchen, you know the way, and Fritz'll give you a pork tenderloin sandwich with onion grass."

He looked wistful. "I guess I won't let her out of my sight—"

"Pooh pooh. My dear fellow. This is a conference

and Mr. Wolfe and I are conferees. Breaded pork tenderloin and steaming black coffee?"

So he headed for the kitchen and I herded the Balkans into the office.

I was afraid Wolfe might be skittish, confronted with two Montenegrin females at once, but he stood up and greeted them like a man. I had chairs already arranged. It was the first time I had seen Neya in anything but her fencing costume with robe. She was natty in a dark-brown suit and brown oxfords, with no foreign touch as far as I could see, but my interest in women's clothes is not technical. Her eyes were as black as two prunes in a dish of cream, but there was a little flush on her cheeks, which may have been from the cold outdoors.

She said, with the eyes aimed at him, "You are Nero Wolfe."

Wolfe nodded just perceptibly. He was leaning forward with his elbows resting on the desk and his fingers linked together. Having seen him scrutinize a lot of people, I was aware that he was putting on a special and rare performance.

She said, "You sent a policeman to bring me here. I don't understand that."

"Inspector Cramer sent him."

"But you must have permitted it." There was a swift movement of her head; a characteristic arrested toss that I had observed that afternoon. "Or suggested it."

"Yes, Miss Tormic. I arranged it. A certain fact was exposed which required immediate action in order to save Mr. Goodwin from arrest. He is my confidential assistant, and I wouldn't welcome the ignominy of bailing him out of jail. Or perhaps instead of a fact, it's a lie. We'll find out. I thought it better to do so in the presence of Inspector Cramer, and besides, I want to see how you behave under pressure."

"I can stand pressure."

"Good. We'll see."

She smiled at him. When her mouth was composed the don't-touch-me was in command, but when she smiled it was all come-hither. "Have you told him that I am your adopted daughter?"

Wolfe frowned and turned to me. "Is the man who brought them in the kitchen?"

"Yes, sir. It's Stebbins. You know Sergeant Stebbins."

He nodded. "Nevertheless, Miss Tormic, I think we'll discuss that later. I haven't told the police that you are my daughter. For the present, it is desirable that I should not be suspected of so intimate a prejudice. Do you agree to that?"

"I should think . . ." She hesitated. The smile had gone. "Of course I'll do whatever you say, but . . ." She smiled again. "I'd like to have that paper back, the record of adoption which you signed. I want to hang onto that. I admit it's pure selfishness, because I know what it might mean to be the daughter of Nero Wolfe. I proved that by sending for you when I got into trouble. Of course, since I've never seen you since I was three years old, I can't be expected to show violent affection and throw my arms around you and kiss you—"

"No indeed," Wolfe agreed hastily. "There's no question of . . . it's a matter of responsibility and that's all. My responsibility. I was sane, in the legal sense, when I assumed it. As for the record of adoption, I would prefer, if you don't mind—but that's probably Mr. Cramer. Unless it's Madame Zorka."

"Zorka!" exclaimed Carla Lovchen in surprise.

But it was Cramer, ushered in by Fritz. He glanced sharply around, offered a curt collective greeting, and, finding his usual chair occupied by Neya Tormic, took one at the left of Carla Lovchen.

"Where's the Zorka woman?" he demanded.

"Not here yet," I told him.

"Where's Stebbins?"

"In the kitchen eating our food."

He grunted and looked at Carla, "I told him to bring Miss Tormic."

Carla said, "I came along" in a tone that indicated an intention to stay.

"I see you did. Well, Mr. Wolfe?"

"We'll wait for Madame Zorka. In the meantime, what did the commissioner learn from the consul general?"

Cramer glowered at him.

"Oh, come," Wolfe said testily, "don't degrade discretion into secretiveness. If either of these girls killed Mr. Ludlow, they certainly knew who he was. The fact that you have found that out might frighten them into betraying something. If they didn't kill him, what's the difference?"

Cramer growled, "Tomorrow's papers will have it anyway. I suppose. They always do. Ludlow was a confidential agent of the British government."

"Indeed. What was he doing at the fencing studio? Working or playing?"

"The consul doesn't know. Ludlow reported direct to London. They're trying to get someone in London now. It's five o'clock in the morning there. I told you before that this looks—"

He stopped to let me answer the phone. It was a call for him, and I made room for him to take it at my desk.

After he had listened a while he used profanity again. That made it evident he had got more than a minor irritation, since he had old-fashioned ideas about swearing in front of ladies, and he had strong principles to which he steadfastly adhered when they didn't interfere with his work. Finally he cut the connection, banging the thing into the cradle, went back and sat down, and sighed clear to his belt.

He glared at Wolfe and demanded, "What was the big idea of getting this Zorka down here? Spill it!"

Wolfe shook his head. "Wait till she gets here. Was that her on the phone? Isn't she coming?"

"Coming hell. She's skipped!"

"Skipped?"

"Gone! Left! Departed! And you knew she was going to! You had me send a man up there on a run-around! Damn you, Wolfe, I've told you twenty times that some day—"

"Please, Mr. Cramer." Wolfe was frowning in distaste. "I beg you, sir. I don't make a game of run sheep run out of a murder. I hadn't the faintest notion that Madame Zorka intended to skip. She telephoned here—what time, Archie?"

I glanced at my pad. "11:21."

"Thank you. And told us something. Archie told her he would get Miss Tormic and call on her at her apartment, from where she was talking. Then we made a brief investigation and decided it would be better to have the matter discussed with you present. As you know, I never go out on business, so we asked you to bring them here. Since her phoning here was by her own volition, and since she expected Archie and Miss Tormic to call, it is odd that she should leave her apartment."

"Yeah. Especially with a bag and a suitcase."

Wolfe's brows went up. "But I presume you were having her followed?"

"No! Why should we? Have I got a million men on the squad to tail everybody on the premises every time there's a homicide? Nuts! I sent a man to get her and bring her here. She wasn't there. Downstairs they told him that she went out with a bag and suitcase ten minutes before he arrived."

"Any trail?"

"They're after it."

"Pfui." Wolfe looked around at us. "Well. Here we are. Under the circumstances, the best thing we can do is to proceed without her."

"Go ahead," Cramer said grimly.

Wolfe leaned back and half closed his eyes and Miss Tormic was possibly unaware that he was watching her like a hawk. "As I say, Madame Zorka phoned here at 11:21. She stated that shortly after the murder was discovered, when everyone was together up there in the office, she saw Miss Tormic put something into the pocket of Mr. Goodwin's coat, which was hanging on a rack. She hadn't mentioned the incident to the police and her conscience was bothering her because she thinks murder is terrible. So she had decided to phone Mr. Goodwin and tell him that she intended to inform the police at once—"

Cramer barked at Neya, "What did you put in Goodwin's pocket?"

She kept her eyes leveled at Wolfe and paid no attention to him.

Wolfe said in his tone of authority, "Just a moment. I arranged this meeting and I'm handling it. Archie told Madame Zorka he would get Miss Tormic and go to see her. Of course he was stalling. He went to the hall to investigate, and there was something in the pocket of his overcoat which he had not put there. He didn't take it out. He left it there undisturbed, and it was decided to phone you and get Miss Tormic and Madame Zorka down here. That's all so far. Archie, go get the coat."

I went to the hall and removed it from the hanger and took it back and laid it on Wolfe's desk, with the guilty pocket uppermost.

Wolfe said, "Please, Mr. Cramer. It seemed preferable that you should have the first look at it."

Even when he said that he didn't look at Cramer, but kept watching Neya. Cramer advanced and stuck his hand in the pocket and pulled the thing out. I was right at his elbow, beside myself with curiosity as to what it might be. He stared at the rolled-up bunch of canvas clenched in his fist, then put it down on the desk and unrolled it. The stains were now the color of dark mahogany. As the little metal doodad was disclosed to our gaze I permitted myself an ejaculation of astonishment.

Wolfe said, "I suspected that. Your two missing objects, Mr. Cramer. Aren't they?"

Cramer said to me through his teeth, "So that's why you took a powder."

I gave him a cold hard eye. "Guess again. You heard what Mr. Wolfe said—"

He wheeled on Neya. "You!" he said with his jaw still clamped. "Let's have it." He grabbed the glove, with the *col de mort* nested in the palm, and stuck it under her nose. "Did you put that in Goodwin's pocket?"

She nodded her head. "Yes, I did."

That unclamped his jaw. He goggled at her and I guess I joined him. She was all right. Her hands were clasped tight on her lap and she sat stiff, but she certainly showed no signs of hysteria. Cramer opened his mouth to speak, then shut it again, tramped to the door and pulled it open and bellowed:

"Stebbins! Come here!"

Purley came trotting, with a startled and embarrassed look on his big face because he was trying to chew and swallow at the same time. Cramer motioned to the chair he had been occupying and growled, "Sit down there and take your notebook."

"Wait a minute," Wolfe put in. "Are you charging Miss Tormic?"

"No." Cramer didn't look at him. "I'm asking her. Any objections? If so, I can take her downtown."

"None at all. I prefer it here. We're four to two."

"I don't care if you're a hundred to two." Cramer exhibited the objects to the sergeant. "Put down that I showed her this canvas gauntlet and this steel thing with a point and asked her if she put them in Goodwin's overcoat pocket and she replied, 'Yes, I did.'" He confronted Neya Tormic. "Now. You state that you put these two things into Goodwin's overcoat pocket while it was hanging on a rack in the office of Miltan's studio not long after Ludlow's dead body was discovered. Is that right?"

"Yes."

"Did you kill Percy Ludlow?"

She said in a good clear voice, "You've asked me that before and I said no."

Carla Lovchen blurted, "She can explain—"

"Shut up please!—Do you still say no?"

"Yes."

"Did you take this steel thing off of the end of the épée after it had gone through Ludlow's chest?"

"No."

"Did you take it off the épée with this glove on

your hand and then discover there was blood on the glove and you would have to get rid of both of them?"

"No. I never—"

"When did you take this thing out of the cabinet in Miltan's office?"

"I didn't take it out."

"You put these two things in Goodwin's pocket, didn't you?"

"Yes."

"You had them then, didn't you?"

"Yes."

"Where did you get them?"

"I found them in the pocket of my robe—the green robe I put on over my fencing costume."

"What do you mean, you found them?"

"I just mean that. Isn't that a good word? Found?"

"Sure, it's a swell word. It's a beaut. How and when and why did you find them?"

"Just a moment, Mr. Cramer." It was Wolfe, in a tone that meant business. "Miss Tormic is a stranger in this country. Either I advise her to say nothing whatever and I get a lawyer for her, or I will tell her one or two things myself. At this point."

"What do you want to tell her?"

"You will hear it." Wolfe wiggled a finger. "Miss Tormic. It is unlikely that you will be charged with murder as long as the alibi furnished by Mr. Faber is unimpeached. That is, remains good. You can, however, be put under arrest as a material witness—a device to prevent you from running away—and then be released under a bond to appear when needed. You have been asked to give a circumstantial account of your connection with the instrument of murder, which you have admitted was in your possession shortly after the crime was committed. Your words are being taken down by a stenographer. If you give that account, you will be committed to it as the truth, so it had better be the truth. If you refuse to give it, you will probably be arrested as a material witness. You must decide for yourself. Have I made it clear?"

"Yes," she said, and smiled at him. "I think I understand that all right. There's no reason why I shouldn't tell the truth—it's the only thing I can do, now." She shifted her eyes to Cramer. "It was in the office when we were all in there, waiting for the police to come. I put my hand in the pocket of my robe and there was something in there. It's a big pocket, quite big. I started to pull it out to see what it was, but the feel of it told me it must be a fencing glove. I tried to think what to do. I knew it shouldn't be there—I mean I knew I hadn't put it there. For a minute I was scared, but I made myself think. Mr. Ludlow had been killed in the fencing room where I had been fencing with him, and there I was with a wadded-up glove in my pocket, and if we were searched . . ." She up-turned a palm. "I looked around for a place to put it and saw Mr. Goodwin's coat. I knew it must be his, because the others were all upstairs in their lockers, and I knew he had come there anyway to get me out of trouble—so I went over to it and when I thought no one was looking I took it out of my pocket and put it in his."

"*Very* much obliged—"

"Shut up, Goodwin! Do you realize what you're trying to tell me, Miss Tormic?"

"I . . . I think I do."

"You're trying to tell me that you had a bulky thing like that in your pocket and didn't know it."

"So am I," I put in. "The same goes for me."

"I know damn well it does! Did I ask you to close your trap? What about it, Miss Tormic?"

She shook her head. "I don't know—of course I was excited. It's a loose robe and it's a big pocket. I had it on—you saw it."

"Yeah, I saw it. So you admit you concealed evidence of a crime?"

"Is that . . . wrong?"

"Hell, no. Oh, my, no. And do you know who put it in your pocket?"

"No."

"Of course you don't. Or when?"

"No." Neya frowned. "I have thought about that. I left the robe in the locker room, lying on a bench, when I went to the end room to fence. After I left Mr. Ludlow there and met Mr. Faber in the hall, I stopped in the locker room to leave my pad and glove and mask, and put on the robe and went with Mr. Faber to the alcove. Whoever put the glove in my pocket, I don't think they did it until afterwards, because I think I would have noticed it. After the porter started to yell, we were all running around and jostling against each other—and I suppose someone did it then . . . that's the only way I can explain how it might have happened—"

"And you knew nothing about it."

"I knew nothing about it until I felt something in my pocket there in the office."

"And you were scared. You were just simply perfectly innocent."

"Yes. I was. I am."

"Sure. But though you were perfectly innocent, you didn't tell the police about it, and you weren't going to tell about it, and you never would have told about it, if Madame Zorka hadn't reported that she saw you do it and you were afraid to deny it!" He was yapping into her face at a range of thirty inches. "Huh?"

"I—" She swallowed. "I think I might. But the way I thought about it, I thought Mr. Goodwin would find it in his pocket and turn it over to you, and it wouldn't matter whether you knew it had ever been in my pocket or not."

"Then you thought wrong. Mr. Goodwin doesn't turn things over to the police. Mr. Goodwin climbs a fence and runs home to papa and says see what I got, and papa says—"

"Nonsense!" Wolfe cut in sharply. "We'll dispose of that point now. You know what I told you; I don't need to repeat it. Granted that your supposititious assumption is correct, that Archie knew it was in his pocket and ran away with it, and that we concealed it from you, you can't possibly establish it as a fact, so why the devil waste time harping on it? Especially in view of a fact that is established, that when Madame Zorka's phone call caused us to investigate the overcoat pocket, we immediately communicated with you."

"You had to!"

Wolfe grimaced. "I don't know. Had to? Ingenuity can nearly always create an alternative if none exists. Anyway, we did. And if we hadn't, but had proceeded without you, your two missing objects would still be missing, for when Archie and Miss Tormic called on Madame Zorka she would have been gone, and the compulsion of her threatened exposure would have been removed. So you owe your possession of those two objects to us. You owe your knowledge of a suspicious circumstance, Madame Zorka's flight with a bag and suitcase, to us. And you owe your knowledge of the manner in which the criminal disposed of the glove and *col de mort* to the courageous candor of my client."

Cramer, standing, stared down at him, and as far as I could see his face was not glowing with gratitude.

He said, "So she's your client, is she?"

"I told you so."

"You said tentatively. You said you'd decide when you had met her."

"I have met her."

"All right, you've met her. Is she your client?"

"She is."

Cramer hesitated, then turned slowly and looked down at Neya. His gaze had concentration, but no acute hostility; and I suppressed a grin. I knew what was eating him. He was well aware that the time had yet to come when he would successfully pin a murder charge on any man, woman or child whom Nero Wolfe had accepted as a client, and he was strongly tempted to call it a day then and there as far as Neya Tormic was concerned and throw in another line. He even, half unconsciously, favored Carla Lovchen with a sidewise suspicious glance, but he returned to Neya and, after a moment, wheeled again to Wolfe.

"Faber gives her an alibi. Okay. But you don't need to be told that an alibi works both ways. What if Faber thought she needed one and so he provided it? And she thought she needed it to, and accepted it and confirmed it? Without maybe realizing that while Faber was giving her an alibi, what he was really doing was arranging one for himself?"

Wolfe nodded. "An old trick, but still a good one. That's quite possible, of course. Will you have some beer?"

"No."

"You, Miss Tormic, Miss Lovchen?"

He got their declinations, pressed the button and went on. "This thing's messy, Mr. Cramer. It looks as if I'm going to have to find out who killed Mr. Ludlow, unless you do it first yourself. You certainly aren't going to get anywhere badgering my client. Look at her. I'll have a little talk with her after you leave, and one thing I shall tell her is to hang onto the Faber alibi, for the present, even if it was fabricated by him. True, it protects Faber, but it also protects her. If and when you can point a suspicion at Faber, especially a motive, let me know and we'll discuss the alibi business."

"You suspect her of lying yourself!"

"Not specifically. Anyone would tell a lie, at least by acquiescence, rather than stand trial for murder. By the way, about this Mr. Faber. You are entirely wrong in your suspicion that he wasn't a stranger to me. I never saw him or heard of him in my life before today. Is he by any chance another confidential government agent?"

Cramer eyed him. "How did you know that if he was such a stranger to you?"

"I didn't. Mere conjecture. If I had known it I wouldn't have asked. Not British, is he?"

"No."

"Of course not. He might as well display an emblem on an arm band. Archie and I don't like him. It's a pity my client's alibi depends on him; I would prefer to establish her innocence without that. Do you suppose the attack on Ludlow was the eagle clawing the lion?"

"I don't suppose. It was a human being murdering a man."

"Yes, it was that, all right." Wolfe glanced up at the clock. "It's well past midnight, and I want to have a little talk with Miss Tormic. Is there anything else you want to ask her?"

"She's an alien. I ought to have her under bond."

"She won't skip, at least not tonight, and we can arrange for the bond tomorrow if you insist on it."

Cramer grunted. "She's important. She had the murder weapon in her possession. I'd like to have her come to my office tomorrow morning at nine o'clock and see Lieutenant Rowcliff."

Wolfe frowned. "Mr. Rowcliff is the officer who came here once with a warrant and searched my house."

"Yeah. You don't forget that, do you?"

"No. Neither do you—Come in . . . Yes, Fritz?"

On account of the barricade of chairs, Fritz had to talk over the top of Neya Tormic's head. He was stiffly formal, as was his invariable custom when there were ladies present, not from any sense of propriety but from fear. Whenever any female, no matter what her age or appearance, got inside the house, he was apprehensive and ill at ease until she got out again.

"A gentleman to see you, sir. Mr. Stahl. He was here this afternoon."

Wolfe said to show him in.

Chapter 8

The G-man was wearing the same suit and the same manners, and the only visible change was that he had had his shoes shined. Cramer took one look at him, let out a grunt, and propped himself against the edge of my desk.

The G-man apologized in his educated voice. "I didn't know you were engaged, Mr. Wolfe . . . I don't want to interrupt—"

"I'll be engaged for some time. Do you need to see me alone?"

That seemed to stump him. He frowned and took a quick survey of the crowd. "Perhaps not," he decided. "It's only . . . about that statute requiring the registration of agents of foreign principals."

"What about it?"

"Well—it is necessary to make sure that you understand the requirements."

"I think I do understand them."

"Perhaps. Section 5 of the Act says, 'Any person who willfully fails to file any statement required to be filed under this act, or, in complying with the provisions of this act, makes a false statement of a material fact, or willfully omits to state any material fact required to be stated therein, shall, on conviction thereof, be punished by a fine of not more than $1000 or imprisonment for not more than two years, or both.'"

"Yes, I understand that."

"Perhaps. Another section of the Act defines an agent of a foreign principal to mean any individual, partnership, association or corporation who acts or engages as agent or representative for a foreign principal, and a foreign principal is defined to mean the government of a foreign country, a person domiciled abroad, or any foreign business, partnership, association, corporation, or political organization."

"Say it again."

He repeated it.

Wolfe shook his head. "I don't know. I don't think I need to register under the act. I am agent for a young woman named Neya Tormic. She is foreign. But she is not a business, partnership, association, corporation, or political organization, nor is she at present domiciled abroad."

"Where is she?"

"Right there."

The G-man looked at Neya; in fact, he studied her. Then he switched to Wolfe and studied him. Finally he slowly shook his head. "I don't know either," he declared. "It's a situation I haven't met. I'll have to get an opinion from the attorney general. I'll let you know."

He bowed with perfect aplomb, turned, and departed.

I tittered.

Cramer threw up both hands, pawed the air, and headed for the door. Halfway across he turned to announce, "I heard every word of that and I don't believe it. If I had it on a phonograph record and played it all day I still wouldn't believe it. And in spite of that, I believe in law enforcement. Come on, Stebbins. Bring that glove and that thing. Miss Tormic, there'll be a man at your apartment at 8:30 in the morning to bring you to my office. You'll be there?"

She said she would, and went out with the sergeant at his heels.

Wolfe poured beer and drank. I covered a yawn.

Neya Tormic asked, with her forehead wrinkled, "Was it silly of me to admit it like that? I thought—it seemed to be the only thing I could do."

Wolfe wiped his lips, leaned back, and looked at her. "Anyhow, it was one thing to do, and you did it. Was it the truth?"

"Yes."

"Is Faber's story, which you have confirmed, and which gives you both an alibi, also true?"

"Yes."

"You realize, I suppose, that without that alibi you would probably now be under arrest, charged with murder."

"Yes."

"Did you know that Ludlow was an agent of the British government?"

"Yes."

"And that Faber is an agent of the German government?"

"Yes."

"Are you a government agent, or is Miss Lovchen?"

"No."

"Do you know who killed Ludlow?"

"No."

"Have you any idea?"

"No."

His eyes darted aside. "Did you kill Ludlow, Miss Lovchen?"

"No, sir."

"Have you any idea who did?"

"No, sir."

Wolfe sighed. "Now. Take those orders. Mr. and Mrs. Miltan, Driscoll, Gill, Barrett, Miss Reade, Madame Zorka. Do you know whether they were involved with Ludlow, either politically or personally?"

Neya's eyes shifted to Carla and then returned to Wolfe. She opened her mouth, closed it, and then spoke. "I don't know how much involved. They all knew each other. We haven't been there very long ourselves."

"Did you first meet Ludlow and Faber at Miltan's?"

"Yes."

"How did you learn they were government agents?"

"Why . . . they told me."

"Indeed. Just told you to make conversation?"

"They . . . well, they told me." She smiled at him. "Under certain conditions—I mean, a man is apt to tell a girl things if the conditions are such that he feels like it."

"Were you intimate with Mr. Ludlow? Are you intimate with Mr. Faber?"

"Oh, no." Her nose seemed to go up. "Not intimate."

"Yet they told you—never mind. You say you are not a government agent. Are you a political agent? Did you come to this country on a political mission?"

"No."

"Did you, Miss Lovchen?"

"No, sir."

"You're both lying."

They stared at him. Neya's chin went up. Carla's eyes narrowed, which left them still wide enough for ordinary purposes.

Wolfe snapped, "As an intrigante, Miss Lovchen, you are incredibly maladroit. Twice since you entered this room you have glanced at the place on the bookshelves where my copy of *United Yugoslavia* stands. I know you put that paper there. I've removed it and put it somewhere else."

Neya merely continued to stare, but Carla jumped up, with her face white, and started to sputter at him, "But I—I only meant—"

"I know." He showed her a palm. "You only meant to leave it there a while for safekeeping. It's even safer where I put it. The reason I mention it—"

"Where is it?" Neya Tormic's eyes were two épées going through him and her tone was a dagger whizzing at him. She was up and at the edge of his desk in one swift movement that reminded me of the lunge Miltan had made with his championship sticker to show me how it was done. She threw the dagger again, at short range: "Where is it?"

She turned, because Carla was up too and had grabbed her arm. She shook herself loose, but Carla seized her elbow again and told her sharply, "Neya— Neya! Sit down! Neya—you know—"

Neya spouted a torrent at her that I would have had no symbols for if I had been at my notebook. Carla returned it, but not in a torrent; she was cool and controlled.

Wolfe said, "I understand Serbo-Croat."

They both said, "Oh!"

He nodded. "I used to knock around. I did some

work for the Austrian government when I was too young to know better. And I was in your country in 1921, and adopted a daughter—"

"I want that paper."

"I know you do, Miss Lovchen. But I won't even discuss it, let alone return it to you, unless you children sit down and behave yourselves. None of this jumping up and caterwauling; I don't like it; besides, it won't do you any good. Sit down!"

They sat.

"That's better. I mentioned that paper only to show you how I knew you were lying when you said you aren't in this country on a political mission—and by the way, I suppose you lied to the police too? Of course you did. Now that the paper's been mentioned—where did you get it, Miss Lovchen?"

"I . . ." She fingered her skirt. "I got it."

"Where and how? Is it yours?"

"I stole it."

Neya snapped, "You did not! I stole it myself!"

Wolfe shrugged. "Split the honors. Who did you steal it from?"

"From the person who had it."

"From the Princess Vladanka Donevitch?"

"I won't tell you."

"Good. That's better than trying to lie. Is the princess in New York now?"

"I won't tell you anything about that paper."

"You are in danger. You are actually in peril of your life. Faber's unsupported alibi is the only thing between you and an indictment for murder. Do you want my assistance in the removal of that danger?"

"Yes." It looked for an instant as if she were going to smile at him, but she didn't. "Yes," she repeated, "I do."

"Are you prepared to pay me? My usual fee? Several thousand dollars, for instance?"

"My God, no." She glanced at Carla and back at him. "But . . . I might."

"But when you sent Miss Lovchen here in the first place, you expected me to help you because you are my adopted daughter, didn't you?"

She nodded. "I thought you might feel—"

"I carry this fat to insulate my feelings. They got too strong for me once or twice and I had that idea. If I had stayed lean and kept moving around I would have been dead long ago. You are aware that I have no proof that you are my daughter. You sent Miss Lovchen here with that record of adoption bearing my signature. Another paper. Did you steal that too?"

Carla ejaculated something indignant. Neya was on her feet, with her eyes flashing. "If you think I did that, there's no use—"

"I don't think you did that. I just don't know. I asked you to stop jumping up. Please sit down, Miss Tormic. Thank you. I used to be idiotically romantic. I still am, but I've got it in hand. I thought it romantic, when I was a boy, twenty-five years ago, to be a secret agent of the Austrian government. My progress toward maturity got interrupted by the World War and my experience with it. War doesn't mature men; it merely pickles them in the brine of disgust and dread. Pfui! After the war I was still lean and I moved around. In Montenegro I assumed responsibility for the sustenance and mental and physical thrift of a three-year-old orphan girl by adopting her. I did something else there too, which advanced my maturity, but that has nothing to do with you. I saw that girl's ribs. The something else I did finished Montenegro for me, and I left the girl, I thought, in good hands, and returned to America."

Wolfe leaned back and let his lids down a little. "You go on from there, please."

Neya said, "You left me in Zagreb with Pero Brovnik and his wife."

"That's right. Your name?"

"My name was Anna. When I was eight years old they were arrested as revolutionaries and shot. I don't remember that very well, but I know all about it."

"Yes." Wolfe looked grim. "And for three years the money I continued to send to Zagreb was appropriated by someone in Brovnik's name, and when I got suspicious and went over there, in spite of the fact that I was no longer lean, I got nowhere. I couldn't find the girl. I got no satisfaction about the money. I got put in jail, and the American consul got me out and I was given ten hours to leave the country." He made a face. "I have not been in Europe, nor in jail, since. Where were you?"

"I was eleven years old then."

"Yes. I can add. Where were you?"

She looked at him a while before she spoke. "I can't tell you that."

"You'll either tell me that or march on out of here and not come back. And I have the paper which you stole and your friend left in my book for safekeeping. Now don't start caterwauling."

Carla said, "Tell him, Neya."

"But Carla! Then he'll know—"

"Tell him."

"And tell the truth," Wolfe advised, "or I'll know that, and I'll know it even better after I've cabled Europe."

She told him. "When the Brovniks were arrested

I was sent to an institution. A year later I was taken out by a woman named Mrs. Campbell."

"Who was she?"

"She was the English secretary of Prince Peter Donevitch."

"What did she want with you?"

"She visited the institution and she took a liking to me. My ribs didn't show then. She wanted to adopt me, but she couldn't, legally, on account of you."

"Why didn't she communicate with me?"

"Because . . . her connection with Prince Donevitch. The kind of friends you had had in Yugoslavia, like the Brovniks. They knew you would make trouble, and they didn't want trouble from an American."

"No. You can't take an American out and shoot him. So she just stole the money I sent for three years."

"I don't know anything about that."

"Where is she now?"

"She died four years ago."

"Where did you go then?"

"I continued to live there."

"With Donevitch?"

"In that house."

"Did young Prince Stefan live there?"

"Yes, he—he and his sisters."

"And his wife?"

"After—of course. When he was married, two years ago."

"Were you treated as one of the family?"

"No." She hesitated and then said more emphatically, "No, I wasn't."

Wolfe turned abruptly to Carla Lovchen and snapped at her, "Are you Stefan's wife? The Princess Vladanka?"

Her eyes popped open. "Me? *Boga ti!* No!"

"You had that paper which you put in my book."

Neya said, "I told you I stole that paper. I don't always lie."

"Where did you steal it, Zagreb or New York?"

She shook her head. "I can't tell about that paper. Not even—no matter what you do."

He grunted. "Your secret political mission. I know. Die first. I used to play that silly dirty game myself. But since you lived in the same house with the Princess Vladanka, you must know her pretty well. Are you and she friends?"

"Friends?" Neya's forehead showed a crease. "No."

"What's she like?"

"She is clever, beautiful, selfish and treacherous."

"Indeed. What does she look like?"

"Well . . . she is tall. Her arms move like snakes. Her face is like this." Neya described an oval with her fingers. "Her eyes are as black as mine—sometimes blacker."

"Is she in Zagreb now?"

"She was when I left. It was said she was going to Paris to see old Prince Peter and then to America."

"You're lying."

She looked straight at him. "Sometimes it is necessary to lie. There are some things I can't tell."

"Ha, over your dead body. The curlicues of some old bandit's trademark engraved on your heart, and what do you get out of it? When do you expect to finish this political errand you're working on?"

She looked at him, at Carla, back at him, and said nothing.

"Come, come," he insisted impatiently. "I merely ask when. Is the end in sight?"

"I think so," she admitted. "I think it will be . . . To-morrow."

"It's past midnight. Do you mean this day?"

"Yes. But I must have that paper. You have no right to keep it. When that imbecile, that Driscoll, made the trouble about his diamonds being stolen, I thought the police might come and search everything, even my room where I live. I thought of you, the American who had adopted me when I was a baby; I had brought the record of adoption with me when I left Zagreb; Mrs. Campbell had given it to me before she died. So Carla and I decided the paper would be safer with you than anywhere else, and we decided how to do it so she could easily get it again. Then you refused to help me and she had to return and let you know who I am." She stopped and smiled at him, but she was so anxious that the effort was a little cock-eyed. "I must have that paper now! I must!"

"We'll see. You admit you stole it. So you expect to accomplish your mission this day."

"Yes."

"You realize, of course, that the police won't let you leave New York until they're satisfied their murder case is solved."

"But I . . . you said yourself my alibi—"

"That doesn't solve the case. Don't you do anything silly. If you do complete your errand, don't try sneaking aboard a ship disguised as a Nereid. Who is Madame Zorka?"

They both stared at him in surprise.

"Well?" Wolfe demanded. "You know her, don't you?"

Carla laughed. It sounded quite natural, as though something really had struck her as funny. Neya said:

"Why . . . she's nobody. She's a dressmaker."

"So I understand. Where did she get that name? The name of the daughter of King Nikita of Montenegro."

"But Queen Zorka has been dead—"

"I know that. Where did this dressmaker get the name?"

Carla laughed again. "She must have found it in a book."

"Who is she?"

Neya shrugged and upturned her palms. "We know nothing about her."

Wolfe eyed them a moment and then sighed. "All right. It's late and you ought to be in bed, since you have to get up early to visit Mr. Rowcliff. That smile ought to help with him. When you are through there, come here, and I'll see you at eleven o'clock and give you that paper."

"I want it now!"

"You can't have it now. It isn't here. I will—"

Neya jumped up. "What did you—where is it?"

"Stop screaming at me. It's safe. I'll give it to you at eleven o'clock. Sit down—no, don't bother to sit down; you're going. Remember now, don't do anything silly. As for you, Miss Lovchen, I would advise you to do nothing whatever except eat and sleep. I say that on account of your performance yesterday when you hid that paper in my book—asking Mr. Goodwin if I had read it and did I study it and was he reading it. Unbelievable!"

Carla flushed. "I thought . . . I was casual—"

"Good heavens! Casual? I still suspect you meant us to find it, though I can't imagine what for. Well, good night—By the way, Miss Tormic, about your being my client. I'll return that adoption paper to you in the morning along with the other; it seems likely that it belongs to you; but I am cautious and skeptical and I don't like misunderstandings. You are my client only so long as it remains established that you are the girl whose ribs I saw in 1921. I am your protector, but if it turns out that you have duped me on that, I shall be your enemy. I don't like to be fooled."

"I doubt if I could fool you if I wanted to." She met his eye and suddenly smiled at him. "You can feel my ribs if you want to, but as for looking at them—"

"Oh, no. No, thank you. Good night. Good night, Miss Lovchen."

I went with them and extended the courtesies of the hall, and when they were out I shot the night bolt on the door. Then I went back to the office and stood and looked down at Wolfe's colossal countenance, immobile with closed eyes, and treated myself to an unrestricted stretch and yawn.

"*Hvala Bogu,*" I declared. "I like Montenegrin girls, but it's time to go to bed. They're all right. I offered to take them home and they refused to let me. In spite of which, I have to run up to 48th Street before I turn in, to get the damn roadster I left there. This is a very peculiar case. I've got a feeling in my bones that there is going to be a strange romantic twist to it by the time we get through. I have an inner conviction that when the full moon comes I'll be standing right here in this office asking you formally for the hand of your daughter in marriage. You've got something there, gospodar. Only you'll have to help me break her of lying."

"Shut up."

"Shall I go up for the roadster?"

"I suppose you'll have to." Wolfe shuddered. Out into the night like that. "What time will Saul be here in the morning?"

"Nine o'clock."

"Phone him and tell him to bring that envelope."

"Yes, sir. Are you really going to hand it over to her?"

"I am. I want to see what she is going to do with it. Will Fred and Orrie also be here at nine?"

"Yes, sir. Who do you want to tail whom?"

"Tailing may not be necessary. On the other hand it may be, for her protection. Mr. Faber wanted that paper."

"Not only did he want it, he knew where to look for it." I yawned. "And since Carla put it there, did she tell him about it? Or did he learn it from a member of your family?"

"I have no family."

"A daughter is commonly considered to be a member of one's family. In this case it would hardly be too much to say that a daughter *is* a family." I made my voice grave and respectful. "When I marry her I guess it will be unavoidable for me to call you Dad."

"Archie, I swear by all—"

"And I would be your heir in case you die. I would be the beneficiary on your life insurance. We could play in father and son golf tournaments. Later on you could hold the baby. Babies. When the time comes for the divorce—now what the hell!"

The doorbell was ringing.

Chapter 9

At half past one in the morning, with me yawning my head off and an outside errand still to do, the doorbell should ring.

I went to the front and unlocked, leaving the chain bolt on so that the door only opened to a five-inch crack, and peered through at the male figure standing there.

"Well?"

"I want to see Nero Wolfe."

"Name, please?"

"Open the door!" He was a bit peremptory.

"Tut tut," I said. "It's after office hours. If you don't like your own name, make up one. But it had better be a good one, at this time of night."

"My name is Donald Barrett."

"Oh. Okay. Hold that pose. I'll be back."

I went to the office and told Wolfe. He opened his eyes, frowned, muttered something, and nodded. I returned to the front and let the nightwalker in, flunkeyed for him, and escorted him to the office. In the bright light he looked handsome and harassed, with his white tie somewhat crooked and his hair disarranged. He blinked at Wolfe and said he was Donald Barrett.

"So I understand. Sit down."

"Thanks." He lodged his sitter on the edge of a chair in a temporary manner. "This is a frightful stink, this thing."

Wolfe's brows went slightly up. "This thing?"

"This—up at Miltan's. Ludlow. It's murder, you know."

"I believe it is. You were among those present."

"Yes, I was, damn it. Of course you got that from this fellow you sent up there."

"Excuse me," Wolfe murmured. "I thought you two had met. Mr. Barrett, this is Mr. Goodwin, my assistant."

"Oh, we met. We spoke a few words. He was guarding the door and I asked him to let a young lady through to keep an important appointment and he wouldn't do it."

Wolfe nodded. "That was Miss Reade."

"Oh? He told you that too?"

"Mr. Goodwin tells me everything."

"I suppose he would. Naturally. He was damn bullheaded about letting Miss Reade out. He said the worst thing she could do was to leave the place and start the cops looking for her, and then, by God, he gets out himself somehow and starts them looking for him!"

"I know. He goes by whim." Wolfe was sympathetic. "Is that what you came to see me for? To reproach me for Mr. Goodwin's behavior?"

Barrett looked at him suspiciously, but Wolfe's expression was bland. "No," he said, "I just mentioned it. He was damn bullheaded. There was no reason in the world why Miss Reade should have been kept there. As far as I myself was concerned, I was perfectly willing to stand the inconvenience. But I came to see you regarding another . . . well, another angle. This fellow that you sent up there—you sent him to represent Miss Tormic, didn't you?"

"What fellow?"

"Your assistant, damn it!" His head went sidewise in my direction. "Goodwin."

"Yes. I'm not really obtuse, Mr. Barrett, only I like the custom of designating people by their names; it's so handy. Yes, Mr. Goodwin was there in the interest of Miss Tormic."

"That's what he said."

"She agreed, didn't she?"

"Sure. That was all right. But that was about that business of Driscoll's diamonds—the damn fool. What I want to know is, are you still representing her? I mean, in connection with the murder."

"Do you ask that question as a curious friend?"

"Why, I—a friend, yes. It's not just curiosity."

"Well, I am representing Miss Tormic. What moved you besides curiosity?"

"Oh, just . . ." He hesitated. He put his hand up to smooth his straggled hair, shifted in his chair, and cleared his throat. "Frankly, just that I'm a little interested in Miss Tormic and I should hate it . . . you know? Such a frightful stink? I only met her a couple of months ago, and I got her and Miss Lovchen their jobs at Miltan's—and I feel some responsibility about that too. She's a stranger in New York, and I wanted to be sure she has proper and competent advice. Of course, if you're representing her . . ."

"I am."

"That ought to settle it."

"Thank you."

"Provided you . . ." He smoothed his hair, and cleared his throat again. It was plain that he was having trouble getting the cork out. "Provided you appreciate that it's important that she shouldn't be tangled up in the thing at all. For instance, take that rumor that she was seen putting something in that fellow—in Goodwin's overcoat pocket. If that got to the police it would start a hell of a row. Although I don't believe she did any such thing. I doubt if anybody did." He turned to me. "You ought to know. Did you find anything in your overcoat pocket?"

"Sure." I grinned at him. "Driscoll's diamonds."

"No, damn it—"

"Permit me," Wolfe said brusquely. "If we are in possession of any secrets which we think should remain secret in the interest of Miss Tormic, we certainly aren't going to disclose them. Neither to the police nor to anyone else. Including you, sir. If you came here for information of that kind you may expect a famine."

"I am a friend of Miss Tormic."

"Then you should be glad that she has discreet advisers."

"That's all right. Certainly. But sometimes you fellows like to stand in with the police. You know? And it would be bad if they got hold of that talk about her putting something in Goodwin's pocket. They'd go after her plenty and they'd turn her inside out. It was bad enough that she had been in there fencing with Ludlow, and this would make it ten times worse. I wanted to be sure you appreciate—"

"We do, Mr. Barrett. We haven't much native subtlety, but a long experience has taught us things— for instance, never to toss ammunition to the enemy except under compulsion or in exchange for something better." Wolfe's tone was a soothing purr, which made me wonder when and why he was getting ready to pounce. He went on with it: "By the way, I don't suppose you happened to meet Miss Tormic on your way down here just now?"

"No, I didn't. Why? Where was she?"

"She was here for a little talk. She and her friend, Miss Lovchen. They left shortly before you arrived and I wondered if by any chance you had seen them."

"No."

"Have you had an opportunity to talk this thing over with her in much detail?"

"Not much of one. You might say none, really. They questioned the men first up there, and they let me go around eight o'clock. She was still there. I don't know how long they kept her."

"Indeed. Since you are a sufficiently good friend of hers to bother to come down here, it might be thought that you wouldn't have gone off and left her there."

"I couldn't get at her. The place was full of cops and there was one for everybody. Anyway, that's my business. Meaning it's none of yours. You know?"

"Yes, excuse me. You're quite right." Then Wolfe pounced. As usual, there was no change whatever in his tone as his forefinger traced a tiny circle on the polished mahogany of his chair arm. "But I think you'll have to concede that this is my business: where have you hid Madame Zorka?"

Chapter 10

Donald Barrett wasn't especially good; not much above the average man when he is suddenly and abruptly faced with a question which he isn't supposed to know the answer to but does. His jaw loosened, his eyes widened, and his breathing stopped. The first two may be the result of innocent surprise, but not the third. But he was fairly quick on the recovery. He stared at Wolfe and made folds in his smooth handsome brow and demanded:

"Where have I hid who?"

"Madame Zorka."

He shook his head. "If it's a joke you'll have to explain it to me. I don't get it."

Wolfe said patiently, "I'll explain it. Madame Zorka phoned here this evening and said she saw Miss Tormic put something in Mr. Goodwin's pocket and she was going to report it to the police immediately."

"The devil she did!"

"Please don't interrupt. It's wasted. Mr. Goodwin persuaded her to postpone informing the police until he could take Miss Tormic to Madame Zorka's apartment for a discussion of the matter. When he and Miss Tormic arrived some time later, they found the apartment empty; and they learned that Madame Zorka had departed fifteen minutes previously, in a hurry, with a bag and suitcase. Mr. Goodwin then brought Miss Tormic and Miss Lovchen here to see me."

"Well, that—"

"Please. The two young ladies have a talk with me and leave. Soon you arrive. You reveal that you possess knowledge of three facts: that someone says that Miss Tormic was seen putting something in Mr. Goodwin's pocket, that that information has not yet reached the police, and that it has reached me. The first two you might have got hold of in several conceivable ways, but not the third. You couldn't possibly have known that the information had reached me unless Madame Zorka communicated with you after she phoned here."

Barrett was standing up, apparently with the idea that it was time to go. "Rubbish," he snorted. "If that's the kind of deduction—"

Wolfe shook his head and his tone got sharp. "I won't have it, sir. I won't spend an hour working it into your skull that I know what I know. Madame Zorka told you what she had told me. Don't try dodging; you'll only annoy me."

"It would be too damn bad if I annoyed you." He looked and sounded nasty. "What if Zorka did tell me about it? What if that's why I came down here? What's wrong with that?"

"Did she?"

"What if she did?"

"Did she?"

"Yes!"

"On the telephone?"

"Yes."

"And you, being a friend of Miss Tormic, saw that

the only way to make sure that her story would not reach the police was to hustle her away somewhere— and you somehow persuaded her. Then you thought of the possibility that I might pass it on to the police, and came here to plug that hole. Where is Madame Zorka, Mr. Barrett?"

"I don't know. I supposed she was at home until you said Goodwin was told she had gone with her bag and suitcase. I'll tell *you* something. I don't like the way you're handling this and I'm going to tell Miss Tormic so. She ought to have a good lawyer, anyway, and I'll see that she gets one. If she lets you out, how much cash will you take not to peddle this fairy tale to the police about her putting something in Goodwin's pocket?"

I got up and took a step toward him, but Wolfe shook his head at me. "No, Archie. Let me—"

I said, "Excuse me. There are times when you get mad and there are times when I get mad. I'll make a concession. I was going to hit him and then talk, but I'll talk first."

I put my face fourteen inches from Barrett's. "You. I am restraining myself. You have implied that this office has a stooling department. What evidence have you got to back that up? Talk like a man whether you are one or not. I warn you I'm mad. Have you got any evidence?"

"I . . . I didn't mean—"

"Have you?"

"No."

"Are you sorry you said it?"

"Yes."

"Don't say it to oblige me. I'd rather you refused to say it. You *are* sorry?"

"Yes."

"Marshmallows," I muttered, and went back to my chair.

Wolfe said, "You'll have to learn to control that, Archie. Physical duress, unless carried to an intolerable extreme, is a miserable weapon." He wiggled a finger at Barrett. "Not that I object to duress when it's necessary, as it is now. It doesn't matter what it was that moved Madame Zorka to tell you about her phone call to me; the fact is that she did so; nor does it matter what form of persuasion you used on her. It's obvious that you hid her, or at least you know where she is, since it was you who got her to pack up and go—"

Barrett started off. I circled around him on the lope to head him off at the door. Wolfe snapped at his back:

"Come back here! Unless you want everyone sniffing on the trail of Bosnian forest concessions and Yugoslav credits—"

I admit that Wolfe's form of duress was more effective than mine. Mine had made him eat a bite of crow, but Wolfe's apparently drained him of his blood. Three steps from the door he stopped and stiffened, and his cheeks went pasty. He turned slowly then, to face Wolfe. I went back to my chair and sat and enjoyed looking at him.

He wet his lips with his tongue, twice. Then he moved, clear to the corner of Wolfe's desk, and squeaked down at him: "What are you talking about? Do you know what you're talking about?"

"Certainly. About banditry. A euphemism for it is international finance. In this case represented by the well-known firm of Barrett & De Russy."

"And what about it?"

Wolfe shook his head. "I furnish no details, Mr. Barrett. You know them better than I do. The precise amount of the credits held by your firm, for instance, and the extent of its relations with the Donevitch gang. I don't need to supply details in order to blackmail you, which is all I'm after. I merely want to see Madame Zorka, and I'm sure you'll help me on that rather than have this Yugoslav foray exposed to a lot of disconcerting curiosity."

Barrett, motionless and silent, gazed at him. Southwest of his ear, above the edge of his starched white collar, I could see the tendons on his neck standing out. Finally he squeaked again:

"Who are you working for?"

"For Miss Tormic."

"I asked you, who are you working for? Rome?"

"I am working on a murder case. My client is Neya Tormic. My only interest—"

"Oh, skip it. Do you think I'm a boob?" The international financier put the tips of eight fingers on the desk and gave them some weight. "Look here. I understand perfectly that no matter who you're working for, you wouldn't be tipping me off just for your health. If you'll put this damn pet gorilla of yours on a leash, I'm quite willing to discuss details and terms— subject of course to consultation with my associates—"

"Pfui." Wolfe was disgusted. "I might have known it would make you ugly. Now how the devil am I going to convince you that my only concern is the welfare of my client?"

"I don't know. If I were you I wouldn't try." Barrett's voice had lost its squeak and assumed a tone that might have sold me on the idea he was really tough if I hadn't already caught a glimpse of the yellow. "I don't know how far you're in, but I presume you know what you're doing. If you do, I don't need to tell you that it's too dangerous a game for anybody to try any private hijacking."

"I said blackmail."

"All right, blackmail. Who are you selling out and what's your price?"

I let it pass. If he was going to wholesale his insults, it would save trouble to wait till he was finished and then collect in a lump sum.

Wolfe leaned back and sighed. "Will you sit down, sir?"

"I'm all right standing."

"Then please back up. I'm not comfortable with my head tilted. Now listen. Get it out of your head that I represent any interest, either friendly or hostile to you, in your Balkan enterprise. I don't. Then, you wonder, how did I learn of it? What's the difference? I did. Next you must somehow manage to believe that I do not want a slice of the loot. Incredible and even immoral as that must seem to a man of your instinct and training, I don't. I want just one thing. I want you to conduct Mr. Goodwin to Madame Zorka, wherever you have put her, and he will bring her here. That's all. Unless you do that, I shall send information at once, to three different quarters, of your firm's projected raid on the property of the people of Yugoslavia. You know better than I do the sort of hullabaloo that would start. Don't complicate matters by assuming for me a cupidity and corruption beyond the limits I have set for myself. You're suffering from an occupational disease. When an international financier is confronted by a holdup man with a gun, he automatically hands over not only his money and jewelry but also his shirt and pants, because it doesn't occur to him that a robber might draw the line somewhere. I beg you, understand that I want Madame Zorka and nothing else. Beyond that I do not and shall not represent any threat to you—unless, of course, it should turn out that it was you who murdered Percy Ludlow."

Wolfe shifted his eyes to me. "Archie, I'm afraid there's no help for it. Mr. Barrett will take you to Madame Zorka. You will bring her here."

"What if she's skipped town?"

"I doubt it. She can't have got far. Take the roadster and go after her. Hang onto Mr. Barrett."

"That's the part I don't like, hanging onto Barrett."

"I know. You'll have to put up with it. It may be only—" He switched to Barrett. "Where is she? How far away?"

The financier was standing there trying to concentrate, with his gaze fastened on Wolfe and his lips working. He made them function: "Damn you, if you let this out—"

Wolfe said curtly, "I've told you what I want, and that's all I want. Where is she?"

"She's—I think—not far away."

"In the city?"

"I think so."

"Good. Don't try any tricks with Mr. Goodwin. They make him lose his temper."

"I'm coming back with them. I want to talk—"

"No. Not tonight. Tomorrow perhaps. Don't let him in, Archie."

"Okay." I was on my feet. "For God's sake, let's step on it, or my bed will think I'm having an affair with the couch. I only wish I was."

He didn't like going, leaving Wolfe there within three feet of a telephone and all that intimate knowledge of Bosnian forests buzzing in his head, but I eased him into the hall and on out into the November night.

I had rather expected to find a Minerva town car waiting at the curb, considering his category, but there wasn't anything there at all, and we had to hoof it to Eighth Avenue before we could ambush a taxi at that ungodly hour. We piled in, me last, and he told the driver Times Square.

As we jolted off I surveyed him disapprovingly. "Don't tell me you left her standing on the sidewalk."

Disregarding that, he twisted himself on the cushion to face me in a confidential manner. "See here, Goodwin," he demanded, "you've got to help me. I'm in a bad hole. It wouldn't have done any good to try to persuade Wolfe that I don't know where Zorka is, because he was convinced that I do. But the fact is, I don't know."

"That's too bad."

"Yes. I'm in one hell of a fix. If you go back and say I told you I couldn't take you to her because I don't know where she is, he'll do what he threatened to do."

"He sure will. So I won't go back and say that."

"No, that wouldn't do. If I couldn't persuade him I don't know, I can't expect you to. But we could work it this way. We can drop in somewhere and have a couple of drinks. Then, say in half an hour or so, you go back and tell him I took you to an address—pick out any likely address—and we went in expecting to find Zorka and she wasn't there. You can describe how astonished and upset I was—you know, make it vivid."

"Sure, I'm good at that. But you haven't—"

"Wait a minute." The taxi swerved into 42nd Street, and he lurched against me and got straight again. "I know you'll get the devil for going back without Zorka, but you can't help that anyway, because I don't know where she is. I wouldn't expect you to help me out of this just for the hell of it. Why should you? You know? How about fifty dollars?"

I have never seen a worse case of briber's itch.

I made a scornful sound. "Now, brother! Fifty lousy bucks with a big deal in international finance trembling in the balance? A century at least."

The driver called back, "Which corner?"

Barrett told him to stop at the curb and leave his meter on. Then he stretched out a leg to get into his trouser pocket, and extracted a modest roll. "I don't know if I happen to have that much with me." He peered and counted in the dim light. Glancing through the window, I saw an old woman in a shawl headed for us with a box of chewing gum. I wouldn't even have to leave the cab.

"I've got it," Barrett said.

"Good. Gimme, please. I can concentrate on the details better with the jack in my jeans."

He handed it over. Without bothering to count it, I shoved it through the window at the old woman and told her, "Here, grandma, two packets and keep the change." She passed them in, took the currency and gave it a look, gave me a swift startled glance from bleary old eyes and shuffled off double-quick. I offered a packet of gum to Barrett and said, "Here, one apiece."

Instead of taking it he sputtered, "You goddam lunatic!"

I shook my head. "Nope, wrong again. You sure do make a lot of mistakes, mister. That little gesture I just made, that wasn't original—I first had the idea upstate in a cow barn and the beneficiary was a guy in overalls with a pitchfork." I stuck a piece of gum in my mouth. "Maybe this will keep me awake. That's enough horseplay and, besides, Mr. Wolfe is waiting. Lead me to Zorka."

"Why you dirty cheap—"

"Oh, can it! What's the address?"

"I don't know. I don't know where she is."

"Okay." I leaned forward to the driver. "Go to 48th Street, east of Lexington."

He nodded and got in gear.

Barrett demanded, "What are you going to do? What are you going to Miltan's for?"

"I left my car there. I'm going to get it and drive it home, and tell Mr. Wolfe the sad news, and then, I suppose, help him until dawn with phone calls and so on. He never puts off till tomorrow what I can do today."

"Do you mean to say that after taking my money and giving it to that hag—"

"I mean to say exactly that. Either you quit stalling and squirming and take me to Zorka, or I go back to Nero Wolfe and watch him throw the switch. I ought to be asleep right now. You claim you don't know where Zorka is. My employer claims you do. I have no opinion. My mind is open, but I follow instructions blindly. Take me to Zorka or pop goes the weasel."

The taxi bumped across Sixth Avenue and scooted ahead for Fifth, along Bryant Park. Nearing the library, he called to the driver: "Stop at the curb and leave the meter on." As we rolled to a standstill I said, "You'd better keep the rest of your dough to pay the fare with."

He sat and glared at me in silence. Finally he blurted, "Look here, I can't take you to her. I can't do that. I'll tell you what I'll do. You wait right here, and I'll take another cab and be back here with her inside of twenty minutes."

I stared at him. "The reason I don't talk," I told him, "is because I'm speechless. Holy heaven!"

"What's wrong with that? I give you my word—"

"I don't want it. Cut the comedy and let's go."

He glared some more. I permitted it for a full minute and then got impatient. "I'll count up to twenty-nine," I said, "one for each year of my life and one to grow on and one to get married on, and then—"

"Wait a minute." He was approaching the pleading stage. "The reason I can't take you to her is a personal reason. I don't intend to try any deception, I can't. You know damn well the hole I'm in. What about this? You go with me to a phone booth, and I'll call her up and tell her to meet us—"

I shook my head emphatically. "No. A thousand times no. Quit trying to wiggle off the hook. How do I know but what you've got a code with her to use in emergencies? Remember I'm ignorant. I don't even know but what Wolfe has got it figured out that she killed Ludlow and, in that case—" I shrugged. "I'm only a puppet and I'm under orders. For God's sake, shut up and let's go."

He curled his fingers to make fists. "I can just open this door and beat it. You know?"

"Go ahead. Don't let me stop you. Then I could phone Wolfe and go on home."

"But goddam it, if you hear me phone—"

"Shut up. I'm bored stiff."

He gave me one more good long glare and then leaned forward and gave the driver an address on Madison Avenue, not ten blocks away. The driver nodded and got going again.

He had enough left to pay the fare. It wasn't a modern apartment house we stopped in front of, but an older building whose days of pride were in the past. The ground floor was a trinket shop, dark of course. Barrett got out a key and unlocked a door that let us

into a small public corridor, went to the rear of it, and
with another key admitted us into a miniature elevator of the drive-it-yourself variety. That took us up
five stories, and then we had to climb a flight of stairs.
The layout wasn't exactly shabby, though it was far
from ostentatious. From the top of the stairs he
preceded me through a sort of vestibule and used a
third key on a wide solid-looking door. I followed him
in and he shut the door and turned to call out:

"Yoohoo!"

An answer came: "Back here, Donnybonny!"

I could already smell perfume, and the tempera-
ture even there in the foyer must have been close to
ninety. I copied his example when he took off his coat,
but when he scowled at me and said, "Wait here a
minute," I disregarded it and went along behind him
into a large and dazzling room full of heat, synthetic
smells, thick rugs, divans and cushions, miscellaneous
stuff, and a pair of damsels. They were sprawled out,
one on a divan and the other on a chaise lounge.

Zorka, a loose red thing around her, started a wave
of greeting at Barrett and then halted it in mid-air as
she saw me. Belinda Reade, nothing at all around her,
called, "How's my Donny—*Oh!*" And grabbed for a
pale blue negligee that was draped over the back of
the divan.

Chapter 11

Barrett growled at me, "Didn't I ask you to wait?"

"It doesn't matter," I soothed him. "When my mind is on business—"

"Why!" Belinda Reade cried in innocent delight, "it's the detective man! Have a drink?"

She was working on one herself, and the ingredients for plenty more were handy on a little table. Zorka was having one too; she had raised herself to her elbow on the chaise longue and was smiling at me foolishly, without any intention, apparently, of saying anything.

Barrett said, "Be quiet, Bel. This fellow came . . ." He turned to Zorka. "He came for you. My God, look at you. Both of you." He frowned at her and switched to me: "You explain it to her."

"Thees ess no time," Zorka declared in an injured tone, "for explanations."

"Have a drink," Miss Reade insisted. "I have never had a drink with a detective, and especially such a darned good-looking detective." She patted the divan and tugged at the negligee to cover a knee. "Sit here by me and have a drink."

"Don't be a damned fool," Barrett told her.

Zorka tittered. "She only wants to make you jealous, Donald. Because you make her jealous of the Tormic girl."

"Bah," said Miss Reade. "Have a drink! What's your name?"

"Call me Archie." It struck me that a little reinforcement might help, so I stretched for the bottle and a glass. Then I drew back and turned to Barrett. "But excuse me. If you're the host . . ."

"This is Miss Reade's apartment," he said stiffly. "But you came here—"

"*Please* have a drink," the lady begged me.

"Thanks, I will." I poured a good one and tossed it off, and then advised Barrett, "You ought to have a shot yourself. You're under a strain." I confronted Zorka. "The idea is this. After you phoned me at Nero Wolfe's office and told me—"

"What? After what?"

I went closer so she could focus easier. "After you phoned and told me you saw Miss Tormic putting something in my overcoat pocket—"

"But I didn't! I? I phoned you?" She waved her glass at Belinda, spilling a drop or two on the rug, and said in a hurt tone, "Don't let him have another drink! He says I phoned him!"

"Maybe you did, darling. You phone so many men. I wouldn't blame you for phoning him. I like him."

"But I didn't!"

"Well, you should have." Belinda used the blue eyes on me. "Have a drink, Percy."

"Not Percy, Archie. Percy was the one that got murdered."

"Oh." She frowned at me. "That's right. That's why we started drinking, to forget about it. Brrrh." She shivered. "And I called you Percy! How funny! Don't you think that's funny, Donnyhoney?"

"No," Barrett declared curtly. "This fellow—"

"But of course it's funny! I *like* Archie, and why should I call him Percy?" She shivered again. "It was perfectly terrible! Simply awful! The porter yelling and Percy lying there on the floor, and the police and—" She stopped and stared at me with her lips parted. "Why! I forgot! You son-of-a-gun! It was you that wouldn't let me out of that door! You dirty bum!"

Barrett tapped me on the shoulder. "You know, you came—"

"Yeah, I know." I faced Zorka. She had the fixed smile on again. I would have given an hour's sleep to know how many drinks she had had. "About your phoning me," I said. "Maybe I was just trying to brag. It's my one weakness, bragging about women phoning me. The fact is, I came along with Donald Barrett to save him some trouble. I had to come to 48th Street anyway, to get my car. He told me he had asked you to come and spend the night with Miss Reade, but after the talk we had that wasn't necessary, so he supposed you would want to go home. Isn't that right, Barrett?"

"I didn't agree—"

"Isn't that right?"

"Well . . . yes."

"Sure it is. So if you'll just put on a coat—you don't need to bother to dress—we can take your bag and suitcase—"

"What for?" she demanded.

"Why, if you're going home you'll want your luggage—"

"I'm not going home."

"My God, it's nearly daylight—"

"I'm not going home. Am I going home, Belinda?"

"You are not. Even if you were, you wouldn't go with him. I don't like him. Didn't you hear me say I remembered that I don't like him?"

I poured myself another drink, drank it, sat down on the end of the chaise longue next to Zorka's feet and considered the situation. It had various aspects, the basic problem being whether she was or was not honestly stoozled. If she was, she wouldn't be worth a damn to Wolfe even if I got her there. But I had my reputation to consider. Over a period of years Wolfe had sent me many places many times, to bring him everything from a spool of thread to a Wall Street broker, and I had batted mighty close to a thousand. Besides that, if I went back without her I knew what Wolfe would say: and in addition to that, her silly smile aggravated me.

I stood up and told Barrett in a cold inflexible tone, "It's up to you, brother. You got her here, now you can get her out."

"He didn't get me here," Zorka said. "I came here myself."

"How do you expect me to get her out?" Barrett demanded. "Carry her?"

Zorka said, "Nobody had better touch anybody. Especially you, you good-looking bum."

Barrett said, "I brought you here. That's all I agreed to do. I didn't agree—what's the idea?"

I ignored him and continued on around the head of the divan to where a red-enameled phone was resting on a long narrow table. He scowled at me while I dialed a number. Belinda commanded him, "Tackle him, Donnydarling. Knock him down and walk on him. Don't let him use my phone. Don't let him use anything—"

A voice sounded in my ear: "This is Nero Wolfe."

I said, "Hello, Police Headquarters? Give me Inspector Cramer of the homicide squad."

Wolfe's voice said, "Indeed. Go ahead."

Barrett leaned across the divan at me and started to expostulate. I waved a hand at him to subside, and talked again:

"Hello, Homicide Division? I want to talk to Inspector Cramer. Oh, he has. Who is this talking? Sergeant Finkle? I guess you'll do. This is Archie Goodwin of Nero Wolfe's office. I want to report a development in the Ludlow mur—"

Barrett's hand shot out and pushed the cradle down and held it.

"Don't be a sap," I told him politely. "Even if I don't want to start a roughhouse—"

"What are you going to tell him?"

"Where he can find a woman who says she saw Miss Tormic put something in my pocket and is now saying she didn't say it."

"You're a goddam fool. You're supposed to be protecting Miss Tormic."

"I know I am. But in the long run the truth is the best protection against—"

"Truth, hell. Do you realize they can trace that call?"

I shrugged. "I presume so. If they do they'll ring back. Then, if they don't get satisfaction, I presume they'll send somebody here and it would be bad tactics not to let them in. And of course if they find Zorka and me here—"

He had his jaw clamped. "You dirty treacherous—"

I shrugged

Miss Reade said, "I am darned sick and tired of hearing about that Tormic! As far as I'm concerned, Archie—"

"Be quiet!" Barrett told her savagely. "You know damn well—" He bit it off and wheeled to Zorka. "You'll have to go, and go quick! Get a move on!"

"But," she protested, "you told me—"

"I don't care what I told you! This double-crossing—" He grabbed her shoulder and got her upright. He was pretty masterful in a real emergency. "Where's your coat? Where's your shoes and stockings? To hell with stockings. Shoes!"

He raced to the far end of the room and through a door. I went in the opposite direction, to the foyer, and got my hat and coat and put them on. Then I opened the closet door, thinking to help, but stood bewildered at the array of furbearing animals hanging there. I thought what's the difference, and reached for one, but felt my elbow seized from behind and heard Belinda's voice:

"Hey, no you don't, that's my mink! Get out of the way!"

She pushed past me, her open negligee doing practically nothing to conceal distractions, and emerged with a mink coat that looked all the same to me. I took it and trotted back in. Zorka, shod, was on her feet, and Barrett was tying the girdle of the red gown. She swayed a little while we got the coat on her and buttoned it up to her chin, but navigated well enough when I hooked onto her arm and escorted her to the foyer. Miss Reade was standing there holding the outer door open. As we passed through Barrett told her, "I'll have to take them down. If the phone rings, don't answer it. I'll be right back."

She stumbled on the stairs, but I had a good hold and we got her into the elevator without mishap. Barrett pushed the button and we descended. At the ground floor he preceded us along the corridor and opened the street door.

"Do you want me to help—"

"No, thanks. If they trace that call, my advice—"

"Go to hell."

The door shut and I was alone on the sidewalk with my booty. She was clinging to my arm and at intervals was saying something that sounded like "Oops." I squeezed her hand reassuringly and started to convey her gently in the direction of Grand Central, but had negotiated less than half a block when a taxi appeared and I flagged it. Getting her in was more a matter of strength than strategy. She was floppy on the cushion, and I held her against me as we bounced along and around a corner towards Lexington Avenue. She was now murmuring something like "Urpees."

The roadster was still there, like a faithful dog waiting for its master. The taxi driver was sympathetic and helpful, and with his assistance it was an easy matter to make the transfer. As we were boosting her in she started to kick, but with a firm tone and a firm hand I got her onto the seat and the door closed. The driver nodded his thanks for the moderate tip I gave him and offered advice: "Taking her out, if she gets nasty, work from behind. That way she can't reach your face and she's not so apt to bite."

"Okay. Much obliged."

I climbed in and started the engine and rolled. As I rounded the corner to head downtown she said, "Gribblezook." I replied, *Hvala Bogu.* Apparently it was satisfactory, for she relaxed into the corner and shut up. A couple of times en route I opened my mouth to inform her where we were bound for and what she had to look forward to, but a glance at her made me decide I'd be wasting my breath. The traffic was at

home in bed where it belonged, and I made good time
down to 35th and then cross-town.

I stopped at the curb in front of the house, grabbed
her shoulder and straightened her up, and called her
name. No response and her eyes were shut. I shook
her. I turned her loose and she flopped in the corner as
runny as mush. I pinched her thigh, a good one, and
she didn't flinch. I pulled her up straight and shook her
again, and her head bounced onto my shoulder and
stayed there, and then rolled off. "Hell," I muttered,
"it's only ten yards to a touchdown," and I climbed out,
pulled her across to my side, got my shoulder under
her, and histed her up. She was as dead as a bag of
oats. I distributed her weight better, something
around 120, and crossed the sidewalk, staggered up
the steps, and rang the bell two shorts and a long. In
a minute the door opened as far as the chain and
Fritz's voice came through:

"Archie?"

"Yeah. Open up."

The door swung open and I entered. After one
glance at my cargo Fritz staggered back a step.

"*Grand Dieu!* Is she dead?"

"Naw, she's not even sick. Lock the door."

The door to the office was standing open and I
went through sidewise to keep from knocking her
head against the jamb. Wolfe was there reading a
book. He looked up and saw what I had, made a face,
dog-eared a page and closed the book, and sat and
shook his head. A glance at the couch showed me that
it was still covered with the maps which he had spread
all over it three days previously with instructions that
they were not to be touched, so I put her down on the
floor, in the middle of the rug, straightened my back to

remove a kink, pointed an unwavering finger at her, and said casually: "Madame Zorka."

He folded his arms. "What's the matter with her?"

"Nothing."

"Did you hit her?"

"No."

"Don't be an ass. You don't carry women around and lay them on the floor when there's nothing wrong with them. Is she unconscious?"

"I don't think so. Her contention is that she is in a drunken stupor, but I think she's playing charades. I found her in a penthouse love nest on Madison Avenue. Barrett furnishes the nest and Belinda Reade the love. You know? Belinda was there and Zorka was her guest. Zorka denied that she had made any phone call to this office and she refused to leave. I made a phone call to work up pressure and she came. She is almost certainly listening carefully to what we are saying. She'll smother in here with that fur coat buttoned up."

I stooped and unfastened the coat and flung it open. Wolfe got to his feet, walked around the desk, and stood frowning down at her.

"She has no stockings on."

"Right."

"What's that thing she wearing? A dress?"

"Oh, heavens, no. I think it's a drinking gown."

"And you think she's shamming?"

"I do."

"Well." He turned and called, "Fritz!" Fritz was right there. Wolfe told him, "Bring a dozen ice cubes."

I knelt down beside the patient and felt her pulse, and then pried open her eyelid and took a look at the iris, and announced that it would be perfectly safe to proceed with the experiment. Wolfe, looking down at me, nodded gravely. Fritz appeared with the dish of ice cubes and Wolfe told him to give them to me. I took a cube and laid it on her cheek and it slid off. I picked it up and carefully placed it at the base of her neck, in the little depression where the shoulder began, and it stayed nicely. Then I gently but firmly lifted her arm, held it up with my left hand, and with my right hand got another cube and as modestly as possible worked it under the edge of the red robe until it was snug in her arm pit; and let the arm down.

The reaction was so sudden and violent it startled me into spilling the rest of the cubes all over the rug, and her knees in my belly nearly spilled me too. She didn't stop at sitting up, but scrambled to her feet, with Wolfe retreating to make room for her. She shook herself, more of a spasm than a shake, and the ice cube emerged from under the hem of the gown to the floor. She goggled around at us, perceived a chair, and sank into it.

"What—what—" she stammered.

"Wrong line," I told her. "Say, 'Where am I?'"

She groaned and pressed both palms against her forehead. Wolfe, having waited until Fritz had retrieved all the cubes, moved back to his chair and lowered his fundament. He regarded her sourly for a full minute of silence and then spoke to me.

"And what," he demanded resentfully, "would you suggest that we do with her?"

"Search me. It was you that wanted her."

"I don't want her like that."

"Send her home." I added emphatically, "In a taxi."

"We can't send her home. The police are looking for her, and one will be posted at her door, and I want to talk to her first."

"Go ahead and talk to her."

"I want to ask her some questions. Is she capable of coherence?"

"Capable, yes. But I doubt if she'll cohere, with ice or without. Go on and try it."

He looked at her. "Madame Zorka, I am Nero Wolfe. I would like to discuss something with you. When were you last in Yugoslavia?"

With her face covered with her hands, she shook her head, moaned, and muttered something not even as intelligible as gribblezook.

"But, madame," Wolfe said patiently. "I'm sorry you don't feel well, but that is a very simple question." Then he spouted some lingo at her, a couple of sentences, that may have been words but not to me. She didn't even shake her head.

"Don't you understand Serbo-Croat?" he demanded.

"No," she muttered. "Zat I do not onderstand."

He kept at it for a solid hour. When he wanted to be, he could be as patient as he was big, and apparently on that occasion he wanted to be. I took it all down in my notebook, and I never filled as many pages with less dependable information. There was no telling, when he got through, whether she had ever been in Yugoslavia, how and when she had acquired the name Zorka, or whether she had actually ever been born or not. It seemed to be tentatively established that she had once resided in a hotel in Paris, at least for one night, that her couturière enterprise had been installed within the year on the street floor of the Churchill with the help of outside capital, that her native tongue was not Serbo-Croat, that she was not on intimate terms with Neya Tormic or Carla Lovchen, that she had known Percy Ludlow only slightly, and that she had taken up fencing to keep her weight down and was not an expert. Wolfe did succeed in extorting an admission that she had made the phone call to our office, but it was an empty triumph; she couldn't remember what she had said! She just simply couldn't remember.

At twenty minutes past four Wolfe arose from his chair with a sigh and said to me: "Put her to bed in the south room, above mine, and lock the door."

She rose too, steadying herself with her hand on the edge of his desk, and declared, "I want to go home."

"The police are there laying for you. As I told you, I have informed them of your phone call. They'll take you to headquarters and be much more insistent than I have been. Well?"

"All right." She groaned.

"Good night, madame. Good night, Archie." He stalked out.

It was two flights to the floor above his, and I was in no mood to elevate her that far by brute force, so I trotted up and got the elevator after he had ascended, and took it down and got her. Fritz, half asleep and half displeased, went along to make sure that the bed was habitable and that towels and accessories were at hand; and for the honor of the house he brought with him the vase of cattleyas from Wolfe's desk. She may have had no nightie or slippers or toothbrush, but by golly she had orchids. Fritz turned the bed down and, me steering her, she got seated on the edge of it.

Fritz said, "She's forlorn."

"Yep." I asked her, "Do you want me to help you off with your coat or anything?"

She shook her head.

"Shall I open the window?"

Another shake.

We left her there. From the outside I locked the door and put the key in my pocket. It was ten to five, and a dingy November dawn was feebly whimpering "Let there be light," at my windows when I finally hit the mattress.

At eight o'clock in the morning, bathed and dressed but bleary-eyed and grouchy, I took a pot of coffee up to her. When my third and loudest knock got no response, I used the key and went in. She wasn't there. The bed was just as Fritz had turned it down. The window on the left, the one that opened onto the fire escape, was standing wide-open.

Chapter 12

I descended a flight to Wolfe's room, tapped on the door, and entered. He was in bed, propped up against three pillows, just ready to attack the provender on the breakfast table which straddled his mountainous ridge under the black silk coverlet. There was orange juice, eggs *au beurre noir*, two slices of broiled Georgia ham, hashed brown potatoes, hot blueberry muffins, and a pot of steaming cocoa.

He snapped at me, "I haven't eaten!"

"Neither have I," I said bitterly. "I'm in no better humor than you are, so let's call it a tie. I just went up to take our guest some coffee—"

"How is she?"

"I don't know."

"Is she asleep?"

"I don't know."

"What the devil—"

"I was starting to tell you and you interrupted me. Please don't interrupt. She's gone. She didn't even lie down. She went by the window and the fire escape, and presumably found her way to 34th Street by the passage we use sometimes. Since she descended the fire escape, she went right past that window"—I pointed—"facing you, and it must have been daylight."

"I was asleep."

"So it seems. I thought maybe with a woman in the house, and possibly a murderess, you might have been on the qui vive—"

"Shut up."

He took some of the orange juice, frowned at me half a minute, and took some more.

"Phone Mr. Cramer. Give him everything."

"Including my trip to the love nest?"

He grimaced. "Don't use terms like that when my stomach's empty. Including everything about Madame Zorka, Mr. Barrett, and Miss Reade, except the subject of my threat to Mr. Barrett."

"Bosnian forests."

"All of that to be deleted. If he wants a transcript of our talk with Madame Zorka, furnish it; he's welcome to it. He has resources for investigating those people and for finding Madame Zorka. If he wants to see me, eleven o'clock."

"Your daughter's coming at eleven."

"Then noon for Mr. Cramer if he wants it." He swallowed more orange juice. "Phone Seven Seas Radio and ask if they have anything for me. If they haven't, tell them to rush it to me when it comes. Make an appointment for me to talk with Mr. Hitchcock in London at nine o'clock."

"Do you want a record—"

"No. Who is downstairs?"

"No one has come yet. They ought to be here any minute."

"When Saul comes, put the envelope in the safe. I'll see them as soon as I'm through talking to Mr.

Hitchcock. Send Saul up first, then Fred, then Orrie. Have you had your breakfast?"

"You know damn well I haven't."

"Good heavens. Get it."

I went down to the kitchen and did that, after first calling Seven Seas Radio and arranging for a wire to London at nine. With my breakfast I consumed portions of the *Times*, specializing on the report of the Ludlow murder. They had my name spelled wrong, and they were pretty stale for a paper that had gone to press at midnight, for they said that the police were looking for me. As Cramer had predicted, they had the low-down on Ludlow's being an agent of the British government, but there wasn't any hint of Montenegro or Bosnian forests or Balkan princesses. On an inside page there was a spread of pictures and a two-column piece about the murder in Paris that the *col de mort* had figured in some years before.

When Saul and Fred and Orrie came I shooed them into the front room to wait, since I had jobs to do. After my second cup of coffee and what preceded it, I felt better and was almost cheerful by the time I got Inspector Cramer on the wire to relate the sad story. He hadn't had much more sleep than me, and was naturally disgruntled when he learned that we had had Zorka in our clutches for a couple of hours without bothering him about it, and he got rude and vulgar at the news that she had left before breakfast, but I applied the salve by reminding him how many presents he was getting absolutely gratis. He had no news to speak of himself, or if he had he wasn't handing it out, but he said he would drop in around noon if he could make it, and in the meantime he would like me to type a report, not only of our session with Zorka, but also of the one with Barrett and of my visit on Madison Avenue. That was sweet of him. I felt a lot like a hard morning at the alphabet piano, no I didn't.

As it turned out, I didn't get much typing done. The talk with Hitchcock in London took place at nine o'clock as scheduled, and of course I didn't listen in, since Wolfe had said no record. Then I sent Saul up to meet Wolfe in the plant rooms, having first procured the envelope and stowed it away in the safe. The instructions for Saul must have been complicated, for fifteen minutes passed before he came back down and calmly requested fifty bucks expense money. I whistled and asked who he was going to bribe and he said the District Attorney. Wolfe rang me on the house phone and said to keep Fred in storage for the present and to send Orrie Cather up. Orrie's schedule must have been a simple one, for he returned in no time at all, marched over to me and said:

"Give me about three thousand dollars in threes."

"With pleasure. I'm busy. How much in cold cash?"

"Nothing, my dear fellow."

"Nothing?"

"Right. And please don't disturb me. I shall be spending the day on research at the public library. Hold yourself in readiness—"

He dodged the notebook I threw, and danced out.

I put a sheet in the typewriter and started, without any enthusiasm, on the report for Cramer, but had only filled a third of a page when it occurred to me that it would be fun to locate Zorka without moving from my desk. I pulled the phone over and dialed a number. The ringing signal was in my ear a long while before there was a voice. It sounded disconsolate.

"Hullohullohullo!"

I made mine vigorous but musical. "Hello, Belinda?"

"Yes. Who is this?"

"Guess."

"I'm in no condition to guess."

"It's Archie. Archie the good-looking bum. I want to warn—"

"How did you get this number? It's private and it's not listed."

"I know, but I can read, can't I? I saw it on your phone when I used it. I want to say three things. First, that I think you're very very beautiful and if you ever ask me to come and read aloud to you I will. Second, I forgot to thank you for the drinks. Third, I want to warn you about Zorka. About a thousand cops are looking for her, and if they come and find her there it will get you in a lot of trouble, and I'd be glad to—"

"What are you talking about? How are they going to find her here when you took her away?"

"But she went back there."

"She did not. Where is she?"

"She started for your place about five o'clock."

"Well, she didn't get here."

"That's funny. What do you suppose happened to her?"

"I have no idea."

A click in my ear ended it. So much for that. It sounded very much as if Zorka had not returned to Madison Avenue. I wrote three more lines of the report and the doorbell rang and I went up to the front and opened up.

It was Rudolph Faber.

I admit it was Wolfe's house and I was employed there, and courtesy is courtesy, but he hung up his coat himself. That was the effect that guy had on me. I let him precede me into the office because I didn't want him behind me, and he required no invitation to take a chair. I had explained in the hall that Mr. Wolfe was never available in the morning until eleven o'clock, but I seated myself at my desk and rang up the plant rooms, and in a moment Wolfe answered.

I told him, "Mr. Rudolph Faber is here."

"Indeed. What does he want?"

"To see you. He says he'll wait."

"I doubt if I can see him before lunch."

"I told him so."

"Well. Let's see." A pause. "Come up here. Better still, call on Mr. Green. Before leaving, give him a good book to read, and see what happens."

"A really good book?"

"The best you can find."

I hung up and swiveled to face the caller. "Mr. Wolfe needs me upstairs, and he suggested that I should give you a book to amuse yourself with while I'm gone."

I went to the shelves and got down *United Yugoslavia* and returned and handed it to him. "I think you'll find it very interesting, especially—"

He stood up and threw the book on the floor and started for the exit.

I trotted around and got between him and the door, faced him, and said urgently, "Pick it up!" I knew at the time that it was childish, but in the first place the impulse to make some kind of alteration on the supercilious look of his face was absolutely irresistible, and in the second place I had been permanently impressed by what I had been reading in the papers about certain things being done by certain people in certain parts of the world. I did give him a second chance by telling him again to pick it up, but he kept right on coming, apparently expecting me to melt into a grease spot. I said calmly, "Look out, here it is," and put it there. I didn't aim for the chin because there wasn't any and I didn't want to pay a hospital bill. Instead, I took his left eye with a right hook and most of me behind it.

The door connecting with the front room opened a crack and Fred Durkin stuck his head in.

"Hey, need any help?"

"Come on in. What do you think?"

He walked over and stood looking down at Faber. "I'll be darned. How many times did you hit him?"

"Once."

"I'll be darned. And you with a name like Goodwin. Sometimes I'm inclined to think—was your mother ever in Ireland?"

"Go suck an orange. Stand back and give him room."

Faber got up by degrees. First on his hands, then on his hands and knees, and then slow but sure on up. He turned slowly, and looked at me, and I looked away on account of the expression in his eyes. It embarrassed me so much it damn near scared me, to see such an expression in the eyes of a man who had merely been knocked down. Naturally, it had been my intention to request him to pick the book up when he got upright again, but I didn't do it. When he got under headway towards the door I stepped aside and let him go, and asked Fred to go to the hall and let him out. I picked up the book and put it away and sat down and rubbed my knuckles and worked my fingers open and shut a few times, and then phoned Wolfe a communiqué. All he did was grunt.

I worked my fingers limber enough so I could resume at the typewriter, but that report was hoeing a hard row. In addition to my deep-seated reluctance to spoiling white paper just to furnish a cop with reading matter, there were constant interruptions. A phone call from Miltan the épée champion. All he wanted was information and I had none to give him. One from a guy in town from St. Louis who wanted to discuss orchids with Wolfe, and an appointment was made for next day. One from Orrie Cather for Wolfe and, a little later, one from Saul Panzer, both of which I was invited to keep out of.

Towards eleven o'clock there was a phone call from the Emperor of Japan. At least it might as well have been. First a woman asked for Mr. Wolfe, and I asked who was it and she said Mr. Barrett and I said put him on and she said hold the wire. I waited a while. Then a man said he wanted Mr. Wolfe, and I said is this Mr. Barrett, and he said authoritatively, no, it isn't, put Mr. Wolfe on, please, and I asked who it was that wanted to talk to Mr. Wolfe, and he said Mr. Barrett, and I said put him on and he said hold the wire. That kind of a shenanigan. There was more to it than that, but after a terrific and exhausting struggle I finally heard something definite, in a leisurely cultivated male voice:

"This is Barrett. Mr. Wolfe?"

"Donald Barrett?"

"No, no, John P. Barrett."

"Oh, Donald's father. Of Barrett & De Russy?"

"That's right. Mr. Wolfe, could you—"

"Hold it. This is Archie Goodwin, Mr. Wolfe's confidential assistant."

"I thought I had Wolfe."

"Nope. I wore 'em out. Mr. Wolfe will be engaged until eleven o'clock. I'll take any message."

"Well." Hesitation. "That will do, I suppose. I would like to have Mr. Wolfe call at my office as soon after eleven as possible."

"No, sir. I'm sorry. He never makes calls."

"But this is important. In fact, urgent. It will be well worth his while—"

"No, sir. There's no use prolonging it. Mr. Wolfe transacts business only at his office. He wouldn't go across the street to receive the keys to the Bank of England."

"That's ridiculous!"

"Yes, sir. I've always said so. But there's no use discussing it, except as an interesting case of cussedness."

For ten seconds I heard nothing. Then, "Where is your office?"

"506 West 35th Street."

"Mr. Wolfe is there throughout the day?"

"And night. Office and home."

"Well . . . I'll see. Thank you."

Wolfe came down from the plant rooms a few minutes later, and after he had run through the mail, tested his pen, rung for beer, and glanced at the three pages of the report I had managed to finish, I told him about it. He listened impressively and thanked me with a disinterested nod. Thinking a little prodding was in order, I observed that he was in the case anyway, on account of family obligations, spending money right and left, and that it was therefore short-sighted and unintelligent not to permit Miss Tormic to have a co-client, when the co-client was of the nature of John P. Barrett, obviously anxious to join in the fun and ready to ante. I told him about the hundred bucks of Barrett dough which had already passed through our hands and said what a pity it would be to stop there, but before I could really get worked up about it I was interrupted by the arrival of the client herself.

Fritz announced Miss Neya Tormic and escorted her in.

She greeted Wolfe in a hurry and me not at all, and without taking time to sit down demanded of him: "The paper? Have you got the paper?"

She looked drawn and she acted jerky.

Wolfe said, "Yes, it's here. Please sit down, won't you?"

"I . . . the paper!"

"Give it to her, Archie."

I went to the safe and got it. It was still in the envelope addressed to Saul Panzer. I removed it, tossed the envelope into the wastebasket, and handed the paper to her. She unfolded it and inspected it.

Wolfe said, extending his hand, "Let me see it, please."

That didn't appeal to her. She made no move to comply. He frowned at her and repeated his request in a crisper tone, and she handed it over but kept her eyes glued to it. He gave it a glance, folded it up, and asked her:

"Where is Miss Lovchen?"

"I suppose she's at the studio. She said she was going there."

"Surely there'll be no fencing lessons there today."

"I don't know. That's what she said."

"You saw her this morning?"

"Of course. We live together in a little flat on 38th Street." She put her hand out. "Give me—"

"Wait a minute. I don't know why I assumed that Miss Lovchen would accompany you here this morning—it was stupid of me to do so, but I did. Anyway, it was she who left this paper here, and I'd rather return it to her. If she—"

"I'll take it to her."

"No, I think not. Here, Archie. Go along with Miss Tormic to Miltan's and deliver this to Miss Lovchen. I like it better that way—"

"That's absurd!" the client protested. "What's the difference whether it's me or Carla?"

"None, perhaps. But this suits me better. It's neater." He handed the thing to me and then regarded her gloomily. "I hope you know what you're doing. I hope you have some idea of what's going on. I haven't. Mr. Faber has come here twice for the purpose of getting hold of that paper."

"Oh." She compressed her lips. "He has?"

"Yes. The second time was only a little more than an hour ago, and Mr. Goodwin lost his temper and hit him in the eye. So . . . I presume you girls realize that possession of that document—"

"We realize it."

"Very well. Do you still expect to complete your . . . errand . . . today?"

"Yes."

"When and where."

She shook her head.

He shrugged. "Did you keep your appointment with Mr. Cramer this morning?"

"Yes, but not with Mr. Cramer. A man came and took me down there, and two men talked with me. That's where I came from, here."

"You told about finding those things in your pocket and so on."

"Yes."

"Did they ask about your political mission— anything of that sort?"

"Why, no, they don't know anything about that."

"Were you followed when you left there?"

"I—" She bit it off. In a moment she said, "I don't

think so." Her head jerked at me and back at him. "If you're going to insist—I haven't much time. I must see Carla anyway, but if he's going—"

Wolfe nodded. "All right. Pfui. Archie, give that paper to Miss Lovchen in the presence of Miss Tormic."

I suggested, "Fred's in the front room—"

"No. You do it."

"Cramer's due in half an hour."

"I know. Hurry back."

I ushered her out. The roadster was still at the curb in front where I had left it. We climbed in and I warmed up the engine a minute, and rolled. She was completely don't-touch-me. Whatever her mind was on, it certainly wasn't on me, and during the short ride to 48th Street I accepted that as the status quo.

Across the street from Miltan's a little group was collected on the sidewalk, and in front of the entrance a flatfoot was pacing a short beat. He gave us an eye as we went in, but made no attempt to interfere. Inside was no sign of life in the hall or reception room, but a murmur came from the rear and we went back there to the large office. Jeanne Miltan was in a chair at a desk, with two squad dicks, each with a notebook, seated facing her. Her husband, looking haggard and hopeless, was pacing the floor, shaking his head at himself. As we entered one of the dicks looked up and barked:

"What do you want?"

I waved a friendly hand. "Okay, private business."

Neya intercepted Miltan and asked, "Is Miss Lovchen upstairs?"

He groaned. "No one is upstairs. We are deserted. We are ruined. Mr. Goodwin, can you tell me—"

"I'm sorry, I can't tell you a darned thing. Has Miss Lovchen been here this morning?"

"She came and stayed a while, but she left."

"How long ago?"

"Oh, my God, I don't know—half an hour." He clapped a hand to his head and stared at Neya. "She said to tell you something if you came—"

Jeanne Miltan's voice sounded: "She went home, Miss Tormic."

"That's it," Miltan agreed. "She said to tell you she went home. That was all. She went home."

"What do you want with her?" a dick demanded.

"Sell her a chance on a turkey raffle. Come on, Miss Tormic."

We went back out to the sidewalk. Halting there, I asked her, "You said 38th Street? East or west?"

She smiled at me. "It's silly for you to go. It's so silly. Why don't you just give it to me?"

"I'd love to," I assured her. I didn't see any sense in antagonizing her if she was my future wife. "I really would." We were moving along to the roadster. "But here's my car and I have to go downtown anyway. Besides, if I don't follow instructions I'll get fired. What's the address?"

"404 East 38th."

"Okay, that'll only take—excuse me a minute." I had caught a glimpse of something comical. "Climb in," I told her, "I'll be right back."

I left her and went down the sidewalk to where a taxi had parked twenty feet behind the roadster. My glimpse had been of the passenger inside ducking out of our sight. As I lifted a foot to the running board the driver said:

"Busy."

"Yeah, so I see." I stretched my neck to get a better view of Fred Durkin huddled on the seat. So Wolfe was putting a tail on his own client. "I just wanted to save you some trouble. 404 East 38th Street."

I returned to the roadster and got in and started off, telling Neya that I had merely exchanged the time of day with a Russian nobleman friend of mine who was driving a taxicab for his health. She said nothing. Apparently she was concentrating again on Balkan history, or whatever kind it was she was making. I retaliated by concentrating on my driving.

There was space for me directly in front of 404. It was an old house, one of a row, that had been done over into inexpensive flats by blocking off the stairs and sticking in some partitions. Eight steps up to the stoop, then a vestibule with mailboxes and bell buttons, then the door into the narrow hall. It wasn't even necessary for Neya to use her key on the door, because it had stopped an inch short of closing and all I had to do was push it open. I let her go ahead. She led me up two flights of stairs with just enough light to keep you from groping, went to a door towards the front, and opened her bag and started fishing for a key. Then she thought better of that and pushed the button, and I could hear a bell ringing inside. But nothing else was heard, though after an interval she rang the bell again, and then again.

She muttered, "He said she was coming home."

"So he did. Got a key?"

She opened her bag again, and this time produced the key. She used it herself, pushed the door open, went in four paces with me on her heels, and stopped in her tracks, jerking her head up and freezing there. Over her shoulder I could see what she saw: the body of a man sprawled on the floor in a very unlikely attitude; and the face, which was the one I had undertaken to alter with my fist two hours previously.

Before I could stop her she jerked her head up higher and yowled into space:

"Carla!"

Chapter 13

I said resentfully, "Will you kindly close your trap?"

She didn't move. I got in front of her and took a look at her face. She didn't seem to be prepared for more clamor, so I went and squatted for a quick survey of the corpus. A quick one was enough. I glanced up at her again and saw that she was breathing through her nose. I rocked on my heels for half a minute, gazing at the chinless wonder and using my brain up to capacity. Then I stood up and said:

"The first and worse thing seems to be that I've got that goddam paper in my pocket."

She met my eye and said with her lips barely moving, "Give it to me."

"Sure. That'd be swell."

I walked around a table to get at one of the windows, which fronted on 38th Street, and opened it and poked my head out, and saw what I hoped to see. I pulled my head in and asked her, "How's your nerve?"

"My nerve's all right."

"Then come over here."

She came, nice and steady, and I told her to look out the window with me.

"See that gray and white taxicab at the curb in the middle of the block?"

"Yes."

"Go down there and you'll find a man inside. Ask him if his name is Fred Durkin and he'll say it is. Tell him I want him up here quick, but no more than that because the driver will hear you. Come back up with him and use your keys. I'll be watching from the window, and if you get an impulse to scoot off—"

"I won't."

"Okay. Step on it. You're a good brave girl."

She went. In a few seconds, from my post at the window, I saw her descend the stoop, trot to the taxi, open the door and speak to its inhabitant, and come back with Fred. Not sure of what a Montenegrin female might do under stress, I stayed at the window until they both entered the room. Fred stopped short at sight of the casualty on the floor.

"I'll be damned," he said, and looked at me.

"No," I said, "not guilty this time. Nobody will ever sock him again." I pulled the paper from my pocket. "Here's something important. I discovered this corpse and I can't leave it, and after certain events that happened yesterday they're apt to frisk me to the skin when they come. Take this—hey, you little devil!"

Neya had lunged like a champion with an épée, grabbed the paper from my fingers and sprung back. She stood there clutching it.

"Jesus," I said, "you're like a streak of lightning! But you're dumb. You've got to stay here too and I'll see that you do. When the cops come they'll go through this place, including us, extra special for today considering yesterday. They would love to have that paper and they'll have it. Hand it to Fred. Well?"

Her breast heaved.

"Don't be dumb, damn it! The only chance of getting it out of here is for him to take it! Hand it over!"

Fred stuck out a hand. "Gimme, lady."

"What will he do with it?"

"Take care of it." She didn't move. I stepped over and yanked it out of her fingers and passed it to Fred. "Go down and dismiss your taxi," I told him, "and take the roadster and go to the office. If Wolfe's alone, give him that paper. If he isn't, go to the kitchen and have Fritz bring Wolfe to the kitchen and give him the paper there."

"Do I tell him—"

"I'll phone him. If and when you're questioned, tell them just what happened, leaving out the paper. I'm sending you to the office because I know I'll be held up here God knows how long, and with me absent Wolfe will need you. Okay?"

"Okay." He turned to go.

"Hold it. Stay there by the door a minute." I began darting around. I took a look behind a sofa and even under it, and opened a closet door for a glance inside, and had my hand on the knob of another door leading to the rear of the flat when Fred growled:

"Hey, what about prints?"

"To hell with prints. I've got a right to look for a murderer, haven't I?" I went on through, and kept moving, bothering only with places big enough to hide a man or woman. It didn't take long, since there was only a bath, a kitchenette, and two small bedrooms. I trotted back to the front and told Fred, "All right, one two three go," and he beat it.

I looked at Neya. "You're starting to tremble. You'd better sit down."

She shook her head. "I'm all right. But I . . . I . . . Carla. Where is she?"

"Search me." I had gone around the table to where the phone was and lifted it from its cradle.

"But wait—please! Why can't we . . . just leave? Just go and find her?"

"Sure. Splendid." I started dialing. "You certainly get charming ideas. Like the one yesterday, stuffing that junk in my pocket. Just lock up and go, huh? With those babies at Miltan's knowing we started for here and Fred's taxi driver—"

The phone told me, "This is Nero Wolfe."

I kept my voice down. "Hullo, boss. Let's be discreet."

"Oh, yes."

"Cramer there?"

"Yes."

"Well, leave it open so that if you want to you can say it was the Salvation Army. We went to Miltan's and Carla had been there but left for home. We came on here, 404 East 38th. Got the address?"

"Yes."

"Old house, walk-up, two flights. Neya let us in with her key. Rudolph Faber was lying on the floor dead. Hole through his coat, left breast. Shirt soaked with blood inside. No weapon. Carla not around on quick inspection. I'm phoning from right here, this room, and Neya is standing here—"

"One moment. I was empowered with reservation—"

"That's all right. Fred was tailing us and Neya went down for him and I gave it to him and he's on his way with it now. He can be traced here easy and so can we. The place has been frisked by someone in a hurry—drawers standing open, things scattered on the floor and so on. The number of this phone is Hammond 3-4505. Do you want me to keep on talking?"

"No."

"Do you want to ring off and let your genius work and I'll call again in three minutes?"

"No. You had better stay there, both of you. Mr. Cramer is here and I'll tell him about it. Hold the wire."

I heard him telling Cramer, and I heard noises which were presumably the inspector turning somersaults. Then a voice in my ear not Wolfe's.

"Goodwin!" Cramer yapped.

"Yes, sir, speaking."

"You stay there, hear me?"

"Yes, sir."

That was all, except the click. I hung up and walked to Neya, took her elbow and steered her to a chair, and put her in it.

"They'll be here in five minutes. Or less. This time Inspector Cramer will get here first. And this time you're connected up. Here in your own front room. What are you going to tell him?"

Her eyes met mine. They didn't waver, but she was having trouble with her chin. She shook her head. "What can I tell him?"

"I don't know. What can you?"

"Nothing."

"Not enough. Under the circumstances. Did your friend Carla do it?"

"I don't know."

"Did you?"

"You know I didn't!"

"I do not. Is there a lot of stuff around here about

Bosnian forests and Barrett & De Russy and secret codes—"

"No, nothing. I am very careful."

"Yeah, this looks like it. All I'm saying, if you try telling Cramer that you know nothing about Faber and you can't imagine why in the world he came here to get killed, you'll find yourself out on a limb. If you tell the truth, that won't be it, and if you decide on lies, you'll have to do a lot better than that. One little fact is that whoever killed Faber deprived you of your alibi for the murder of Ludlow. I'm not trying to scare you, I'm only trying to make you grab hold—"

The phone rang and I went and got it.

"This is Hammond 3-45—"

"Archie. Mr. Cramer will be there shortly."

"Goody!"

"How is Miss Tormic?"

"She's all right. She says her mind's a blank?"

"Shock?"

"No, just ignorance."

"When she is questioned about anything except her movements since ten o'clock this morning—which is the time Mr. Faber left this house alive—she will decline to reply except in the presence of her attorney. That is amply justified in the circumstances."

"I'll tell her that."

"Do so. I'll arrange for Mr. Parker to represent her. What does she say about Miss Lovchen?"

"More ignorance. The first thing she did when she entered the room and looked at the floor was let out a yell for Carla."

"I see. That's too bad. By the way, where did you put those germination records on the oncidium hybrids? I want to check them over."

"Christalmighty," I said bitterly. "Here's your

daughter sizzling on a spot, and here am I with blood on my fingers off of Faber's shirt, and you prate—why don't you try doing a little work for a change—"

"I can't work with nothing to work on. Get away as soon as you can. Where did you put those records?"

I told him. He thanked me and rang off. I looked at Neya, sitting there with her jaw clamped and her fingers twisted, and observed grimly, "You certainly picked a lulu for an adopted daddy. Do you know what he's doing? Checking up on orchid seeds he planted a year ago! Incidentally, he says you are to answer any questions the cops ask about your movements since ten o'clock this morning. All other questions, refuse to answer until you see a lawyer. He's getting one."

"A lawyer for me?"

"Yes."

A police siren sounded through the window I had left open.

Chapter 14

At five minutes past two Wolfe sipped the last drop of his luncheon coffee, put down his cup, and made two distinct and separate oral noises. The first was meant to express his pleasure and satisfaction in the immediate past, the hour spent at table; the second was a grunt of resigned dismay at the prospect of the immediate future, which was embodied in the bulky figure of Inspector Cramer, planted in a chair in the office. He had arrived on the stroke of two and was waiting.

Wolfe and I went in and sat down. The end of the unlighted cigar in Cramer's mouth described a figure 8.

"I hate to hurry your meal," he said sarcastically.

Wolfe eructed.

The inspector turned the sarcasm on me. "Have you had any new ideas about the purpose of your going there with Miss Tormic?"

I shook my head. "No, sir. As I told you, we merely went there to get Miss Lovchen."

"And what were you going to do with her?"

"We were going to bring her to see Mr. Wolfe. To go over things."

"Had she suddenly developed paralysis of the legs?"

"Please, Mr. Cramer," Wolfe murmured. "That's childish and you know it is. Flopping your arms around is no way to discuss anything. If Archie and Miss Tormic were engaged on a mysterious errand, you don't suppose you're going to squeeze it out of him, do you?"

With his fingers entwined, Cramer rubbed his thumb tips together, back and forth, with the cigar in his mouth aimed at the ceiling.

Finally he said, "I've been sitting here thinking."

Wolfe nodded sympathetically. "It's a good room to think in. The faint sounds from the street are just right."

Silence.

Cramer said, "I'm not a fool."

Wolfe nodded again. "We all feel like that occasionally. The poison of conceit. It's all right if you keep an antidote handy."

"Hell, I'm not conceited." The inspector removed the cigar. "What I chiefly meant about not being a fool, I meant that I'm sitting here because I doubt very much if I'll get a start on this case anywhere except right here in this room."

"Well, as I say, it's a good room to think in."

"Yeah. I'm not talking about thinking. I'm talking about you. This case is a hush-hush and I don't know why, and as sure as God made little apples you do know why. I don't expect you to blurt it out, but you've given me a hint before and you might do it again. I wouldn't be surprised if you know right now who killed Ludlow and who killed Faber."

"You're wrong. I don't."

"Well, you know something about it that I don't

know. Take your client, for instance. Why is that girl your client? Can she pay the kind of fee you charge? She cannot. Then who's going to pay you? You know that, don't you? You're damn right you do. You go in for fancy tricks only when someone makes it well worth your while. For example, that Durkin that works for you that was there in the taxi. And Goodwin admits he called him up to that room and then sent him away in his car. Your car. I'm betting the Lovchen girl went with him."

"Nonsense. Fred came directly here alone."

"You say."

"Well, ask Fritz, who opened the door—"

"Nuts. What good does it do to ask questions of anybody who works for you? But we'll find Lovchen, and we'll find Zorka too, don't think we won't."

"You've found no trace of them?"

"Not yet. We will. We had a tail on Lovchen, but he hasn't reported and we don't know where he is. Another thing, you had Zorka right here in this house, on the grill—"

"She was drunk."

"She wasn't too drunk to climb down a fire escape. According to you." Cramer brandished the cigar at him. "Do you realize that this time I could actually slap a charge of obstructing justice on you?"

"I doubt it. Why don't you try?"

"For a damn good reason. Because the commissioner and the district attorney are both on the soft pedal."

Wolfe's brows went up. "They are?"

"Yes. Didn't I say it's a hush-hush? It's exactly the kind of thing that makes my guts turn over. I'm a cop. I am paid a salary to go and look at dead people and decide if they died as the result of a crime and, if they did, find the criminal and fasten it on him so it will stick. That's the job I'm paid to do. Ninety-nine times out of a hundred I get official cooperation as required, but once in a while a bunch of politicians or influential citizens will try to rope me off. I don't like being roped off by anyone whatever." He stuck the cigar in his mouth and laid his heavy fists on the chair arms. "I do not like it."

"And you are being roped off from this case?"

"I am. The British consul phoned the commissioner to express his deep concern at the violent death of a British subject, and his earnest hope and so forth. The commissioner saw him at eleven o'clock last night, and the consul was communicating with London as soon as possible. This morning I ask the commissioner for the dope, and he says the consul can furnish no information regarding Ludlow's activities, but of course it is to be hoped that justice will be done. Like it is to be hoped we'll have a mild winter. Then, a little later, talking with the district attorney, I suggested that he might phone the British embassy in Washington, and he vetoes it and says he doubts if it would be fruitful to pursue an investigation along that line. I damn near went ahead and phoned Washington myself!"

"Why didn't you?"

"Because I'm too old to look for another job. Besides, it wouldn't have been fruitful. But what I did this morning, within five minutes after I got there on 38th Street, I phoned right from that room to the German consul general and asked him about Faber, and he had the brass to tell me that he hadn't the faintest notion what Faber was doing in New York! After telling me last evening, in connection with Ludlow, that he could vouch for Faber absolutely! I phoned the German embassy in Washington then and there, and got the same run-around. What the hell right have countries got to send guys to other countries to do things they're ashamed to talk about? Even when the guys get murdered?"

Wolfe shook his head.

Cramer glared at him a while in silence and then announced abruptly, "I sent a cable to a place in Yugoslavia called Zagreb."

Wolfe murmured, "Indeed."

"Yes, indeed. That's the town those two girls came from. It's the address on their passports. They say they came over here because America is the land of opportunity. They were asked, in that case why didn't they enter on the quota instead of visitors' visas. They said they wanted to see what it was like first."

"Cautious." Wolfe grunted. "You cabled, of course, to learn if they might be suspected of a grudge against the British Empire. I doubt if you'll get much. If they're working for the Yugoslav government, of course you won't. If for someone else—Zagreb is the Croatian capital, and the authorities there certainly wouldn't help you any. May I ask why you picked on those two girls especially?"

"I didn't. I picked on everybody. But it isn't surprising if I pick on 'em now, is it? With one of 'em evaporated? And Faber stabbed to death right in their flat? Is Tormic still your client?"

"She is."

"If she's innocent it's a mistake not to let her talk."

"I don't think so."

"I do." Cramer discarded his cigar and leaned back. "I'll tell you frankly, I don't think she did it. Chiefly for two reasons, and one is that she's your client. I admit that's a reason. The other is that Faber's death takes away her alibi for Ludlow. She wouldn't be that dumb.

But. She left headquarters at a quarter past ten this morning and she was tailed. She took a taxi. At Canal Street she suddenly hopped out of the taxi and into the subway. It was so unexpected that the tail lost her in the shuffle because a train was just pulling in and she made it and he didn't. So what did she do between then and the time she got to your office, ten after eleven?"

"What does she say?"

"She says she told the taxi driver to take her to your place, but she suddenly decided that she would have time to go to Miltan's and see Miss Lovchen about something if she took the subway, so she did. Then she decided she wouldn't have time after all, so she got out at Grand Central and phoned Miss Lovchen instead, and then took a taxi here."

"She phoned Miss Lovchen where? Miltan's?"

"Yes. And she did. Miltan answered the phone himself and recognized her voice and called Miss Lovchen. About a quarter to eleven."

"What does she say she phoned Miss Lovchen about?"

"She says it's none of my business."

Wolfe sighed. "Well, disprove it."

"Sure. I know. I said frankly, I don't think she did it."

"Who do you think did? Miss Lovchen?"

"How the hell do I know?" Cramer sat up and made fists again. "Haven't I made it plain that I don't know a damn thing? I can't even put anyone in that room between ten o'clock, the time that Faber left here on his feet, and the time Goodwin and Miss Tormic went there and found him. We can't find anyone that saw anybody go in or out of the building. We're still trying it, but you know that game."

He banged a fist and demanded, "And what if we

do? What if I had stood there on the sidewalk myself and saw her go in with Faber and come out again without him? What good would that do me? When the question comes up, what did she kill him for, or Ludlow either, what do I say then? Huh? Or anybody else! It is customary, before you turn a murder case over to a jury and ask them for a conviction, to give them some slight hint of what the motivation was. They like it better that way. And where it stands now, I could give just as good a motive for Goodwin here, and say he did it with his jackknife when he went there with Miss Tormic, as I could for anybody else."

I protested, "I don't carry a jackknife. A penknife."

"Maybe your field's too narrow," Wolfe suggested. "Have you considered—"

"I haven't got any field. As far as I'm concerned, it's wide open. Naturally, we're checking up on everyone that was at Miltan's last evening. Young Gill was at his office. One out. Miltan and his wife were at their place. Three out. That leaves six in, of that bunch. Driscoll went for a walk at half past ten and got to his office at eleven thirty. Donald Barrett says he was at his office, Barrett & De Russy, but it hasn't been confirmed yet to make it tight. Lovchen and Tormic and Zorka. Two of those disappeared. Belinda Reade left her apartment shortly after ten o'clock to go shopping and hasn't been located."

"The weapon?"

"Hasn't been found. He was stabbed in the left breast with a blade long enough to reach the heart, and it was withdrawn in a few minutes, but not immediately, judging from the amount of bleeding. He was also struck a severe blow, before he was stabbed, on the left eye. A very hard blow with something blunt and hard and heavy. Very unlikely that he could have got it falling, and anyway, if it had happened at the

moment he was stabbed to death it wouldn't look the
way it does. It indicates that there was a struggle—
what's the idea?"

I had doubled up my right fist and displayed it in
front of his nose.

"Blunt and hard and heavy," I declared.

"Huh? What—"

"Yes, sir. It was me. He got obnoxious here in this
office and I plugged him. I tell it because you may dig
up someone who saw him soon after, and I don't want
to be accused of withholding evidence."

Cramer's chin slowly sunk to his breastbone. It
looked like a slow motion of Jack Dempsey preparing
to wade in. Then, also slowly, he put the tip of a
forefinger to his nose and rubbed up and down, gently
and rhythmically, meanwhile surveying me through
narrowed lids. It was quite a while before he said
thoughtfully:

"You wouldn't stab a guy."

"No, sir," I agreed brightly, "it wouldn't be in
character—"

"Shut up. But what if you and Tormic went there
and found him there going through things. You got
mad and socked him. Tormic got mad and stuck a knife
in him. You sent for Durkin and made him a gift of the
knife and he left with it. You phoned here and I was
here."

"It sounds pretty plausible," I conceded, "but
you're confronted with the question of motive again.
What was it that infuriated Tormic to the point of
croaking him? Another trouble is that Fred Durkin
was here in the office when I plugged him." I shook my
head. "That theory is full of holes. I'm in favor of
crossing it off—"

The phone interrupted me. It was a call for

Cramer. I gave him room to take it at my desk. He talked for a full ten minutes, everything from noncommittal grunts to elaborate detailed instructions, and when it was finished returned to his chair.

He regarded me with a cold eye. "You know, son," he said finally, "you have one or two good qualities. In a way I even like you. In another way I could stand and watch your hide peeling off and not shed any tears. You have undoubtedly got the goddamnedest nerve of anybody I know except maybe Nero Wolfe. Tormic is down at headquarters, with that lawyer you got for her, refusing to answer questions. I've got half a notion to try that old gag on her. I think I'll phone Rowcliff to tell her that you have admitted that Faber was on his feet when you and she got there, and you knocked him down."

"Go ahead," I urged him. "It will be interesting to see how it works out. But as far as my nerve is concerned, I never have had, do not now have, and never will have, enough nerve to risk one teeny-weeny chance of sitting in the frying-chair."

"Yesterday afternoon you fled the scene of a murder with the weapon used for the crime."

"Not knowingly. To begin with, I didn't fled, I merely went. And I did not know that culdymore was in my pocket."

Cramer leaned back, sighed, and began rubbing his nose again.

The door opened. Fritz entered, approached, and said:

"Mr. Cather, sir."

Wolfe's chin went up. "Show him in."

I could tell from the tone of Wolfe's voice that there was a possibility that Orrie was bringing home a chunk of important bacon, but a glance at Orrie's face told me that he didn't have it. Wolfe obviously reached the same conclusion, for he said, more a statement than a question:

"No result."

Orrie stood with his overcoat on and his hat in his hand. "No, sir."

Wolfe grimaced. "Did you find the—things I suggested?"

"Yes, sir. More too. There were mentions—I saw the name—in a lot of articles and sometimes in headlines, but that was all. Of course I couldn't read—"

"That wouldn't help any. No pictures."

"No, sir. I went through every possible thing at the library, and I tried the other places. The *Times* thought they would have one, but they didn't. I'm on my way now to the consulate and I just stopped by here instead of phoning—"

"Don't go to the consulate. I phoned there and it's hopeless. Mr. Cramer and I are both out of humor with consulates. Have you been to Second Avenue?"

"No, I was going there last."

"Try it. You might find it there. It is possible that Mr. Cramer has arranged that anyone leaving this house shall be followed. If so, shake him. I don't want the police in on this. Not yet."

Orrie grinned. "That will be a pleasure." He tramped out.

Cramer said in a tone of disgust, "Horse feathers."

"It wouldn't be the first time you've tried that stratagem," Wolfe observed mildly. "Anyway, it's not as annoying as your former attempts at bulldozing. Thank heaven, you seem to have given that up. Are you through amusing yourself with Archie?"

"Amusing myself? Good God!"

"You must have been. You couldn't very well have been serious. Will you have some beer?"

"No, thanks—yes I will too. I'm thirsty."

"Good." Wolfe pushed the button. "Did I understand you to say that you were having Miss Lovchen followed?"

"Yes. A double tail. One of them phoned in at ten forty that she had left the house at 38th Street and gone to Miltan's, and was in there then, and we haven't heard from them since. Their instructions are to report in every two hours if they can do so without danger of losing contact."

"I see. It's very handy to have so many men."

"Yeah. It would be if more of them were worth a damn. There are over a hundred of them on this case right now. Sifting out up at 38th Street. Looking for the thing he was stabbed with. Getting backgrounds. Tailing. Looking for Lovchen and Zorka. Checking alibis. I'm expecting any minute to be told to pull a bunch of them off. Hush-hush." The inspector set his jaw. "But until I get direct orders to the contrary, I'm going to proceed on the theory that the people who pay my salary don't want any kind of a murderer to get any kind of a break. That's why I'm sitting here chinning with you. This is the one place where I might get a line on whatever it is that the goddam consuls and ambassadors are so bashful about . . . much obliged."

He took the beer Wolfe had poured for him, gulped, licked the foam from his lips, and gulped again.

He sat back holding the half-filled glass. "Let me ask you something. If you had your pick of everybody, everybody in or near New York, to be brought in here right now, for you to ask questions of about this case, who would it be?"

"Thank heaven," Wolfe declared, "I can answer that unequivocally. Madame Zorka."

The phone rang. It was for Cramer again and he took it at my desk. It was a short conversation this time, and when he disconnected and went back to his chair he had a satisfied grin on his mug.

"Well, well," he said. "I call that pretty good. No sooner asked for. They've got Zorka and I told them to bring her here."

"Indeed." Wolfe was filling his glass again. "Where did they find her?"

"In a room at the Brissenden. Registered phone. Arrived at ten minutes past five this morning."

"I hope," Wolfe muttered, "that she has something to wear besides that red thing she had on last night."

"Huh? I beg your pardon?"

"Nothing. Soliloquy—Yes, Fritz?"

Fritz was in again. He had the salver this time, and crossed to Wolfe. Wolfe took the card, read it and frowned.

"The devil," he said. "Where is he?"

"In the hall, sir."

"Please put him in the front room, close the door, and come back."

As Fritz went Wolfe addressed the inspector:

"I don't suppose you have an errand somewhere else."

"Neither do I," Cramer said emphatically. "I've told you ten times I like it here. If I once got out you might not let me in again unless I brought a warrant."

"Very well. Then I'm afraid—Oh, Fritz. Will you please take Mr. Cramer up in the elevator and ask Theodore to show him the orchids?" He smiled at the inspector. "You haven't been up there for a long while. I'm sure you'll enjoy it."

"I'll love it," Cramer declared, and got up and followed Fritz out.

Wolfe handed me the card and I read, "John P. Barrett."

The sound came of the elevator door clanging, and Wolfe said, "Bring him in."

Chapter 15

The appearance of Donnybonny's father in the flesh fitted the sound of his voice on the telephone. He was the kind many people call distinguished-looking and I call Headwaiter's Dream. He was around fifty, smooth-shaven, with gray eyes that needed to look only once at something, and was wearing $485 worth of quiet clothes. He shook hands with Wolfe in a pleasant manner, as if there could never be any hurry or urgency about anything in the world.

"You're over here by the river in a corner of your own," he observed genially as he sat down.

Wolfe nodded. "Yes, I bought this place a long time ago and I'm hard to move. You must excuse me, Mr. Barrett, if I say that I haven't much time to spare. I'm wedging you in. Another caller kindly went up to my plant rooms for an interlude. Mr. Cramer of the police."

"Cramer?"

"Inspector Cramer of the Homicide Bureau."

"Oh." Barrett's tone was nonchalant but his eyes, for an instant, were not. "I came to see you on account of some remarks you made last night to my son.

Regarding Bosnian forests, credits held by my firm, and the Donevitch gang. That was your word, I believe—gang."

"I believe it was," Wolfe admitted. "Was there something wrong with my remarks?"

"Oh, no. Nothing wrong. May I smoke?"

Permission received, he got a cigarette from a case which boosted his freight loading from the $485 up to around eight hundred berries, lit, and thanked me for the ash tray I provided.

"My son," he said in a tone of civilized exasperation, "is a little bit green. It's unavoidable that youth should arrange people in categories, it's the only way of handling the mass of material at first to avoid hopeless confusion, but the sorting out should not be too long delayed. My son seems to be pretty slow at it. He overrates some people and underrates others. Perhaps I've tried to rush it by opening too many doors for him. A father's conceit can be a very disastrous thing."

He tapped ashes from his cigarette. He asked abruptly but not at all pugnaciously, "What is it you want, Mr. Wolfe?"

Wolfe shook his head. "Nothing right now. I wanted to see Madame Zorka and your son kindly made that possible."

"Yes, he told me about that. But what else?"

"Nothing at present. Really."

"Well." Barrett smiled. "I understand that as a private investigator you undertake almost any sort of job that promises a fee proportionate to your abilities."

"Yes, sir, I do. Within certain boundaries I have set. I try to keep my prejudices intact."

"Naturally." Barrett laughed sympathetically. "We

can't leave it to anyone else to defend our prejudices for us." He tapped off ashes again. "My son also tells me that you are engaged in the interests of a young woman named Tormic who is a friend of his. At least—hum—an acquaintance. In connection with the murder of that man Ludlow."

"That's right," Wolfe agreed. "I was originally engaged to clear her of a charge of stealing diamonds from a man named Driscoll. Then Mr. Ludlow got killed, and Miss Tormic needed a little help on that too because she was implicated by circumstances."

"And was it from this Miss Tormic that you received information which enabled you to put pressure on my son? You did put pressure on him, didn't you?"

"Certainly. I blackmailed him."

"Yes. With a threat to disclose certain facts. Did you get those facts from Miss Tormic?"

"My dear sir." Wolfe wiggled a finger at him. "You can't possibly be fatuous enough to expect me to tell you that."

Barrett smiled at him. "There's always a chance that you might. Especially since there's no good reason why you shouldn't. Are you under obligation to defend the interests of anyone except Miss Tormic?"

"Yes. My own. Always my own."

"That, of course. But anyone else? I should think there would be no impropriety in your telling me if you represent any interest except that of Miss Tormic. For instance, Madame Zorka?"

Wolfe frowned. "I am always reluctant to make a present of information. Just as you are reluctant to make a present of money. You're a banker and your business is selling money; I'm a detective and mine is selling information. But I don't want to be churlish. In connection with the activities we are speaking of, I represent no interest whatever except that of Miss Tormic."

"And, always, your own."

"Always my own."

"Good." Barrett crushed his cigarette in the tray. "That clears the way for us, I should think. Please don't think I'm fatuous. I've made some inquiries and I find you have an enviable reputation for good faith. I have a proposal to make regarding this little project my firm is interested in. This—um—business you mentioned to my son. We need your services. Nothing onerous, and certainly nothing to offend your prejudices." He pulled a little leather fold from his pocket. "I'll give you a check now as a retainer. Say ten thousand dollars?"

I thought to myself, what do you know about that; Donny-darling got his briber's itch honestly, by direct inheritance. Then I grinned, looking at Wolfe. One corner of his mouth was twisted a little out of line, which mean that he was suffering acute pain. It was a situation he had had to face fairly often during the years I had known him, and the torture involved was in direct proportion to the number of ciphers. Ten thousand bucks would have kept a good man, even Ray Borchers, in Central America for a full year, hunting rare orchids, always with the possibility of finding one absolutely new. Or 5000 cases of beer or 600 pounds of caviar. . . .

He said bravely, but with somewhat more breath than the word should require, "No."

"No?"

"No."

"If I assure you that you will be expected to do nothing that will interfere with the interest you already represent? And in case my assurance doesn't satisfy you, if at any time you find your engagements in conflict you may merely return the ten thousand dollars—"

Wolfe's lip twitched. I turned my head away. But his voice showed that he had it licked: "No, sir. To return that amount of money would ruin my digestion for a week. If I could bring myself to do it, which is doubtful. No, sir. Abandon the idea. I shall accept no commission or retainer from you."

"Is that—um—definite?"

"Irrevocable."

One little vertical crease showed in the middle of Barrett's forehead. With no other sign of fits, he returned the leather fold to his breast pocket, and then regarded Wolfe with what was probably as close to an open stare as he ever got.

"The only recourse that leaves me," he said, with no affability left in his tone at all, "is to draw my own conclusions."

"If you find you must have a conclusion, yes, sir."

"But I confess I'm puzzled. I'm not often puzzled, but I am now. I'm not gullible enough to believe that your interest is only what you profess it to be. I have very good reasons for not believing it besides the fact that in that case there would be no explanation for your refusing my proposal. My son thinks that you are representing either London or Rome, but there are two objections to that: first, no contacts have been reported to us, and second, if that were true why would you have exposed yourself as you did last night? Is it any wonder that we regarded that as an invitation to deal?"

"I'm sorry I misled you," Wolfe murmured.

"But you're not going to tell me whom you're tied up with."

"I have no client but Miss Tormic."

"And you're not prepared to deal with us."

Wolfe shook his head, if not with enthusiasm, with finality.

John P. Barrett stood up. There was a vague sort of vexation on his face, like a man with a feeling that he has gone off and left something somewhere but unable to say either what it was or where he left it.

"I hope," he said, with an edge to his tone, "for your own sake, that you don't happen to get in our way unwittingly. We know who our opponents are, and we know how to handle them. If you're in this on your own and you're trying to play for a haul—"

"Nonsense." Wolfe cut him off. "I'm a detective working on a job. I am not apt to get in anyone's way, or perform any other maneuver, unwittingly. I will say this. There is a possibility that in finishing up my own business I'll be compelled to interfere with yours. If that seems likely to occur, I'll let you know in advance."

Bang went another illusion. I wouldn't have supposed that a man of Barrett's appearance and breeding, and especially with the clothes he was wearing, could do or say anything mean. But the look in his eyes at that moment, and the tone of his voice, were plain mean and you could even say nasty. All he said was, "Don't try it, Mr. Wolfe. Don't try interfering with my business."

He turned to go.

Fortunately I had noticed the sound of Fritz in the hall and, passing Wolfe a signal to hold Barrett a moment, I bounced up and out, shutting the office door behind me, not in Barrett's face, for he had turned at a remark from Wolfe. As I trotted down the hall Fritz was holding the street door open and three people were entering in the shape of a sandwich: a dick, Zorka, and another dick. Without ceremony or apology I hustled them into the front room and shut them in, then trotted back to the office and nearly knocked Barrett off his pins swinging the door against him.

"Sorry, sir, I did it unwittingly."

He gave me a frosty eye and departed. I stayed there on the threshold until I saw Fritz had got him accoutered and dispatched on his way, and then told Wolfe who had come and asked him if he thought Cramer would prefer to go on looking at orchids. He told me to phone up and tell Horstmann to bring the inspector down, and I did so, and then returned to the front room for Zorka. The two dicks started to come along, and I waved them back and said I would take her to Inspector Cramer.

"We'll help you, buddy," they said as if they were twins, and stayed as close to her as they could without being vulgar. Wolfe frowned as the four of us cluttered into the office. In a minute we were a neat half-dozen when Cramer joined us, five full-grown men against one dressmaker. One of the dicks got out a notebook and I arranged myself at my desk with mine. Wolfe leaned back with his clasped hands resting on his meal container, looking at Zorka with his eyes half shut. Cramer was scowling at her.

I had remembered the name of the girl in the Bible she resembled—Delilah. But right then she looked crumby, with puffs under her eyes, scared and nervous, and altogether anything but carefree. I was glad to notice, for Wolfe's sake, that she had snared a dark red woolen suit somewhere, and some shoes and stockings, but it was just like Wolfe to pick on that as the first means of harassing her. Naturally he was sore at her for using his fire escape.

He growled at her, "Where did you get those clothes?"

She looked at the skirt as if she hadn't realized she had it on. "Zeeze—" She stopped, frowning at him.

"I mean the clothes you're wearing. When you left here last night—this morning—all you had on was a red thing. Under your coat. Those things you're wearing now were in the bag and suitcase you took to Miss Reade's apartment. Is that right?"

"You say zey waire."

"Weren't they? Who took them to you at the Hotel Brissenden? Mr. Barrett?"

She shrugged.

Cramer barked, "We can prove that and that's not all we can prove! After those clothes were delivered to you this morning, you put them on and left the hotel, and you were followed."

"Zat ees not true." She set her teeth on her lower lip for a moment, and then went on, "For one sing, if you had me followed you would know where I was and you would not wait so late to get me and bring me here. For anozzer sing, I did not leave zee hotel, not once until zee men came—"

"That won't get you anywhere! Now look here—"

"Please, Mr. Cramer?" Wolfe opened his eyes. "If you don't mind? Remember what you said, that you'd be no better off if you had stood across the street yourself and seen her go in with him and emerge without him. There's no point in running her up a tree if you have no ammunition to bring her down again."

"Have you?" the inspector demanded.

"I don't know, but I'd like to find out."

Cramer pulled out a cigar and stuck it between his teeth. "Go ahead."

Wolfe cleared his throat and focused on her. "Madame Zorka. Is that your name?"

"Of course eet ees."

"I know it's the name on your letterheads and in the telephone book. But were you christened Zorka?"

"Eet ees my name."

"What's the rest of it?"

She fluttered a nervous hand. "Zorka."

"Now my dear young lady. Last night, inferentially at least, you were drunk. But you're not drunk now, you're merely bedraggled. Do you intend to tell us the rest of your name or not?"

"I . . ." She hesitated, and then said with sudden determination, "No. I can't."

"Why can't you?"

"Because I—it would be dangerous."

"Dangerous to whom? To you?"

"No, not to me—as much as uzzer people." She took a deep breath. "I am a refugee. I escaped."

"Where from?"

She shook her head.

"Come, come," Wolfe said brusquely. "Not the place, the city, the village, if you think you can't. What country? Germany? Russia? Italy? Yugoslavia?"

"All right. Zat much. Yugoslavia."

"I see. Croatia? Serbia? Montenegro?"

"I said, Yugoslavia."

"Yes, but—very well." Wolfe shrugged. "How long ago did you escape?"

"About one year ago."

"And came to America? To New York?"

"First Paris. Paris some time, then America."

"Did you bring a lot of money with you?"

"Oh, no." She spread out her hands to reject an absurdity. "No money. No refugee could have money."

"But I understand you have a business here in New York which must have cost a good deal to set up."

She almost smiled at him. "I knew you would ask zat. A friend was very kind to me."

"Is the friend's name Donald Barrett?"

She sat silent a moment, just looking at him, and then said, "But I am foolish. Zaire is no disgrace. Anyway, eet ees known to a few people, and you would ask and find out. Zee kind friend who lent me money ees Mr. Barrett. He ees, what you call eet, silent partner."

"You're in debt to Mr. Barrett, then."

"Debt?" She frowned. "Oh, debt. Yes, very much."

Wolfe nodded. "I sympathize with you, madame. I hate being in debt. Some people don't seem to mind it. By the way, those people in Yugoslavia—those who might be in danger if you told us the rest of your name—are they relatives of yours?"

"Yes, some. Some relatives."

"Are you Jewish?"

"Oh, no. I am very old Yugoslavian family."

"Indeed. Nobility?"

"Well . . ." She pulled her shoulders up and together, and released them again.

"I see. I won't press that. The danger to your relatives—would that be on account of your activities in New York?"

"But I have no activities in New York, except my business."

"Then I don't understand how revealing your name would place your relatives in peril."

"Zat ees . . . eet would be suspect."

"What would be suspect?"

She shook her head.

Cramer growled, "We known damn well she's not

normal. I could have told you that much. When we went through her apartment this morning—"

Zorka's head jerked around at him and she squeaked in indignation, "You went through my apartment!"

"Yes, ma'am," he said calmly. "And your place of business. Anybody that stages the kind of performance you did last night can expect some unwelcome attention. You're lucky you're not down at headquarters right now phoning for your kind friend to furnish bail for you, and that's exactly where you'll be when we're through here maybe." He resumed to Wolfe, "There's not a thing, not a scratch of anything, at her home or office either, that takes you back further than a year ago, the time she came to New York. That's why I say we already knew she wasn't normal."

"Did you find a passport?"

"No. That's another thing—"

"Where is your passport, madame?"

She looked at him. She wet her lips twice. "I am in zees country legally," she declared.

"Then you must have a passport. Where is it?"

For the first time her eyes had a cornered look. "I weel explain . . . to zee propaire officaire . . ."

"There's nothing improper about me," Cramer said grimly.

Zorka spread out her hands. "I lost eet."

"I'm afraid the water's getting hot," said Wolfe. "Now about last night. Why did you phone here and say that you saw Miss Tormic putting something in Mr. Goodwin's pocket?"

"Because I did see eet."

"Then why hadn't you told the police about it?"

"Because I thought not to make trouble." She edged forward in her chair. "Now look. Zat happen

precisely zee way I say. I thought not to make trouble.
Zen I sink, murder ees so horrible, I have no right. Zen
I phone you and say I weel tell zee police. Zen I sink,
Mr. Barrett ees friend of Mees Tormic, so to be fair I
should tell heem what I do, and I phone heem. Of
course he know how I am refugee, how I escape, how
I must not put people in danger—"

"By the way, where did you first meet Mr. Barrett?"

"I meet heem in Paris."

"Go ahead."

"So he say, good God, zee police kestion me so
much, zey must know everysing about me, so dangerous to me and to so many people, so why do I not go
veesit Mees Reade, so I pack my bags—"

There was a knock at the door and Fritz entered.
He advanced and spoke over a dick's shoulder:

"Mr. Panzer, sir."

"Tell him I'm engaged with Madame Zorka and Mr.
Cramer."

"I did so, sir. He said he would like to see you."

"Send him in."

Cramer bellowed, "So it was Donald Barrett that
got you to take a powder—"

"Just a moment," Wolfe begged him. "I think we're
getting a reinforcement."

Nobody seeing Saul Panzer for the first time would
have regarded him as a valuable reinforcement for
anything whatever, but they would have been wrong.
A lot of people had underrated him, and a lot of people
had paid for it. He had left his old brown cap and coat
in the hall and, as he stood there absorbing a couple of
million details of the little group with one quick glance,
everything about him looked insignificant but his big
nose.

Wolfe asked him, "Results, Saul?"

"Yes, sir."

"Definite?"

"Yes, sir."

"Indeed. Let us have them."

"I was going to bring her birth certificate along, but I thought that might make trouble, so I took a copy—"

He retreated a step, because Zorka had leaped to her feet, confronted him, and practically shrieked at him, "You didn't! You couldn't—"

A dick reached for her elbow and Cramer bawled, "Sit down!"

"But he—if he—"

"I said sit down!"

She backed up, stumbled on the other dick's foot, recovered her balance, and dropped into her chair. Her shoulders sagged, and she sat that way.

Saul said, "I didn't have to make any expenditures of the kind you contemplated, but I spent three dollars and ninety cents on a phone call. I thought it was justified."

"No doubt. Go ahead."

Saul took his step back. "First I went to Madame Zorka's apartment. There were four city detectives there making a search, and the maid was sitting in a bedroom crying. I had already decided what to do if I found that, so I merely went in—"

He stopped, with a glance at Cramer and the dicks.

"Go on, don't mind them," Wolfe told him. "If it ruins a modus operandi for you, you'll invent an even better one for next time."

"Thank you, sir. I went in for a minute only, establishing a friendly basis, and got the maid to look at me. Then I went to Madame Zorka's place of business on 54th Street. There were more city detectives there, but aside from that it didn't look promising, and I decided to leave it as a last resort. From a certain source I got three leads on friends and associates, and I spent nearly four hours on that line, counting lunch, but got nothing at all.

"I then, at 2:15, returned to the apartment. I learned downstairs that two of the detectives were still there, so I waited until they left, which was at 2:35, and then went up. I rang the bell and the maid opened the door and I went in. On account of the impression created at my visit in the morning, she took it for granted that I was a city detective, though I did not say so. I merely went in and started searching—"

Cramer growled, "By God, impersonating—"

"Oh, no, Inspector." Saul looked shocked. "I wouldn't impersonate an officer. But I did suspect the maid made a mistake and took me for one, for otherwise she might have objected to my searching the place. I thought if she had it fixed in her mind that I was a city detective, she probably wouldn't believe me anyway if I tried to tell her I wasn't, so I didn't try. And if you won't regard it as impertinent, I'd like to compliment you on the job your men did. You would hardly know the place had been touched, the way they left things, and they must have gone through every inch. And the fact that they had been over it made it unnecessary for me to do any of the superficial things. I could concentrate on the long chance that there was some trick they had missed. It wasn't much of a trick at that, only a false bottom in a leather hatbox. Underneath it I found her birth certificate and a few letters and things. I left it all there after taking a copy of the certificate, and then I went out to a phone booth

and made a long distance call to Ottumwa, Iowa. To
her mother. Just to make sure—"

Zorka blurted at him, "You—you phoned my mother . . ."

"Yes, ma'am, I did. It's all right, I didn't scare her
or anything, I made it all right. Having found out from
the birth certificate that your name is Pansy Bupp,
and having read a letter—"

"What's that?" Wolfe demanded. "Her name is
what?"

"Pansy Bupp." He pulled a piece of paper from his
pocket. "P, A, N, S, Y, B, U, P, P. Her father is William
O. Bupp. He runs a feed store. She was born at
Ottumwa on April 9, 1912—"

"Give me that paper."

Saul handed it over. Wolfe glared at it, ate it with
his eyes, and transferred the glare to her, and it was
one of the few times on record that I would have called
his tone a snarl as he shot at her:

"Why?"

She snarled back, "Why what?"

"Why that confounded drivel? That imbecile flummery?"

She looked as if she would like to stick a knife
through him. "What do you think would happen," she
demanded, "to a Fifth Avenue couturière if it came out
that her name was Pansy Bupp?" Her voice rose to an
indignant wail. "What do you think *will* happen?"

Wolfe, beside himself with fury, wiggled a whole
hand at her. "Answer me!" he roared. "Is your name
Pansy Bupp?"

"Yes."

"Were you born in Ottumwa, Iowa?"

"Yes."

"When did you leave there?"

"Why, I . . . I took trips to Denver—"

"I'm not speaking of trips to Denver! When did you leave there?"

"Two years ago. Nearly. My father gave me money for a trip to Paris—and I got a job there and learned to design—and I met Donald Barrett and he suggested—"

"Where did you get the name Zorka?"

"I saw it somewhere—"

"Have you ever been in Yugoslavia?"

"No."

"Or anywhere in Europe besides Paris?"

"No."

"Is what you said last night—about the reason for your phoning here and then running away to Miss Reade's place—is that the truth?"

"Yes, it is. Like a fool, an utter fool"—she gulped—"I let my conscience bother me because it was murder. If I hadn't done that, none of this . . ." She flung out her hands. "Oh, can it be—can't this be—" Her chin was quivering.

"Miss Bupp!" Wolfe thundered. "Don't you dare! Archie, get her out of here! Get her out of the house!"

"Zat weel be a plaizhoore," I said.

Chapter 16

Wolfe looked up at the wall clock and said, "Ten minutes to four. I'll have to leave you pretty soon to go up to my plants."

We were comparatively peaceful again. The two dicks had departed with Miss Bupp, and Lieutenant Rowcliff had been phoned to expect her at headquarters for a little talk.

Cramer said, "It *could* be a frame, you know. We've tried some of her friends and associates too. We heard she was a Turk, a Hungarian, a Russian Jew, and maybe part Jap. It won't hurt any to check it up."

Wolfe shook his head, grimaced, and muttered, "Ottumwa, Iowa."

"I guess so," the inspector admitted. "Does that shove you off onto a siding?"

"No. It merely . . ." Wolfe shrugged.

"It merely leaves you still waiting at the station, huh?" Getting no answer, he regarded Wolfe a moment and then went on, "As far as I'm concerned, I'm still playing these. If you go up to your plants, I go along. If you go to the kitchen to mix salad dressing—"

"You don't mix salad dressing in the kitchen. You do it at the table and use it immediately."

"All right. No matter what you go to the kitchen for, I go too. It's plainer than ever that you know where the kernel is in this nut and I don't. Take the fact of Donald Barrett chasing this Zorka Bupp away so we couldn't get at her. I would get fat trying to put the screws on Donald Barrett, with both the commissioner and the district attorney having a bad attack of bashfulness. Wouldn't I? But you don't even waste time with Donald. You have his old man, John P., himself, coming right here and walking right into your office. That goes to show."

Wolfe looked at me. "Archie. Find out if Theodore failed to understand that when I send a gentleman to look at orchids—"

Cramer snorted. "Don't bother. I didn't sneak downstairs and take a peek. Rowcliff told me on the phone that he had received a report that John P. Barrett had been seen entering this address at 2:55 this p.m."

"Were you having Mr. Barrett followed?"

"No."

"I see. You have a regiment watching this house."

"I wouldn't say a regiment. But I've said and I say again that right now I'm more interested in this house than any other building in the borough of Manhattan. If you want me out of it you'll have to call the police. By the way, another thing Rowcliff told me, they've found Belinda Reade. She's at a matinee at the Lincoln Theater. Do we want her in here?"

"I don't."

"Then I don't either. The boys'll take care of her. If she can account satisfactorily for—is that for me?"

I nodded, and vacated my chair for him to take another phone call. This was a comparatively short one. He emitted a few grunts and made a few unilluminating remarks, and hung up and returned to his chair. No sooner had I got back into mine than the house phone buzzed. As I pulled it over to me I heard Wolfe asking Cramer if there was anything new and the inspector replying that there was nothing worth mentioning and then, over the house phone, in response to my hello, Fred Durkin's voice was in my ear:

"Archie? Come up here."

I said with irritation, "Damn it, Fritz, I'm busy." Then I waited a minute and said, "Okay, okay, quit running off your face," and got up and beat it to the hall, shutting the door behind me. I went quickly but noiselessly up one flight of stairs, opened the door of Wolfe's room, and entered. Fred Durkin was there on a chair beside the bed, within reach of the phone, where he had been instructed to place himself two hours previously.

He started to grumble, "This is one hell of a job—"

"Don't crab, my boy. From each according to his ability. What is it, Lovchen?"

He nodded. "I didn't call you when he got the report on Zorka, because he told them to bring her here, but—"

"What about Lovchen?"

"Her tail phoned in to headquarters." Fred looked at a pad of paper he had scribbled on. "They followed her to Miltan's this morning, and she left there at 10:53 and went back to 404 East 38th Street—"

"The hell she did. Anyone with her?"

"No, she was alone. She stayed in there only about ten minutes. At 11:15 she came out and went to Second Avenue and took a taxi. She got out at the Maidstone Building on 42nd Street. They were a little behind her as she entered the building, and she popped into an elevator just as the door was closing and they missed it. They couldn't find out from the elevator boy what floor she got off at, and anyway, as you know and I know, that would be bad tailing because she could have taken to the stairs and gone up or down. There are four different rows of elevators to watch in that building, and they were afraid to leave to go to a phone, but just now a cop passed by and they flagged him and had him send in a report. They're sure she hasn't left the building and they want help because the rush hour will be on at five o'clock."

"Is that all?"

"That's the crop."

I made a face. "And Cramer, the louse, said there was no news worth mentioning! He's going upstairs with Wolfe, to the roof. When you hear the elevator go up, you go down to the office and stay there. Take all calls. If anybody comes, tell Wolfe on the house phone. Write out a report of what you've told me, and add to it that I've gone to the Maidstone Building, and send it up to Wolfe by Fritz. If I call in and there's anyone in the office, use code. Got it?"

"I've got it, but why not let me go—"

"No, my boy, this is a job for a master."

I left him there. Descending the stairs as fast as I could without making a hubbub, I went to the kitchen and told Fritz:

"Go to the office and tell Wolfe the goose hasn't been delivered and you've sent me to the Washington Market for it. Tell him I protested and complain bitterly of the language I used. That is for the benefit of Inspector Cramer. Fred has the low-down. Got it?"

"Yes," Fritz hissed.

I left by way of the front hall, grabbing my hat and coat. Outside was no regiment, but there was a dick on the sidewalk not far from the stoop, and another one across the street, and a taxi was parked fifty yards east. Not to mention Cramer's police car, there nosing the hind end of my roadster. I climbed in the roadster and started the engine, called to Cramer's chauffeur, "Follow me to the scene of the crime!" and rolled. I didn't go far, only around the corner and a couple of blocks on Tenth Avenue, and then stopped at the curb, locked the ignition, got out, and stopped the first taxi that came along. I waited a minute to see either the police car or the taxi if they turned in from 35th Street, but apparently my invitation hadn't been accepted, so I hopped in and told the driver 42nd and Lexington.

Entering the marble lobby of the fifty-story Maidstone Building, I felt fairly sappy. I had come because Wolfe had instructed me that if Fred copped any news about Carla Lovchen I was to follow it up, and the only way I could follow it up was to go there. I felt sappy because, observing the extent and complications of the lobby, with the four banks of elevators and the twisting crowds, not to mention such things as stairways and possibly basement exits, it seemed good for even money that she had moved out and on; and also, even if she hadn't, I stood a fat chance of grabbing her and getting away with her under the circumstances. Apparently the tails had already got their reinforcements; I had easily spotted three of them on one quick survey. It was obvious that the lobby was no place for me, even if she walked out of an elevator right into my arms.

I had had one feeble idea on my way up in the taxi, and I proceeded to use that up. The building directory board was in two sections, on two sides of the lobby, one A to L and the other M to Z. I tackled the first section and went over it thoroughly, a name at a time, hoping for a hint or a hunch. I got neither, and moved across to the second section, and there, nearing the end, I saw WHEELER & DRISCOLL 3259. It looked slim, but I went to the information booth and told the guy, "I'm looking for a tenant and don't know his firm. Nat Driscoll. Or maybe instead of Nat, Nathaniel."

He opened his book with weary hands and looked at it with weary eyes and said in a weary voice, "Driscoll, Nathaniel, 3259, thirty-second floor, elevators on the—"

I was gone. My heart had started to pump. I love the feeling of a hunch.

I got out at the thirty-second and walked half a mile, around three corners, to 3259. The lettering on the door said:

WHEELER & DRISCOLL
IMPORTERS AND BROKERS

I opened the door and went in, and right away, even in the anteroom, found myself in the midst of prosperity, judging by the rugs and furniture and the type of employee displayed. She was the kind who without any visible effort conveys the impression that she got a job in an office only because she was fed up with yachting and riding to hounds. Not wanting to frighten anyone into scooting out of any other Wheeler & Driscoll doors into the public corridor, I told her:

"My name is Goodwin and I would like to see Mr. Nathaniel Driscoll."

"Have you an appointment?"

"Nope, I just dropped in. Have you heard about the diamonds? The ones he thought had been stolen from him?"

"Oh, yes." Her lip twitched. "Yes, indeed."

"Tell him my name is Goodwin and Miss Tormic sent me to see him. I represent Miss Tormic."

"I'm sorry. Mr. Driscoll isn't in."

"Has he gone home?"

"He hasn't been here this afternoon."

In the first place, my hunch was still alive and kicking, and in the second place, she wasn't a good liar, even with a common conventional lie like that. I got out my memo pad and wrote on it:

If you don't want the cops busting in here in about two minutes looking for your fencing teacher, let's have a little talk. And for God's sake, don't let her show her face in the hall.

A.G

I grinned at the employee to show there was no hard feeling, and indeed there wasn't. "May I have an envelope?"

She got one and handed it to me, and I inserted the note and licked the flap and sealed it. "Here," I said, "take this to Mr. Driscoll, there's a good girl, and don't argue. Do I look like a man who would come all this way to see him unless I knew he was here?"

Without saying a word, she pressed a button. A boy entered from a door at the left, and she gave him the envelope and told him to deliver it to Mr. Driscoll's desk. I said, "Deliver it to *him*," and then, as the boy disappeared, I went to the entrance door and opened it and stood there where I could see the hall in both directions. There were several passers-by, but no sign of any frantic dash for freedom. I must have stood there all of three minutes before I saw, about fifty feet down the hall, the top of a head and then a pair of eyes protruding beyond the edge of a door jamb. I called in a tone of authority:

"Hey, back in there!"

The head disappeared. It had not shown again when I heard the employee's voice calling my name. I turned. The boy was there holding a door open. He said, "This way, sir," and I followed him into an inner corridor and past three doors to one at the end, which he opened.

The room I entered was at least five times as big as the anteroom and six times as prosperous. I realized that in my one swift glance as I started to where Nat Driscoll stood at the corner of a large and elegant desk, telling him: "If you sneaked her out while I was coming in here, the cops will have her inside of a minute."

With one hand gripping the edge of the desk hard enough to bleach the knuckles, he said, "Unh." He looked as bewildered and terrified as a corpulent uncle who had been inveigled into taking a ride on the Ziparoo at Coney Island.

I looked around. "Where is she?"

He said, "Unh."

There were two doors besides the one I had entered by. I trotted across and opened one, and saw only gleaming tiles and a washbowl and sittery. I closed that and went and opened the other one, and looked into a small room with filing cabinets, a bookcase, and a de luxe secretary's desk. The secretary sat there staring at me with big round blue eyes, and a more glittering stare was bestowed on me from a chair in a corner occupied by Carla Lovchen.

She didn't say anything, just goggled at me. My elbow was grabbed from behind, and I was agreeably surprised to find that Nat Driscoll could grip like that.

I pulled away, and we were both inside the small room, and I shut the door.

I demanded, "What did you figure on doing? Keeping her here till after the funeral?"

Carla asked in a low tense voice, without altering her stare, "Where's Neya?"

"She's all right. For a while anyhow. You were tailed to this building—"

"Tailed?"

"Shadowed. Followed by policemen. There are a dozen of them downstairs now, covering all the elevators and exits."

Driscoll dropped onto a chair and groaned. The blue-eyed secretary inquired in a cool business-like tone:

"Are you Archie Goodwin of Nero Wolfe's office?"

"I am. Pleased to meet you." I met Carla's stare. "Did you kill Rudolph Faber?"

"No." A shiver ran over her, and she controlled it and sat rigid again.

Driscoll mumbled at me, "You mean Ludlow. Percy Ludlow."

"Do I? I don't." I fired at the secretary, "What time did Driscoll get here this morning?"

"Ask him," she said icily.

"I'm asking you. Let me tell you folks something. I may not be your best and dearest friend, but I'm quite a pal compared to the guys downstairs I mentioned. Otherwise I would have brought them up here. That can be done at any moment. What time did Driscoll get here this morning?"

"About half past eleven."

"That was his first appearance here today?"

"Yes."

"What time did he leave?"

"He didn't leave at all. He had some lunch brought in on account of Miss Lovchen."

"She got here at 11:20."

"Yes." The secretary was getting no warmer. "How did you know that? How did you know she was here?"

"Intuition. I'm an intuitive genius." I shifted to Driscoll. "So you didn't kill Faber, huh?"

He stammered, "You mean . . . you must mean Ludlow—"

"I mean Rudolph Faber. A little before noon today he was found in the apartment occupied by Neya Tormic and Carla Lovchen, lying on the floor dead. Stabbed. Miss Tormic and I went there looking for Miss Lovchen, and found him."

The secretary looked impressed. Driscoll's eyes widened and his mouth stood open. I snapped at Carla:

"He was there when you went there. Either alive or dead, or alive and then dead."

"I didn't—I wasn't there—"

"Can it. What do you think this is, hide and seek? They were tailing you. You went in there at 11:05 and came out again at 11:15. Faber was there."

She shivered again. "I didn't kill him."

"Was he there?"

She shook her head and took a deep jerky breath. "I'm not . . . going to say anything. I am going away, away from America." She clasped her hands at me. "Pliz you must help me! Mr. Driscoll would help me! Oh you must, you must—"

Driscoll demanded in an improved voice, "You say Faber was there in her apartment stabbed to death?"

"Yes."

"And she had just been there?"

"She left there about thirty minutes before the body was found."

"Good God." He stared at her. The secretary was staring at her too.

I said briskly, "She says she didn't do it. I don't know. The immediate point is that Nero Wolfe wants to see her before the cops get hold of her. What were you going to do, help her get away?"

Driscoll nodded. Then he shook his head. "I don't know. Good God—she didn't tell me about Faber. She said . . ." He flung out his hands. "Damn it, she appealed to me! She swore she had nothing to do with—Ludlow—but she didn't need to! She has been damn fine with me down there—that fencing—greatest pleasure I ever had in my life—she has been damn fine and understanding! She is a very fine young woman! I would be proud to have her for a sister and I've told her so! Or daughter! Daughter would be better! She came here and appealed to me to help her get away from trouble, and by God I was doing it, and I didn't consult any lawyer either! And by God I'll still do it! Do you realize that she appealed to me? I don't care if her apartment was as full of dead bodies as the morgue, that young woman is no damn murderer!"

"I understand," said the secretary with ice still in her voice box, "that it is perfectly legal to help anyone go anywhere they want to, provided they have not committed a crime."

"I don't give a damn," Driscoll declared, "whether it's legal or not! To hell with legal!"

"Okay." I pushed a palm at him. "Don't yell so loud. The point—"

"I want you to understand—"

"Pipe down! I understand everything. You're a hero. Skip it. Here's the way it stands. You can't go ahead and send her on a world cruise, because to begin with you don't stand a chance of getting her out of here and away, and to end with I won't let you. Nero Wolfe wants to see her. Whatever Nero Wolfe wants he gets or he has a tantrum and I get fired. I have no idea whether she's a very fine young woman or a murderer or what, but I do know that the next thing on her program is a talk with Nero Wolfe, and I'm in charge of the program."

"I suppose," said the secretary crushingly, "that *you* stand a chance of getting her out of here."

"Chance is right," I agreed grimly. "May I use your phone?"

She pushed it across the desk and I asked the anteroom employee to get me a number. In a moment I had the connection.

"Hello, Hotel Alexander? Let me talk to Ernie Flint. The house detective."

In two minutes I had him.

"Hello, Ernie? Archie Goodwin. That's right. How's about things? Fine, thanks, everything rosy, I'm studying to be a detective. Not on your life. Say, listen, I'm pulling a stunt and I want you to do me a favor. Send a bellboy in uniform over to the Maidstone Building, Room 3259. Wait, get this. A small one, about five foot three, and not a fat one. With a cap on, don't forget the cap. With a dark complexion if you've got one like that. Yep, dark hair and eyes. Good. Have him bring a parcel with him containing all his own clothes, everything, including hat. Right. Oh, not long. He can be back there within an hour, only you'll have to give him another uniform. Oh, no. Just a stunt I'm pulling. I'm playing a trick on a feller. I'll describe it when I see you. Make it snappy, will you, Ernie?"

I rang off, took the expense roll from my pocket, peeled off a ten, and tendered it to the secretary. "Here, run down to the nearest store and get a pair of black low-heeled oxfords that will fit her. Like what a bellboy might wear. Step on it."

She looked critically at Carla's feet. "Five?"

Carla nodded. Driscoll told the secretary:

"Give him back that money." He got out his wallet and produced a twenty-dollar bill. "Here. Get a *good* pair."

She took it, handed me mine, and went. She may have been chilly, but she wasn't a goof.

Carla said, "I won't go."

"Oh." I looked at her. "You won't?"

"No."

"Would you rather go to police headquarters and entertain the homicide squad?"

"I won't—I want to go away. I *must* go away. Mr. Driscoll said he would help me."

"Yeah, well, he wasn't quick enough on his feet. Even after all his fencing lessons. Anyway, you would have been nabbed downstairs. Do you realize at all the kind of spot you're inhabiting right now?"

"I realize—" She stopped to make her voice work. "I'm in a terrible fix. Oh—terrible! You don't know how terrible!"

"Wrong again. I do know. Would I be staging a damn fool stunt like this to get you to Nero Wolfe if I didn't?"

"It won't do any good to take me to Nero Wolfe. I won't talk to him. I won't talk to anybody."

Driscoll went over and stood in front of her. "Look here, Miss Lovchen," he said, "I don't think that's a sensible attitude. If you don't want to talk to the police, I can understand that. You may have a reason that's absolutely commendable. But sooner or later you'll have to talk to somebody, and if you're not careful it will be a lawyer, and then you *are* up against it. From what I have heard of this Nero Wolfe . . ."

He was still jabbering away when the phone announced that the bellboy was in the anteroom.

I shooed Driscoll and Carla into Driscoll's room and had the bellboy sent in to me. He looked about right, maybe an inch taller than her, but not too skinny or too husky. He was grinning because he could see it was a good joke. I opened the parcel for him while he took his uniform off, and handed him a couple of dollars and told him:

"Put your clothes on and sit here. It's a nice view from the window. Maybe twenty minutes. A blue-eyed girl will come and tell you when to go. Return to the hotel and they'll give you another uniform to work in. That two bucks was just for your trouble. Here's a finif if its effect will be to keep your trap entirely closed regarding the fun we're having. Okay?"

He said it was, and sounded believable. I gave him the five-spot, gathered up the uniform and cap and wrapping paper, and went to the other room, shutting him in.

Carla, on the edge of the chair, and the secretary, kneeling on the rug in front of her, were busy getting her shoes changed, while Driscoll, with his lips screwed up and his hands in his pockets, gazed down at the operation. Carla stood up and stamped, and said they were all right. I handed the uniform to her and said go ahead but she would have to take off her clothes or it would look bunchy, and told Driscoll:

"Turn your back."

He blushed rosy. "I . . . I can go in there—"

"I forgot you're modest. Suit yourself. Back-turning will do me."

He went and looked through a window, and I,

facing the same way, regarded him suspiciously. It was getting dark outdoors and the lights were on in the room, and under those circumstances a windowpane is a fairly good mirror. I admit I may have been doing him an injustice. I spread the wrapping paper out on his desk and, when the secretary handed me Carla's clothes, including coat and hat, made a bundle and got it tied up.

The secretary said, "Look, it's tight around under the arms."

I looked. "Naturally. What would you expect? I think it'll do. Walk to the door and back." Carla walked. I frowned. "The hips are bad. I mean they're good, but you understand me. Put the cap on . . . No, you'll have to stuff the hair under better than that. There by the left ear. That's it. I believe we'll make it. What do you think?"

The secretary said coldly, "I hope so. It's your idea."

Driscoll crabbed, "It's no good. I'd know her across the street."

"Oh," I said sarcastically, "we wouldn't try to fool *you*. There's hundreds of people going and coming in that lobby and why should they be interested in a bellboy? Anyway, we'll take a shot at it." I got the parcel under my arm and confronted Carla. "Now. We have nothing to fear on this floor. We'll go down in the same elevator. You'll leave the elevator before me at the main floor. Walk straight to the Lexington Avenue entrance and on out, and don't look behind or around. I'll be following you all right. Turn right and keep going on across 43rd Street. Between 43rd and 42nd there'll be taxis at the curb. Hop into one and tell the driver to take you to 37th Street and Tenth Avenue—"

The secretary put in an oar: "You'll be with her—"

"I'll be behind her in another taxi. There's a chance that one of those birds in the lobby knows me and will be curious enough to follow me out, in which case I don't want to be seen going for a ride with a bellboy, especially a bellboy with hips. 37th Street and Tenth Avenue. Got that?"

Carla nodded.

"Okay. Stay there in the taxi till I come. I'll probably be right behind you, but you stay there. If you try a trick, you're done. Every cop in New York is looking for you. Understand?"

"Yes, but I want—I must—"

"What you want is a different matter entirely, like the guy that fell out of the airplane. Will you go to that corner and stay there in the taxi?"

"Yes."

"Right. Good-bye, folks. In ten minutes, not sooner, send the bellboy home. I'll take you on with the épée some day, Driscoll."

He looked as if he was about ready to cry as he shook hands with her. The secretary looked as arctic as ever, but I noticed her voice was a little husky as she wished Carla good luck.

We departed. As she went along the corridor ahead of me on the way to the elevator, she looked kind of preposterous, but of course I saw not only what I saw but also what I knew. The other passengers in the elevator gave her a glance or two, but nothing alarming. At the main floor she preceded me out and marched through the lobby, dodging as necessary in the crowd, and it began to look like everything was jake when a call came from my right:

"Hey, Goodwin! Archie!"

Chapter 17

It was Sergeant Purley Stebbins coming at me. The danger was Carla, but for once she acted as if she had some brains. She certainly heard my name called, but she didn't scream or stop and turn around or break into a run. She just kept on going to the entrance. I saw that out of the corner of my eye as I greeted Purley with a hearty grin.

"Well, well, well!"

"It may be," he growled. "What are you doing here?"

I looked around stealthily to guard against eavesdroppers, put my mouth within two inches of his big red ear, and whispered into it, "None of your goddam business."

He grunted, "It's quite a coincidence."

"What is?"

"Your being here in this building."

I tapped him on the chest. "Now that's funny."

"What's funny?"

"Your saying it's quite a coincidence. It's funny because that's exactly what I was going to say. Mind if I say it? It's quite a coincidence."

"Go to hell."

"Same to you and many of them. May I ask, what

are *you* doing in this building?" I glanced around. "You and all your playmates."

"Go to hell."

"How's the roads?"

"Whatta you got in the bundle?"

"Revolvers, daggers, narcotics, smuggled jewels, and a bottle of blood. Want to look at it?"

"Go to hell."

I shrugged politely, told him I'd meet him at the corner of Fire and Brimstone, and left him.

That was okay. But the danger was, with Carla having such a fixed idea about going away from America, that she might be keeping her promise and she might not. Even so, I didn't jump into a taxi at the entrance. I hoofed it to the corner and popped into Bigger's drugstore and stood there. Since it had another exit on 43rd, anyone Purley sent on my tail would either have to pop in after me or make it to the turn in a hurry where he could see both doors. No one did that. I left by 43rd, crossed the street and entered Grand Central the back way, did another maneuver in the smoking room to make doubly sure, went out to Madison Avenue, jumped into a taxi, and sat on the edge of the seat with my fingers crossed and sweat on my brow until we got to the rendezvous and I saw she was there.

I dismissed my taxi, went to hers and opened the door and beckoned her out, paid the driver and sent him off, and waited until he had rounded the corner out of sight before I steered her down the sidewalk to where I had parked the roadster. She wasn't having anything to say. I told her to climb in and handed her the bundle.

It was only a matter of three minutes across to Ninth, down to 34th, and west to the middle of the block. The day was gone and I stopped at a distance from a street light, shut off the engine, and told her:

"There's an assortment of cops in front of Wolfe's house, so we're going in the back way. Follow me and don't say anything after we get inside the house. Just stay behind me."

"I must know . . ." Her voice quavered and she stopped. In a moment she went on, "I must know one thing. Is Neya there?"

"I don't know. She wasn't when I left."

"Where was she?"

"Police headquarters. Not under arrest, they were questioning her and she wasn't answering. They may have brought her to Wolfe's house or they may not. I don't know. Inspector Cramer is there with Wolfe."

"But you said I would only have to see Mr. Wolfe—"

"I said Wolfe wants to talk with you first. Come on."

I got out and went around to her side and opened the door. She had her teeth sunk into her lip. She sat that way a minute, then climbed out and followed me. I led her down the sidewalk to the entrance to the passageway between a warehouse building and a garage, and along the dark passage until we came to the door in the board fence. It was the door Zorka had used after her trip down the fire escape, only from the inside she had only needed to turn the knob of the spring lock, whereas I had to use my key. I guided her across the court and up the steps to the little porch, and used another key, and entered the kitchen ahead of her. No one was in there but Fritz.

He stared at me. "Now, Archie, you ought to tap—"

"Okay. I forgot. No cause for alarm. Keep Miss Lovchen here on the quiet for about four minutes till I get back."

He stared again, at her. "Miss Lovchen?"

"Right. You'd better hide her in the pantry."

I put the parcel on a chair, went out the way I had

come, through the door in the fence and along the passage to 34th Street, got in the roadster and drove around two corners into 35th Street, and rolled to the curb in front of the house. The police car there had been joined by another one, and the taxi was still parked down a ways, and as I crossed the sidewalk to the stoop I saw the dick there with his foot on the running board, chinning with Cramer's chauffeur. I was in too much of a hurry to toss them anything, because I had one more lap to go. I let myself in, shed my coat and hat, and went to the office.

"Oh," I said, "hello."

There was the explanation of the second police car. Over in a corner was a dick looking bored, and on one of the yellow leather chairs sat Neya Tormic, not looking bored. The way her eyes darted at me, I had to control an impulse to side-step to get out of the line of fire.

The dart was a question and I knew what it was, but I ignored it and spoke to Fred Durkin, who was seated at my desk:

"Get out of my chair, you big bum, and come out here and help me a minute."

He arose and lumbered across, and I steered him into the hall and shut the office door.

"Are Wolfe and Cramer upstairs?"

"Yes."

"Anyone in the front room?"

"No."

"Stand here and hold this doorknob, in case that dick should get a sudden notion to stretch his legs."

He got his paw on it, and I went to the kitchen. Fritz put down a pan he was stirring and came close to me and whispered, "In the pantry." I pushed the swinging door and there she was, on a chair he had put there for her, with the parcel at her feet. I got the parcel and told her to follow me and keep quiet. In the hall Fred was hanging onto the doorknob and I winked at him as we passed. Up one flight of stairs, down the hall six paces, through a door—and I closed it behind us, turned on the light, put the parcel on a table, and shut the window curtains.

"*Hvala Bogu*," I said. "This is Mr. Wolfe's room. Don't leave it. If you open a window bells ring all over the house. It's 5:35 and he will be here shortly after six. You might as well put your own clothes on. That door there is a bathroom. Okay?"

She just looked at me, and I saw she was concentrating so hard on keeping a stiff jaw that she couldn't even nod her head, so I went on out. At the head of the stairs I called down, "All right, Fred, go back in and try another chair," and then proceeded to the next flight up. Two of them took me to the narrow door at the top which opened into the plant rooms. I had to go all the way through to the potting room to find Wolfe. He was at the bench with Theodore, inspecting some recent sprouts with a magnifying glass, and Cramer was on a stool with his back propped against the wall, chewing on a cigar.

I hoisted myself onto the free end of the bench and sat swinging my legs. In a few minutes Wolfe came to a coma, shook his head disapprovingly at something he saw through the glass, sighed, and muttered at me, "Did you get the goose?"

"Yes, sir."

"Good."

He got busy with the glass again. I swung my legs. After a while the phone rang. Theodore went to his desk to answer it and told Cramer it was for him. The inspector went and grunted into it for three or four minutes, then hung up and returned to the stool. I knew he was glaring at me, but I was interested in the tips of my number nines swinging back and forth.

He said, and I knew what it must be costing him to restrain himself like that, "You, Goodwin." There was even a suggestion of a tremble in his voice. "When did they move the Washington Market to the Maidstone Building?"

"Why," I said in a friendly tone, "that must have been Sergeant Stebbins on the phone! How's that for deduction?"

"Fine." Cramer threw his cigar at the trash basket, missed, went and picked it up and dropped it in, and returned to the stool. "Don't think I'm going to blow up, because I'm not. I'm beyond that. Ten minutes after you left I told Wolfe that Carla Lovchen was trailed to the Maidstone Building this morning and was holed up there, but that was *after* you left as I say. All I'm going to do is ask a simple question. Why did you go to the Maidstone Building?"

I grinned at him. "Here's the first answer that occurs to me. There was a phone call here at noon from a certain party, and it was traced to a public phone at that building. All right?"

"No."

I shrugged. "Get Mr. Wolfe to tell you one."

Wolfe, going on with his work, paid no attention. Cramer said, "I still am not going to blow up. I have planted myself here on two assumptions. The first is that Wolfe has got something on this case that I stand damn little chance of getting unless and until the break comes and he loosens up. The second is, inasmuch as I have never yet found him picking up the pieces for a murderer, that he's not doing that now. If my first assumption is wrong, I'm just out of luck. If my second one is, you are. Both of you. That's all. Now you can take the Maidstone Building and stick it up your chimney. But in case you don't already know it,

Carla Lovchen went in that place on 38th Street at eleven o'clock this morning and came out again in ten minutes. I want her, and I want her plenty. I'm telling you. So if it turns out that she has actually pulled a getaway and you helped her do it . . ."

"The man's mad," I declared.

"Shut up. That's all."

I continued to admire my feet.

At five minutes to six Wolfe put the magnifying glass away in the drawer, gave Theodore a few instructions regarding the sprouts, and announced that it was time to descend. Never having felt full confidence in the capacity of the elevator as posted on its wall, I left it to him and took to the stairs, and Cramer joined me. Two flights down we saw that the elevator had stopped there and Wolfe was emerging. We halted as he approached us.

"I'll go to my room and clean up a little. Archie, will you come with me? We'll be with you in the office shortly, Mr. Cramer. Miss Tormic is there, you know."

Cramer hesitated, looked at him suspiciously, and then tramped to the stairs and started down. We waited till we heard the office door close behind him and then went to the door of Wolfe's room and entered. Carla was in a straight-backed chair by the wall, her shoulders hunched over, her hands clenched in her lap, her chin down; but she was wearing her own clothes. The bellboy's outfit, neatly folded, was on the table.

Wolfe stopped in front of her and said, "How do you do, Miss Lovchen."

She looked up at him for an instant, then let her head fall again and made no reply.

Wolfe said, "I have no time now because I am expected downstairs. Mr. Goodwin told me he brought a goose. He did. Whether you killed Mr. Ludlow and Mr. Faber or not, you are pure imbecile. Most people are, under great stress, but that merely gives you company. I don't know how or where Mr. Goodwin found you, but you must have been making an awful fool of yourself or he wouldn't have found you at all. Even though he is fairly good at finding things. If you think I am severe, it is because I have no sympathy to waste on people who come and ask my help and tell me nothing but lies. For the present you will stay in this room. I'll come back pretty soon and ask you some questions."

Carla raised her head again, moved it once from side to side, and said, "I won't answer any questions. I've decided that. I won't say anything. Not to you or anybody."

"Oh. You won't?"

"No. Nothing. No matter what happens. If I don't say anything, what can anybody do? What can they prove if I don't say anything? Maybe you think I haven't enough will power for it, but I have."

"You might have, for a while. Try it, by all means. It would be an improvement on your conduct so far." Wolfe turned to go. "I'll be back to see you, anyway, or send for you. Come, Archie."

With his hand on the knob he asked, "Are you hungry? Could you eat something?"

"No, thank you."

We went.

The trio in the office was now four; with us, six. The dick was still bored. Fred, the bum, had reoccupied my chair against my expressed orders, but as I entered he moved to another one. Cramer stood over by the big globe, twirling it. Neya Tormic's eyes fastened on Wolfe as he appeared in the door and followed him as he crossed to his desk, sat, and reached for the button. I realized that he was in about as bad a humor as I could remember, because he issued no invitation for anyone to have beer. Neya Tormic said, with her eyes boring holes through him:

"I want to see you alone. To ask you something."

Wolfe nodded. "I know what you want. That will have to wait. You didn't get to finish your errand. Isn't that it?"

"I—" She stopped and wet her lips. "You promised."

"No, Miss Tormic, I didn't. I know you've had a hard afternoon, but surely you remember why you and Mrs. Goodwin were looking for Miss Lovchen. And you didn't find her."

"She's gone."

"How do you know that?"

"This—Inspector Cramer just told me they can't find her."

"Where has she gone to?"

"I don't know."

Wolfe uncapped a bottle of beer and poured. "Anyway," he declared, "that will have to wait. Confound it, everything will have to wait!" He drank until the glass was empty. "Mr. Cramer, you have been hanging around here since two o'clock. You have shown admirable patience and restraint—for instance, regarding Archie's presence at the Maidstone Building—and of course I know why. You want something and you think you can get it here and nowhere else. I tell you frankly, it isn't here. I don't suppose you contemplate spending the night in my house . . ."

I didn't hear the rest of the build-up for sending the inspector out into the night, because the doorbell rang and I went to answer it. Usually I performed that service anyway from six to eight, when Fritz was busy getting dinner, and on this occasion, considering the goose I had left in Wolfe's room, I had a special interest in the possibility of invading hordes. But what I found on the stoop wasn't a horde at all, but merely a youth in a snappy uniform with a little flat package he wanted to deliver to Nero Wolfe. I put out a hand for it, but he said he had instructions to put it into the hands of Nero Wolfe and no one else's. So I took him to the office. He marched across to the desk like a West Point cadet ready for his commission, stood with his heels together and asked politely:

"Mr. Nero Wolfe?"

"Yes, sir."

"From Seven Seas Radio. Sign here, please. The bill, sir. Twenty-six dollars, please."

Wolfe, reaching for his pen, told me to fork over the dough. I did so. The youth uttered thanks, stowed away the cash and the receipt, and preceded me to the hall. I let him out and put the chain on, and went back in.

Wolfe was undoing the package, and Cramer was standing across from him, right against the desk, looking down at it. It certainly was an exhibition of bad manners. Wolfe said:

"You make me nervous, Mr. Cramer. Sit down."

"I'm all right."

"But I'm not. Take a chair."

Cramer grunted, backed into the chair I had ready and lowered himself. Wolfe got the wrapping paper opened up and helped himself to an exclusive look at what was inside. Then he gave a little grunt, folded the paper over it again, and handed it to me.

"Put it in the safe, Archie."

I did so, closed the door and spun the knob, and returned to my chair.

Wolfe heaved a deep sigh and then muttered irritably, "That was the break we were waiting for, Mr. Cramer."

The inspector growled, "The break?"

Wolfe nodded. "A minute ago I said that what you want wasn't here. It is now."

Chapter 18

Cramer, slowly and carefully as if he wanted to be sure of not sitting on an egg, got more comfortable in his chair, resting his back, and lifted a forefinger to rub the side of his nose. Wolfe also was leaning back. His eyes were closed, and his lips began to work in and out. In the silence, the dick in the corner suddenly coughed and I glared at him.

"Hell," Cramer said mildly, "I'm in no hurry."

Apparently everyone took him at his word, for the silence continued for another three minutes, and then Wolfe said without opening his eyes:

"Of your two assumptions, Mr. Cramer, the first at least is correct. I doubt if you could get what I've got. Or, considering the attitude of your official superiors, if you did get it I doubt if you'd be able to use it."

"You'll get no argument from me on that," the inspector asserted. "What have I been saying? And while I know you can handle your affairs without the help of any gratitude from me, still and all—"

"I know. You're being tactful and adroit. You're dripping honey. Pfui. I'll tell you what I'll do. I'll give you what you want, on the condition that you agree without reservation to let me do it my way, without interference or protest."

"Well." Cramer regarded him with narrowed eyes, but it was one-sided, because Wolfe's eyes were still shut. "That's sort of vague. That you'll give me what I want. Who decides what I want?"

"Nonsense. I'm not quibbling. You want the identity of the murderer and the motive. I'll give you those."

"Any evidence?"

"Enough to satisfy you. And some of it I don't think you'll ever get unless you get it here and soon."

"Is it that thing in the safe?"

"Oh, no, you could get that yourself in about twenty-four hours. It took me twenty-five. I'll have to pry off a lid to get the evidence I'm speaking of."

Cramer eyed him a moment longer and said, "Shoot."

"Without reservation, no interference or protest from you."

"Right. Shoot."

Wolfe opened his eyes at me. "Archie, get Mr. Barrett on the phone."

"Donny or Dad?"

"Mr. Barrett Senior."

Neya Tormic blurted, "You mustn't—"

As I got at the phone Wolfe shushed her, and he had to keep on shushing her while I fiddled around with three different numbers before I finally reached the desired party at the Thistle Club. She subsided when Wolfe got on the phone:

"Mr. Barrett? This is Nero Wolfe. I'm calling to fulfill a promise. I told you that if I should find it necessary to interfere with your business I'd let you know in advance. I'm afraid I'm not giving you much notice; I'm going ahead now. No, please, please, that won't help matters any. At my office. Yes. Yes, I'll consent to that. No! If your son is there with you, you'd better bring him along. Yes. We'll be expecting you within fifteen minutes."

He pushed the phone away and got to his feet, and moved in the direction of the door.

Neya Tormic jumped up and grabbed at him. She got his sleeve. "Where—I'll go with you—"

"No, Miss Tormic. I'll be back in a moment. Archie!"

I rose and started over, but before I got there she let him go, and he went on out. I had no idea what her status was, or her intentions either, so I ambled to the door and stood there with my back against it. She didn't go back and sit down, but stood pat, with her eyes leveled at me, or maybe at the door since I don't like to flatter myself. We had held the tableau perhaps three minutes, not more than four, when I felt the door pressing against me and stood aside to let Wolfe re-enter. He halted to hand me an envelope, sealed, with *For Neya Tormic* on it in his writing, and then went on to his desk.

He looked at Cramer and indicated with a thumb the dick in the corner. "What is that man's name?"

"That? Charlie Heath."

"Tell him to obey the instructions I give him."

Cramer twisted his neck. "Here, Heath. Follow orders."

"Thank you." Wolfe regarded the dick, approaching. "Have you a car, Mr. Heath?"

"Yes, sir."

"Good. Take that envelope from Mr. Goodwin and put it in your pocket. No, your inside pocket. Take Miss Tormic in your car and drive—"

Neya was at him: "No! I don't—I'm not going—"

"That will do," Wolfe snapped. "You are going. I do this my way. Have you any cash with you?"

"But I won't—"

"You will! Confound it, how much cash have you?"

"I . . . have a little."

"How much?"

"A few dollars."

"Archie, give Miss Tormic a hundred dollars."

I produced the expense roll and peeled it off, making the roll look pretty sick, and handed it to her and she took it.

Wolfe said to the dick, "Drive to the corner of Fifth Avenue and 35th Street, let Miss Tormic out, give her the envelope, leave her there, and return straight here immediately. You are not to loiter to see what she does or which way she goes. Nor are you to communicate in any way with any other person, either going or returning."

I said grimly, "Send Fred along or let me go."

"Will that be necessary, Mr. Cramer?"

"No. I'm not a complete damn fool. Follow instructions, Heath."

"Yes, sir. I take her to Fifth, drop her, give her the envelope, and come straight back."

Wolfe nodded. "Will you do that?"

"Yes, sir."

"Good." He turned. "Au revoir, Miss Tormic."

"Ah," she said. Her black eyes were piercing him. "You think so?"

"Well . . . a conjecture. It wouldn't surprise me any."

"You . . . you fat fool!"

"Yes, I'm fat. And of course we're all fools. I'm sorry you won't be here to see the end of this. A silly little victory, but it's mine."

"Victory!"

"Yes."

Her lip curled. She turned and started off. I got to

the door and opened it, but before she passed through she halted to fling back at him, *"Teega mee bornie roosa,"* or at least that was what it sounded like. Then she went on, don't-touch-me all over, with the dick at her heels. I let them out, followed them into the November night air, and stood on the stoop to overlook the departure. As well as I could see in the dim light, the dick didn't pass any signal to any colleague, and when they rolled off in the police car they certainly weren't followed.

I stayed on the stoop long enough to be absolutely sure of that, knowing as I did the lengths a cop will sometimes go to on account of his passion for law and order, and was about to check it off and go back in when a big black town car rolled to the curb there below me. A chauffeur jumped out and opened the door, and touched his cap when one of the two men who emerged said something to him. They started up the steps, and I recrossed the threshold and turned to welcome two generations of Barretts. I asked them to wait there a minute and went to the office and told Wolfe:

"Father and son."

"Bring them in."

I did that. John P., who hadn't changed his clothes, took the chair Neya had occupied. His face was all tightened up, and the glance that he shot first at Cramer and then at Wolfe was not what I would call conciliatory. I moved up another chair for Donald. He looked so fierce and truculent that I had a notion to go get him a hunk of raw meat. Nobody had seemed to have any inclination to shake hands like gentlemen.

Wolfe said, "Fred, wait in front."

Fred went.

"Archie, take your notebook."

I took it.

John P. asked, "Are you Police Inspector Cramer?"

"Yes, sir," Cramer told him. "Of the Homicide Bureau."

John P. said to Wolfe, "That's ridiculous. This is a confidential business matter. And telling your man to take his notebook."

Wolfe leaned back and pressed his five right finger tips against his five left ones. "No," he said, "I wouldn't call it ridiculous. Mr. Cramer's presence is surely appropriate, since one of the things you'll want to do is to try to arrange it so that your son will escape an indictment for first-degree murder."

Cramer's head jerked around. Donald gawked, and some of the color leaving his face made him look a little less fierce. John P. betrayed no sign whatever of having heard anything more provocative than a remark about the weather. But he clipped off words and lunged with them:

"That's worse than ridiculous. And more dangerous. That's actionable."

"So it is." Wolfe's tone sharpened. "I'm coming right out with it, Mr. Barrett. My dinner's in an hour, and I don't want to waste time flopping around in a mire of inanities. I hold the cards and I don't have to finesse. Your deal with the Donevitch gang is done for. Accept that. Swallow it. I want to go on from that—"

"I'd like to see you alone." John P. stood up. "Get them out of here or take me—"

"No. Sit down."

"Sit down for what? You say the deal's done for. Whether it is or isn't, I'm not talking on that basis. There's nothing to talk about. Come, Donald."

He started off. Wolfe's words hit him in the back:

"Within an hour a warrant will issue charging your son with murder! It will be too late to talk to me then!"

Donald was up and following his leader. But his

leader suddenly wheeled, strode back to confront Cramer, and demanded:

"You're a responsible police officer. This blackmailing threat is made in your presence. Do you know who I am? . . . Well?"

That was a fizzle, in spite of the fact that Cramer hadn't the faintest idea of what was going on. I wouldn't have given an unconditioned guarantee on his brains, but there was nothing wrong with his guts.

"Yeah, I know who you are," he said calmly. "Sit down and give him rope. He owns this house and about a million dollars' worth of orchids. It's a good thing you've got me here as a witness in case you try for damages."

Wolfe snorted irritably. "Get out if you want to and take the consequences. You're acting like a schoolgirl in a pet. Can't you see I've got something to say and the best of your alternatives is to sit down and listen to it? Do you take me for a maudlin blatherskite?"

Donald blurted, "He's a goddam bluffer—"

A look from his father cut him off, and a jerk of his father's head ordered him back to his chair. Donald sat down. John P. did the same and told Wolfe curtly:

"Say it."

"That's better." Wolfe got his finger tips together again. "I'll make it as brief as I can since you already know it and all Mr. Cramer needs at present is the outline." He gave the inspector his eyes. "You might as well have the name of the murderer to begin with. I promised you that. The Princess Vladanka Donevitch."

Cramer grunted. "I don't know her."

"Yes you do. We'll get to that. Her home is in Zagreb, Croatia—Yugoslavia. She is the wife of young Prince Stefan. They like the Nazis. Most Croats don't. The Donevitch family agree with other Croats in their hatred of Belgrade. Belgrade is trying to make up its mind whether to be dominated by Germany, Italy, France, or England. Germany, Italy, France, and England are doing all they can to hasten the process. The attitude of the Croats is Germany's biggest obstacle. She is trying to buy them, with the Donevitch gang as selling agents. The other countries are competing—"

Cramer growled, "I'm a New York cop."

"I know, and most of the money in the world is in New York, or controlled from here. That's why people come here from all directions with things like this." Wolfe reached in to his breast pocket, pulled out a paper and extended it to Cramer. "Keep that; it's evidence. You can't read it. It is signed by Prince Stefan Donevitch and it empowers the princess, his wife, to conclude certain transactions in his name—"

John P.'s lips twitched. "Where did you get that?"

"That doesn't matter, Mr. Barrett. Not now." Wolfe went on to Cramer, "Specifically, transactions regarding concessions of Bosnian forests and the transfer of credits held by a firm of international bankers, Barrett & De Russy. The princess came to New York incognito, under an alias, and started negotiations. Because secrecy was essential on account of American restrictions regarding the export of capital in the form of loans, and I suspect other skulduggery besides the violation of those restrictions, she even went to the trouble of pretending to be an immigrant and getting a job in a fencing school. I don't suppose many persons were aware of her true identity, but certainly three were: Mr. Barrett here and his son, and a man named Rudolph Faber who was assisting in the negotiations as a secret agent of the Nazi government. You see, Barrett & De Russy have financial relations with the Nazis."

Donald began explosively, "We merely act—" but a glance from his father shut him up again.

Wolfe nodded. "I know. Money and morals don't speak . . . But a British agent named Ludlow got onto it. He not only got onto the princess and what she was up to, he even threatened—I don't know how, but possibly by informing the American government—to ruin the deal. And that just at the moment when all details had been decided and it was ready for consummation. So she killed Ludlow. I want to make it plain that the princess did that herself. A friend, another young woman, had come from Zagreb with her, also under an alias, but she had no part in the murder. You understand that, Mr. Cramer?"

Cramer muttered, "Go on."

"There isn't a lot to go on with. Rudolph Faber knew what the princess had done and he blackmailed her. Up to last evening he had been merely a negotiator, a bidder; that made him boss. He imposed terms on her, and I imagine they weren't generous; he didn't strike me as a generous man. He forced her to tell where that paper was and he tried to get it. The paper was of course vital. I presume, Mr. Barrett, it was to be attached to the agreement you were drawing up, to validate it?"

John P. didn't answer.

Wolfe shrugged. "So she killed Faber. She made an appointment to meet him in her own apartment and stabbed him. God only knows what she thought she was going to do next. There is no way of telling what goes on in that kind of a head. She seems to be as heedless and harebrained as a lunatic. She may have counted on the taciturnity of governments and international financiers regarding their privy intrigues, but what the devil did she take me for, a goat on a chain? A creature like that is outside the realm of calculation. I wouldn't have been surprised if she had tried to stab me. Were you able to deal with her on a rational basis, Mr. Barrett?"

John P. was regarding him steadily. "I'm waiting for you to say something."

"That's about all there is."

"Bah. You've made a lot of loose accusations, with nothing to support them."

"There's that paper."

"You stole it."

"I didn't, but what if I did? There it is, for evidence."

"Damn flimsy evidence for two murders."

"I know." Wolfe wiggled a finger at him. "See here, Mr. Barrett, you're making a blunder. I made a serious threat. I said that a warrant would issue charging your son with murder. I meant, of course, as accessory, which is the same thing. It's obvious that he knew the Princess Vladanka had killed Ludlow. You probably knew it too, but I have no proof that you tried actively to cheat the law. I have got proof that your son did, and three witnesses: Belinda Reade, Madame Zorka, and Mr. Goodwin, my assistant."

"That was only—"

"Quiet, son." John P. didn't move his eyes from Wolfe. "What else?"

"Nothing to stun you with, I'm afraid. Frankly, sir, I have no bomb to explode under you. But the point is this. Mr. Cramer here doesn't like murder. He doesn't like to see it practiced with impunity under any circumstances whatever, but in this case he was impeded by a wall of reluctance which he couldn't possibly have breached. By luck I had made a hole in the wall and I've let him through, and if you knew him as I do you would realize that he can't be chased out again. He has it now and he'll hang onto it, unless you can get him ditched, which I doubt. He has that paper and he'll arrest the princess, so your deal's off anyway.

He has enough to take your son as a material witness. With that paper, he can get a court order to examine your records and correspondence. But you know as well as I do what this will mean if you try to fight it. If you try to shield a murderer from the penalty she has earned. The fact is—"

I missed some then because I had to answer the doorbell. It was Charlie Heath. He started for the office as if he owned the place, but I blocked him off and demanded, "Would you mind explaining what it was that took so long?"

"I'll report to the inspector."

"He's busy and you'll wait in here." I opened the door to the front room, where Fred Durkin was sitting with a magazine. "What used up all the time?"

"Nothing used it up. I mean I got back ten minutes ago. I've been out front."

"You have."

"I have."

"Okay. Wait here."

I went back to the office and ran into a scowling match, and took advantage of it to report the return of Heath. All Cramer did was to favor me with five seconds of his share of the scowl. Wolfe didn't even look at me. Apparently he was still trying to undermine Barrett without a bomb and was finding it hard digging.

"No," he said, "I wouldn't expect that. We don't expect much from you, Mr. Barrett, in any event. But you seem to have overlooked one thing, at least. You seem to be ignoring the existence of a person who knows as much about all this as the princess herself does. Including your part in it, and your son's part. I mean, of course, the friend who came here with the princess from Zagreb."

"Maybe he's ignoring it," Cramer put in, "but I'm not. And you let her go, and gave her money to go with. That was cute."

"No," Wolfe asserted, "I did not."

Cramer stared. Wolfe said, "Archie, get that package from the safe and give it to Mr. Cramer."

I went and got it and handed it over. Cramer started to unfold it.

"That," Wolfe said, "is the photograph of the Princess Vladanka Donevitch, radioed from London. If I had only got it this morning—"

Cramer jumped up, sputtering, "What kind of a goddam run-around—this is that Tormic—"

"Now, please!" Wolfe pushed a palm at him. "Yes, it is Miss Tormic. I agreed—"

"And she's—and by God, you had one of *my* men take her and turn her loose—"

"I did. What else could I do? She was sitting here in my office, thinking she was my client, under my protection. I didn't agree to catch the murderer for you, I agreed to disclose the identity and the motive. If you'll take my advice, the simplest way to get her—"

But Cramer wasn't taking advice. He nearly knocked me out of my chair, getting at the phone. Father and son sat tight. Wolfe looked up at the clock and heaved a sigh. Cramer got his number and began spouting orders to someone. I picked up the radiophoto of the princess and laid it on Wolfe's desk, and gathered up the wrapping paper and put it in the wastebasket.

Cramer finished and stood up and yapped at Wolfe, "If we don't get her I'll—"

"It was a bargain," Wolfe snapped.

"One hell of a bargain." He moved for the door, turned, and spoke to the Barretts, "I'll want to see you. If you try setting a fire under me, I'll give you all I've got." He went and I was right behind him. While he grabbed his coat and hat I got Heath from the front room, always glad to get cops out of the house, from flatfoots on up. I followed them out to the stoop, leaving the door ajar, and watched the army that had been surrounding the house being called into action. Cramer waved them in and gave them curt and crackling orders. His own car had to back up a few feet before it could nose around the rear of the Barrett town car. The taxi down the street rolled up, then it and Heath's car sped away. Cramer's car started, then stopped, and my name was called:

"Hey, Goodwin, come here!"

I trotted down the steps and past Barrett's car on over to him. Cramer leaned from the window:

"I want that picture. Understand?"

"Sure we're through with it," I told him obligingly, and stood at the curb and watched their tail light as they headed for the corner.

I watched them too long.

What happened, happened quick, but even so I might have headed her off if I had turned two seconds sooner. She came from inside the tonneau of Barrett's car, leaping out, and went like a bat out of hell across the sidewalk, up the steps and through the door I had left ajar. I was after her, and I am not old enough to be incapable of rapid movement. I was starting up the steps as she hurtled through the door, and by the light in the hall I saw a glittering streak from something she had in her hand. I gave it all I had then, but I couldn't catch lightning. When I was at the door she was swerving into the office. As I made the office she was halfway across it and her hand was up with the shining blade, and Wolfe was there in his chair with no time to move, and I had no gun, and all I could do was yell and keep going.

I do not know how Wolfe did it and I never will know, though he has kindly explained it to me several times. He says that when he heard the commotion in the hall he stiffened into attention, which is the most incredible part of it; that when he saw her leaping in with the dagger flashing he grabbed a beer bottle with each hand; that when she was upon him he struck simultaneously with both hands, with his left at her descending wrist and with his right at anything at all. I don't know. I do know that something broke her right wrist and something cracked her skull.

When I reached them he was still sitting in his chair with a beer bottle in each hand and she was on the floor back of his chair, flat on the floor, with her legs twitching spasmodically. I looked at him for blood and didn't see any. Fred Durkin busted in from the front room. Fritz came running from the kitchen. Father and son stood there white and speechless. I couldn't see anything wrong with Wolfe, but I asked him in a voice that sounded funny to me:

"Did she get you?"

"No!" he bellowed. He couldn't get up because her body against his chair kept him from shoving it back to make room.

I knelt down to take a look at her. Her legs had stopped twitching. I couldn't feel any heart. It was close quarters, with her there between Wolfe's chair and the wall, and I squirmed around to get on the other side of her. As I did so I heard a voice from the middle of the room:

"Excuse me for walking right in, Mr. Wolfe, but the door was standing open. I was on my way uptown and I dropped in to say that we may expect a ruling from the attorney general on that point in about a week— the matter of registration as the agent of a foreign principal when the—"

I raised myself up enough to see the face of Stahl the G-man looking polite but stern. Then I sat back on my heels and howled with laughter.

Chapter 19

Wolfe said in a tone of exasperation, "Fritz tells me nothing on your tray was touched. Confound it, you have to eat something!"

Carla shook her head. "I can't. I'm sorry. I can't."

I had brought her down to the office. The clock on the wall said 11:20. The chairs were back in place.

Wolfe sighed. "It's nearly midnight. Mr. Goodwin is yawning. You may go now whenever you want to. Or I'll ask one or two questions if you feel like telling the truth."

"I can tell the truth—now."

"It would have been just as well . . ." His massive shoulders went up a sixteenth of an inch and down again. "I would like to know if you were aware that that woman was a maniac."

"But she wasn't—" Carla stopped for repairs to her voice. "I never had any idea . . ." Her hand fluttered and dropped again to her lap.

"Were you in fact her friend?"

"Not—no, not her friend. It wasn't like that. When Mrs. Campbell died I was left dependent on the Donevitch family. Then Prince Stefan married her and she came there and in no time she was head of things.

She treated me as well as I could expect, since I was not a Donevitch. I didn't dislike her. I was a little afraid of her and so was everybody else, even Prince Stefan. When she decided to come to America she selected me to come with her, and I thought then that the reason she did that was because she knew about you and she thought she might need to use you. One reason I thought that was because she told me to bring that adoption paper along—"

"Yes. Excuse me. Get it, Archie."

I went to the safe and dug it out and handed it to him. He unfolded it to glance at it, folded it up again, and passed it over to her. She looked at it a second as if she was afraid it might bite, and then reached out and took it.

"I came with her because I had to—and anyway I wanted to," she went on in a better voice. "It was an adventure to come to America. I knew all about—what she was coming for. She trusted me. I knew she would do dangerous things—but I never thought of anything like murder as a thing she would do. When Ludlow was killed I suspected she had done it, but I didn't know. I asked her last night, and she told me I was a fool. Then when I went there this morning and saw Faber, of course I knew she had done that and the other one too. I was frightened and I couldn't think. I couldn't answer questions about her—I couldn't betray her—but I couldn't lie for her any more either. I tried to run away—and I couldn't use my head—and in a strange country—and I was stupid—"

She stopped, and her hand fluttered and fell to her lap again.

In a moment Wolfe said gruffly, "It is faintly encouraging that you are aware that you were stupid."

She offered no comment. He demanded:

"What are you going to do?"

"I . . ." She shook her head. "I don't know."

"Well, I suppose you are legally my daughter. That puts some responsibility on me."

Her chin went up. "I'm not asking any—"

"Pfui! Don't. I know. Confound it, you've been dependent on someone all your life, haven't you? Are you going back to Yugoslavia?"

"No."

"Oh. You're not."

"No."

"What do you want to do, stay in America?"

"Yes."

"As a spy for the Donevitch gang?"

There was a flash in her eye. "No!"

"Where are you going to sleep tonight? In that apartment on 38th Street?"

"Why, I . . ." A shiver went over her. "No," she said, "I . . . I don't think I could. I couldn't go back there. Somewhere else. Anywhere. I have a little money." She got to her feet. "I can go—"

"Nonsense. You'd get run over or fall into a hole. You haven't eaten anything and your brain isn't working. I hope it turns out that you've got one. I'll have Fritz fix up another tray for you—"

"No, I couldn't, really I couldn't . . ."

"Well, you must sleep and in the morning you must eat. You are in no condition now, anyway, to make any sort of intelligent decision. We'll discuss it tomorrow. If you decide to stay in America and not to tear that paper up I suppose your name will be Carla Wolfe. In that case—Archie, what the devil are you grinning about? Baboon! Take Miss—take my—take her upstairs to the south room! And tell her if she undertakes to use the fire escape not to tumble through my window as she goes by!"

I arose. "Come on, Miss my Carla."

Ten minutes later I went back to the office. I hadn't heard the elevator so I knew he was still there. Not only was he still there but he had just received a fresh consignment of beer.

I took a good stretch accompanied by a yawn. "Well," I observed good-naturedly, "that was a damn profitable case. You turned loose of about four centuries not counting loss of brain tissue, and what you got out of it was one shapely responsibility and nothing else."

He put down his empty glass and said nothing.

"There is one thing," I announced, "that I would like to have cleared up now, once and for all. I was at fault in one respect and only one. I should not have left the front door ajar when I went down to the sidewalk when Cramer called me. Aside from that, I couldn't help it. The nervy little devil had come along to the Barretts' chauffeur five minutes before we went out and told him she was supposed to meet his employer there, and he opened the door for her so she could wait inside the car. Two dicks saw it, though they didn't recognize her in the dim light, and they kindly said nothing about it. She was out of the car, behind my back, and starting up the steps before I knew she was there. There wasn't a chance in the world of catching her."

Wolfe shrugged. "I managed without you," he murmured in an absolutely insufferable tone.

I gritted my teeth, and as soon as I had got it swallowed, yawned. "Okay," I said sleepily. "There are, however, one or two little questions. What was in the envelope you gave that dick to give her?"

"Nothing. Only a sentence saying that she was not my client, and, under the terms as stated, never had been."

"And what was it she said as she went out? *'Teega mee bornie roosa,'* or something like that."

"That was her native tongue."

"Yeah. What does it mean?"

"*'Over my dead body.'*"

"Is that so." I humphed. "She called the turn then. I guess that's all I need, except maybe one thing. Such items as her claiming your help by using Carla's adoption paper for herself—I get all that. But I'll be darned if I can see why Ludlow said she went to the locker room to get his cigarettes. Him a British spy and her a Balkan princess? Why did he—"

"He didn't. She went to the locker room to steal something from his coat. Probably that paper which she sent here the next morning to be hid in a safe place, because he had previously stolen it from her. And he was letting her know that he knew that."

Wolfe sighed, pushed back his chair, and manipulated himself to his feet. "I'm going to bed." He got halfway to the door, but stopped again. "By the way, remind me tomorrow to ask Mr. Cramer for that hundred dollars. I wish I could cure myself of those idiotic romantic gestures."

"Oh, that hundred?" I patted my pocket. "I've already got it. That was the first thing I did."

The World of
Rex Stout

Now, for the first time ever, enjoy a peek into the life of Nero Wolfe's creator, Rex Stout, courtesy of the Stout Estate. Pulled from Rex Stout's own archives, here are rarely seen, some never-before-published memorabilia. Each title in "The Rex Stout Library" will offer an exclusive look into the life of the man who gave Nero Wolfe life.

Over My Dead Body

Following is a short review of *Over My Dead Body* from the *Saturday Review*.

Their verdict? "Swell"!

The Criminal Record

The Saturday Review's Guide to Detective Fiction

Title and Author	Crime, Place, Sleuth	Summing Up	Verdict
OVER MY DEAD BODY *Rex Stout* (Farrar & Rinehart: $2.)	Nero Wolfe is back to solve mystery of who stuck épée through customer in N. Y. fencing school, followed by another lethal impalement.	Stooge Archie Goodwin at funniest, and two murders plus transplanted Balkan intrigue can't get him—or his boss—down.	Swell
THE AFRICAN POISON MURDERS *Elspeth Huxley* (Harpers: $2.)	Reign of terror on mid-African farm culminates in two gruesome killings and almost finishes Vachell of C. I. D., who unsnarls case.	Obscure venom, maniacal mutilations, deadly bush fire, thrilling climax compose major opus—at which purists may raise eyebrows.	Top-flight
THE CASE OF THE DEADLY DIARY *William DuBois* (Little, Brown: $2.)	N. Y. newspaper owner pushed from lofty window. Scandal-mongering columnist conked. Gossip gal plugged. Star reporter solves all.	Feverish activity from Manhattan start to Florida finish. Author plays premier clue bit too close to vest. Otherwise jake.	Good grade